MW00331091

To My Baby Sister, Barba!
Thanks for your Support!
Love you,
Arlyon Thomas

THE CAT ON SALTER'S POINT

──────────

By Anita Dixon-Thomas

THE CAT ON SALTER'S POINT

Copyright © 2016 by Anita Dixon-Thomas

All rights reserved. No part of this book may be reproduced or transmitted in any form or by any means without written permission from the author and/or Publisher.

Published by Tavares Entertainment, LLC.
Book cover design by GT Smith
Edited by Gary G. Tavares
Printed in the United States of America

Gary G. Tavares
Tavares Entertainment, LLC.
3320 S. Cobb Dr. SE #21
Smyrna, GA 30080
678-437-4496

ISBN: 978-0-9833292-7-5

Dedication

I dedicate this body of work to my beautiful mother, Juanita Dixon. A loving and gracious spirit, who is my greatest and true fan.

Acknowledgments

I owe a debt of thanks to my sisters, Cheryl, Crystal and Barbara, my best friends, Patty Weathers-Brownlee and Gail Bonner and my daughter Tierri. Finally, my social worker colleagues, Donna Sanders, Paula Barrett, Melissa Collis-Abdulla and Rona Boykin for showing their support while I developed this fascinating, entertaining story. Giving me their invaluable, needed, constructive advice at a moment's notice. All of you deserve credit for the success of this project and your participation and faith in my ability to write such an entertaining story will always be appreciated and valued. Thanks to all of you.

Chapter One

It's March sixth of the year nineteen eighty-four, early in the morning, around four o'clock. A full moon glares down from the dark, clear sky and the air, crisp and chilly is cold to the bone. Salter's Point Regional, an intimidating fortress looms behind an iron gate on the edge of a rocky cliff just outside of Salter's Point. A modest, sleepy town, an hour away from the city of Seattle. A thin white mist hovers low over the hospital's dark outline, its eerie appearance resembling a haunted house. Every three seconds, a faint light flickers in and out in the hospital's clock tower. The light's humble illumination barely gracing the dark misty sky.

A man in black slides out of his red Porsche and slams the door shut. He shudders at the sight of the gloomy looking fortress. Its massive structure, towering high above him, seems to take up the entire sky. He cringes when he sees bats swarming high over his head. Their wings flapping loud like waves of rushing water. The night creatures circle in and out around the hospital's clock tower and then they settle on the clock's narrow ledge lining up like huge black crows on a picket fence. Then in one swift movement, one by one, the bats flip upside down. Their naked bodies suspended in mid-air. A permanent fixture against the foggy sky.

The man cases the area for a split second and then he sprints across the parking lot to the hospital's entrance. He stops and peers through the sliding glass door searching for human activity. The lobby, barely lit, is empty with no sign of life.

With great care, he slides the key in the lock and it clicks twice, opening the door. He tiptoes inside and guides the door to its latch until it clicks shut. And then without hesitation he sprints across the lobby straight to the locked unit. He is familiar with the area. After all he walks this lobby a hundred times a day, either on his way to a meeting or visiting his patients on the unit. When he arrives at the locked unit he forces the key into the lock of the heavy steel door and jiggles it. Within a minute, the lock gives and the door clicks open. When he shoves the door wide open, it moans and cracks, causing him to hesitate. His heart races and his mind tries to grapple why he has never noticed the door creaking so loud before. He stands there for a moment and listens, hoping the noise doesn't draw attention. When he doesn't hear anything, after a few seconds, he lets out a deep sigh and tiptoes inside.

He squints trying to see down the dense lit hall and a cold shiver begins to creep up his spine. A group of dark shadows bounce up and down along the concrete walls in the hall, dancing in a melodic tempo. Their menacing rhythm sinister and lewd. He lingers by the door and listens. His heart bangs hard in his chest as he tries to detect any semblance of a human voice or sign of life. When he doesn't see, or hear anyone, he's decides the coast is clear. He closes the steel door and turns around facing the dark shadows in the hall again, with his adrenalin on speed dial.

Determined to retrieve what he came for, he tiptoes fast down the hall, being careful not to make a sound. The tall dark shadow of his own silhouette moves along the wall with him mimicking his every move. As he tiptoes pass the nursing station, he notices a nurse slumped over in a chair, snoring with his mouth hanging open. His size twelve feet propped high on top the desk.

His big toes play peek-a-boo through ripped dingy white socks while a faint stench of pickles overwhelms the air. Jamie Lee's cat, his size resembling a small bobcat, sits on his hind legs near the nurse's feet. Unfazed by the pickled odor, feverishly licking the thick black fur on his massive hind leg. The man hesitates when the big cat spots him and glares at him. His yellow eyes, intense and disapproving, seem to pierce through his very soul.

He breathes deep, his face dripping with warm perspiration and he wipes the sweat off his brow as he moves pass the nursing station. He tiptoes into the dining area and passes a male patient crumpled up in a chair fast asleep. The cat's yellow eyes follow him, stalking his every move as he makes his way to Susan Cole's room.

Susan Cole, her blond hair twisted high in a ponytail, is there in the room waiting on him with her hands clasped tight in her lap. She sits on the edge of the bed with her packed bag by her side. When Doctor Benny opens the door and peeks inside, her blue eyes light up. She hops off the bed and runs to him as fast as her legs can carry her.

"I thought you would never get here," she said colliding into him and giggling like a school girl. She then hugs him.

"I'm here now," he said embracing her and kissing her forehead. "I told you I would come."

He releases her. "Come on," he whispers pointing to her bed. "Get your bag and let's go."

She snatches her bag off the bed and follows him into the hall. He stops to scout the area in both directions and then he and Susan head for the exit.

When they tiptoe pass the nursing station, she giggles. She is tickled by the nurse's loud snoring, which suddenly stops. Doctor Benny and Susan Cole freeze in place.

They hold their breath staring at the nurse, with their hearts pounding against their chest, as the nurse changes position in the chair. The nurse smacks his lips and yawns. He stops moving for a split second and then he snores again sounding like a soft horn and a stream of clear liquid drools from his mouth.

Doctor Benny glares at his lover. "Susan," he whispers squeezing her hand. "You almost woke Bob up!"

"Ouch," she said snatching her hand away and poking out her bottom lip. "I didn't mean too," she said. "He just looks funny sleeping over there."

"Come on," he said grabbing her hand. "We don't have much time."

He drags her down the hall like a rag doll, passing the big cat, still perched on the desk. His yellow eyes taking in their every move as the couple sprints pass him in the hall. The cat hops off the desk and pursues them, with his stride sneaky, purposeful and quiet. He stalks them, staying three steps behind as they move like lightning down the hall to the exit. When they arrive there, Doctor Benny stops in mid stride and turns and glares at the cat.

The cat stops in his tracks. The hair on his back is prickly and straight. His yellow gaze intense and his white fangs flashing. Warm, sticky sweat drips down Doctor Benny's face while he fiddles with the key. He drops it and the key clangs on the floor like a piece of silverware. "Oh shit!" he said glancing down the hall. Within seconds, he swipes the key off the floor and he unlocks the heavy steel door, shoving it open.

He grabs Susan's hand and pulls her out into the lobby. Once off the locked unit, he guides the heavy steel door shut, being careful not to let it slam. The cat, still crouched in the hall, hisses and flashes his fangs as the door closes in his face. Susan Cole, a tormented soul, has a long history of being abandoned by men she has loved for one reason or another. Her insecure nature and suicidal tendencies motivates her depressed outlook on life. Her personality, borderline sweet and naïve, often draws people in. When she first arrived at Salter's Point Regional, after trying to overdose on Tylenol, she was assigned to Doctor Benny. She soon fell in love with the man. Hanging on his every word. Easily seduced and manipulated by his charm and marginal good looks.

Doctor George Benny, a narcissistic man with emotional boundary issues, latched onto Susan right away after meeting her. He sensed her emotional flaws and used them to his advantage. It wasn't long before he wrapped his seductive web around her and soon manipulated her into a sexual relationship. A role she eagerly accepted. Every day he would summon her to his office under the guise of psychotherapy and then make love to her late into the evening. It was there where the two of them master minded a plan for her escape. The doctor offering his home for immediate shelter and Susan, naïve at best, accepting his offer. Unaware she was accepting a self-imposed prison.

As the two lovers sprint like the wind into the crisp cool night, Doctor Benny sighs, relieved his plan went off without a hitch. Security nowhere in the vicinity, nowhere in sight. The two lovers run like demons across the parking lot to Doctor Benny's Porsche while the cold, whistling wind singes their faces.

The pain so sharp it feels like a bee sting. Doctor Benny, feeling a twinge of guilt, knows full well he has committed a shameful, immoral crime. His relationship with Susan is not only unethical and risky at best, but now it's a threat to his long-standing career. However, for the moment, he doesn't care. He is smitten with her and determined to have her at any cost. Finally, they reach the doctor's Porsche and hop inside. Doctor Benny turns on the ignition and barrels out of the parking lot in lightning speed with Susan Cole snuggled close beside him. The two lovers are excited about their new life together. However, in a few short hours, Susan Cole's mysterious disappearance will be blistering news throughout the hospital community, lasting for a period of several weeks. Forcing the two lovers to operate deep under the radar until one of them, one day, slips up and all hell breaks loose. Their scandalous affair, along with a heart wrenching incident, will haunt Salter's Point Regional for decades to come.

Four hours later, back in Seattle, Rachel tosses and turns in her bed. She contemplates on what to wear to her eleven o'clock interview, which is later that morning at Salter's Point Regional Hospital. She yawns and stretches and then she rolls on her side and squints. The clock on the nightstand reads seven thirty. She switches on the lamp and rolls out of the bed. She trudges over to the window and opens the blinds. It's grey outside and the clouds are angry and threatening rain. A common occurrence in Seattle, Washington. She goes back to her bed and lies down. She grabs her remote off the nightstand and turns the television on. KIRO News is reporting a story of a suicidal patient escaping from a locked unit at Salter's Point Regional. She sits up and turns the volume up. "What the hell?" she shouted as she listens to the report.

"How did that patient escape without being seen?" she wonders shaking her head. She flinches. "I hope that patient hasn't killed herself," she mumbles. "That will be a disaster for the hospital," she said looking worried. "I hope they find her." She glances at her clock. It's now eight o'clock and time is slipping away. She hops out of the bed and rushes around her apartment like a maniac running from one closet to the next and getting her clothes together. Her heart races while she searches each closet for something to wear. Throwing suits, dresses and sweaters on the floor. Thirty minutes later, she's selects a cream-colored blouse, a red dress suit and two-inch brown pumps. She stands back and admires the combination thinking about the nice comments she will receive when she wears her favorite color red. A bold contrast against her coffee latte skin. She smiles at the thought of it, pleased with her selection. She lays the suit on the bed next to her cream-colored blouse and then she glances at the clock. It's now eight thirty. She runs into the bathroom and begins to shower.

Three years ago, Rachel moved to Seattle from California to attend Social Work School at the University of Washington. She ended her relationship with the love of her life. She was hurt after finding him in bed with another woman. For months, her emotions were all over the place. Raw and consumed by his betrayal. Finding inner peace was difficult at first but she pressed on, determined to get over him. Her move to Washington State was her way of distancing herself from such painful memories. A chance to embark on a new chapter in her life. Soon after graduation, she accepts a job at a nursing home in West Seattle. A low paying social worker position.

While there, she continues to search for full time work, in hopes of finding something better and it isn't long before she does. One rainy morning while sitting in Starbucks, having a cup of coffee on the water front near Pike Place Market, she runs across a job announcement in the Seattle Times Newspaper. Salter's Point Regional Hospital, a psychiatric facility, was advertising a social worker position in the classified ads. Excited about the job and its pay, Rachel drives to the hospital the very next day and applies, hoping for an interview. When the hospital finally calls two months later to offer her an interview, she accepts, elated by the possibility of making a decent salary.

Rachel finishes her shower and wraps a towel around her slender body. She stares at the mirror and twists her long black, curly hair in a bun, combing down some of the curls in front to create bangs. She applies her make-up, being careful not to put too much powder on her face. She follows up with a bronze eye shadow to her eye lids and mascara to her lashes to bring out the dark brown color of her eyes. She finishes with a hint of blush and smiles, admiring herself.

She rushes out of the bathroom to her bedroom and glances at the clock again. It is now nine-thirty. She dresses, slips on her heels and checks herself in the full-length mirror across the room. She turns around three times to make sure every piece of clothing is in place. After a close inspection, she is satisfied and then she heads to the kitchen. On the way, she thinks about the interview again. Butterflies dance in her stomach, giving her the jitters. "I need something sweet to get rid of this tension," she said. So, she makes herself a big cup of Starbucks coffee, microwaves a honey bun and within minutes she is sitting at the table enjoying her breakfast.

She glances at her watch again and now it's nine forty-five. She knows it will take at least an hour to drive to Salter's Point Hospital so she drops her dishes in the sink and dashes to the bathroom. She brushes her teeth and then applies a thin layer of red color to her lips. She glimpses in the mirror and smiles at herself, pleased with her overall appearance. She glances at her watch again. It's ten o'clock and time to go. So, she throws on her raincoat, grabs her umbrella and checks herself in the mirror one last time. She then struts out the door.

Chapter Two

The grey sky opens and water droplets the size of moth balls splatter all over the front window of Rachel's red Toyota, as she cruises down Interstate Five on her way to Salter's Point. She flips on the windshield wipers and turns on the radio. Prince's hit song; "When Doves Cry" blasts the air waves. She turns the volume up four octaves and begins bopping her head to the music like a ping pong ball. Singing the Artist's lyrics with her voice loud and screeching. Even with the windshield wipers full blast, the thick precipitation assaults her front window. A watery maze zigzags across it, hampering her vision. She slows down to a snail's pace and she sighs, very relieved she left early enough to navigate through the heavy rain. She maintains the snail-like pace for a few more miles until she reaches the exit to her destination.

As she exits the freeway, the heavy rain tapers off to a light grey drizzle allowing her to pick up speed again. She drives through a residential area and then she crosses some railroad tracks. Soon she finds herself on an open, wide stretch miles and miles ahead into an abyss. The end nowhere in sight. Thirty miles down the road, she finally sees the sign directing her to the town of Salter's Point and then she makes a sharp right. While cruising up the road, she notices tall evergreen trees lining each side of the road. Their elegant branches dusted with silver white dew and their needles glistening like icicles. The sun's blaring rays bring on massive heat, chasing away the clusters of thick grey clouds still lingering in the distant sky.

A man, slender in build, with a red knit hat and dark sunglasses rides his ten-speed bicycle up the winding paved road. His blue jacket flapping high into the cool breeze. When Rachel passes him, he doesn't look up because he's too focused on the road ahead. By the time she reaches the base of the mountain, the rain has stopped. Rachel chugs up the rugged mountain terrain, fighting with the gears. Her Toyota struggling around the slippery curves as she navigates the winding road. She glances to her left and admires the picturesque valley of the evergreen trees below. Their towering majestic presence decorates the mountain's rocky embankment while the sun's intense warmth dries out their water-logged branches. "How beautiful," she whispers taking it all in.

Finally, over the horizon, Rachel eyes the hospital. A few yards off the road. It is an intimidating massive red brick fortress, tucked away behind a black iron gate. She turns left and drives onto the hospital grounds toward the gate. A guard in black signals for her to stop. She heeds him and he approaches her car. She strains her neck, peering over the dashboard, to get a good look at the man. She giggles at the sight of him as he moves closer. Amused by his peculiar, rugged dark looks. The man's thick gray bushy eye brows hang over his deep blue set eyes and the entrenched lines in his face form a complicated road map that seem to disappear into his gray bushy mustache. He resembles Darth Vader in his black uniform and bulky combat boots and when he arrives at Rachel's car, he glares at her. She smiles but he doesn't return the favor.

She takes a deep breath as the tension in the pit of her stomach singes her insides. "Good Morning, Sir," she said rolling down the window. "I have an eleven o'clock interview this morning on East Campus." When he pokes his head in the window, he is so close she can smell tobacco on his breath. She leans over, shifting in her seat, surprised by his lack of personal boundaries. "Who are you here to see?" he asks, with his voice gruff.

"I am here to see Beth Jones," she said sniffling.

"Young lady, I need to see your identification," he said with his tone curt. Rachel pulls her wallet from her handbag and retrieves her driver's license. Her hand trembles as she hands the license to the guard. He snatches it, flashing her a look of disdain. He then turns and hikes back to the glass booth. He makes a phone call and Rachel feels her heart pounding. She contemplates asking the guard for further directions. By the time he finishes his phone call and returns to her car, she has mustered up the courage to ask him for directions, despite the hot nagging tension urging her to do otherwise.

"Sir, could you tell me how to get to East Campus?" she asked, with her voice trembling as she takes her license from him. The security guard frowns and points his bony finger up the road in front of her. "Go through this gate and pass West Campus Hospital. When you reach the top of the hill, you will see a gray building on the right. That building is East Campus Hospital. Now get," he sneers showing two rows of brown stained teeth. He whistles, backing away from the car and he beckons her to proceed through the gate, as Rachel frowns. "What an asshole," she mutters as she rolls up the window. She drives through the gate and sees stretches of red and black rose bushes decorating each side of the road.

On her left are clusters of little white cottages scattered throughout the well- manicured, green lush lawn on one side of the main hospital. "What a beautiful campus this is," she muses. Once over the hill, she eyes East Campus Hospital a few yards on the left. It is a large gray stone building nestled in a grove of pine trees. As she drives into the parking lot, she notices two young men. They are dressed in blue overalls and smoking cigarettes while standing in front of the hospital entrance. She checks them out while she finds a spot and parks her car. Rachel then checks her make-up in the mirror and gets out of the car. With her heart bouncing in her chest like a rubber ball, she is wary of the two men as she moves closer to the hospital entrance. When she struts pass them to the sliding glass door, they step aside, not saying one word. She taps the buzzer and the door slides open. Relieved, she hurries inside and steps to the reception desk.

Rachel's eyes widen as she approaches the desk. Six white wig heads are on top of the counter, lined up in a straight line. Each head has a bundle of black yarn for hair with a red hat and black dots for eyes. Below the eyes is a red smudge for a nose and two inches below the nose are two thick, crooked red lines curled up in a sinister grin. Rachel giggles, as she leans over the counter to search for the receptionist. She is being very careful not to upset the peculiar scene. Soon she notices the receptionist sitting in front of a typewriter across the room, oblivious to Rachel's presence. The woman types fast, as her stubby little fingers click hard in rapid staccato tempo on the typewriter keyboard. Her brown, bee hive hairdo looming high on top of her head.

Her hoop silver earrings jingle loud over the typewriter's rhythm and her outfit is a plain white blouse with black polyester pants, that fit snug on her stocky frame. Rachel clears her throat. "Humph," she said. The woman, still consumed with her typing, doesn't hear her at first. So, Rachel snaps her fingers. "Hi there, my name is Rachel Thomas," she said with her voice high. The receptionist spins around so hard she almost falls out of the chair. Her brown eyes dart back and forth like a wild animal. Her eyes now pinned on Rachel. "Oh, Oh, Oh," she said. "I am so sorry. Have you been standing there long?"

"No, I just got here," Rachel said with her smile warm. "I didn't mean to scare you. I am here to see Beth Jones." The receptionist pats her chest. When she shifts her plumb bottom in her seat, the chair squeaks. "I am Joyce Smith, the receptionist," she said with her voice soft. "Please have a seat. I will tell Beth you are here." "Thank you," said Rachel turning away from the counter. She scans the lobby for a seat. She finds one by the bay window and parks herself on the sofa. She checks out the area. The plain white walls void of pictures give the area a drab, prison-like appearance. She glances at the floor and notices black marks streak across it and on every end table there are ashtrays with cigarette butts. "Messy," she thought, scooting back on the sofa, making herself more comfortable. Minutes later, three male patients in overalls hustle into the lobby mumbling to themselves. They pace back and forth in a robot-like trance staring at the floor. She cringes at the sight of them, with her anxiety in full throttle, as she watches each soul methodically parade in front of her.

She wonders if she's made the right decision in accepting an interview in such an intimidating place. She decides after some thought she could work here. After all, the job offers more money and she could use the extra funds. So, she ignores her uneasy feelings, choosing instead to be optimistic about her upcoming interview. She rehearses possible questions in her head, determined to perform well despite her brewing fear.

Soon Beth Jones appears in the lobby. The supervisor, short and chunky, shines like a Christmas tree ornament. She is in a bright orange tent dress with her flaming red florescent shoes. Her thick, curly, gray hair cradles her round chipmunk face and her bifocal eyeglasses sit on the tip of her pudgy nose. The glasses magnify her big green eyes giving her the appearance of an over-sized jay bird. When she eyes Rachel, she wobbles over to her, with the key ring on her belt jingling like a loud Christmas chorus.

"Good Morning," she grins. "I am Beth Jones, the social worker supervisor here. You must be Rachel Thomas?!"

"Yes, I am," Rachel said smiling and taking the supervisor's hand. They shake hands but Rachel's hand is wet with perspiration. However, Beth didn't seem to notice. "Glad to meet you," Beth said. "Follow me." The supervisor wobbles across the lobby with Rachel keeping one step behind her. The keys on her belt jiggling loud like a pair of cow bells. The supervisor soon stops in front of a gray heavy steel door and snatches her key ring off her belt. She flips through the keys as if dealing a deck of cards until she finds one for the door. She jams the key into the lock and turns it, the door clicks open. Beth leans into the door, pushing it wide open, as she steps on the unit. Rachel, close on her heels, follows her inside.

The heavy steel door slams hard and its weight rattles the walls like a huge earthquake. The hall, foggy with thick grey smoke, has huddles of patients puffing on cigarettes. Each one taking turns blowing puffs of grey smoke into the stuffy atmosphere. Rachel holds her breath, keeping her mouth very tight. Determined not to take a whiff of the stifling air.

Within minutes, they are there and Rachel breathes deep filling her lungs with air. She coughs and notices a black sign etched in white ink hanging high above Beth's door. The sign with a warning "Enter at Your Own Risk." Beth unlocks the door and pushes it quietly aside as if unveiling something scary. She goes inside and gestures for Rachel to follow her. When Rachel steps inside, her dark brown eyes grow big like saucers and she covers her mouth. "A pack rat lives here," she muses.

Books, papers, card board boxes and charts are stacked high on one side of the supervisor's desk. A variety of stuffed animals are scattered on the floor. A deer head, anchored on the wall behind the desk, has white panties and grey socks hanging off one of its antlers. A stench of rotten eggs mixed with stale cigarette smoke reeks throughout the room and Rachel gags.

Beth lights up a Newport cigarette ignoring Rachel's retching. Instead, she beckons for her to take a seat. Rachel, feeling faint, grabs the nearest chair and collapses in it. As soon as her behind hits the wood seat, she hops right up. Cracker crumbs pierce through her clothing, stinging her bottom. "Oh my," she said wiping the crumbs off. She sits back down, her bottom still stinging from the prickly crumbs. Beth, settled behind her desk, opens her drawer and pulls out a snicker's candy bar. She snuffs out her cigarette in a nearby ashtray and bites into the candy bar, tearing off the wrapping.

She then consumes every inch of the candy in a matter of seconds, as her fat cheeks bulge outward like a big hungry chipmunk. Rachel stares at Beth, her eyes wide with fear and braces herself. The supervisor licks her lips and then peers over her bifocals. Her gaze serious and intense. For a moment, she studies the startled social worker with fierce scrutiny and without hesitation she begins the interview.

"Honey, why do you want to work here," she said her voice sharp. Rachel clears her throat, her forehead covered with little beads of sweat. "Humph...... I am very interested in the mental health field," she said. "I think this hospital will be a good place to work." "You don't say," Beth said folding her arms and leaning forward. Her big green eyes peering through her bifocals, checking out every little detail on her potential employee. "Tell me why you think so."

Rachel tells her story while Beth listens and stares at her with fierce intensity. Rachel's heart thumps hard in her chest, but she presses on. Telling Beth about her work at the nursing home and the social work classes she took in college in preparation for the position. Beth rolls her eyes and squirms in her seat and then she pops up like a jack in a box. "Honey, this is no nursing home," she said. "These folks are off their rockers! Are you willing to work with a bunch of crazy ass folks?" Rachel flinches, as every muscle in her body twitches and she wants to leave. However, she stays put, too scared to move. For a moment, she's at a loss for words. Baffled by what to say. Beth cocks her head to the side like a big jay bird.

"Honey, does the cat have your tongue?" she asked, glaring at her with those big green eyes. "Honey, answer my question!" Rachel, her face fiery hot, fidgets in her seat. "I am so sorry! Yes ma'am, absolutely," she said.

Beth claps and grins, swaying from side to side like an excited fan at a football game. Rachel cringes and braces herself. The woman's demeanor is so off it scares her. When the supervisor finally stops clapping and settles in her seat, Rachel is grateful. Beth grabs Rachel's application and reads it. She studies it as if reading a mystery novel and then after a few minutes, although it seems like hours to Rachel, she pops out of her seat again, with a euphoric mood.

"The salary is forty-five thousand dollars a year," she said. "Do you accept this salary, honey?!"

"Yes ma'am," Rachel said, her insides burning like fire. Wishing the woman would stop calling her honey.

"Very well then, you can start Monday morning, March twentieth at eight," Beth said. "You will be assigned to the admissions unit with Doctor Louis."

"Great," Rachel said, relieved the crazy interview is finally over. She slides out of her chair and struts to the door. "I look forward to working with you and Doctor Louis." Beth gives her a sardonic smile and joins her at the door. She swings the door wide open and Rachel steps out into the smoky hallway again. Beth follows her. When they both reach the exit, Beth unlocks the heavy steel door and shoves it open. "See you in two weeks," Beth said. "Okay," Rachel said. She struts pass her and steps out into the lobby, taking in the fresh air. Beth releases the heavy steel door and it slams shut, rattling the walls like an explosive earthquake and leaving Rachel alone in the lobby.

She exhales and shakes her head, glad to be away from Beth and her nasty office. She struts across the lobby to the hospital exit only to stop dead in her tracks when she hears someone yelling in the reception area. A hippie-looking, middle-aged man is cursing and pounding his fist on the counter, with his face red and bloated like a big balloon. He looks scraggy with his long blond matted hair hanging off his shoulders. He has a prickly beard and mustache decorating his bull dog face. On the tip of his nose sits a thin pair of round, gold wired framed glasses that magnify his fiery gaze. The sleeves to his wrinkled white shirt are rolled up to his elbows and his beige pants are four inches above his outdated black loafers. A devout fan of no socks, his ankles are bony and pale. His multi-colored necktie is twisted and hanging on his back and the man, puffed up like a blowfish, spews obscenities at a frightened Joyce. She breaks down and cries.

"Hell, what's wrong with you, woman," he said shaking his thick fist at her. "Stop that crying," he said. "Hiram needs his damn report!" Within an instance, the man punches each wig head, one by one against the wall like a bowling ball barely missing Joyce, who ducks for cover under her desk just in a nick of time. Rachel makes a mad dash to the hospital exit. Running so fast she slips, however she regains her balance and runs out the door. The man stomps each wig head into the floor and tiny pieces of foam fly in the air. Two security guards sprint over to the counter and wrestle him to the floor. They hold him down and he struggles to break free with no success. "Get off me you sons of bitches," he screams. "Get the hell off me!"

Meanwhile, safe outside, Rachel with her nerves rattled, walks in a brisk pace to her car. She wonders who the crazy man is and why he was so angry. In two weeks, she will find out. Her new job will prove to not only be an adventure, but a challenge to her very soul.

Chapter Three

Early Monday morning, fourteen days later, Rachel speeds up the hill in her Toyota to East Campus Hospital. A blanket of white mist hovers over the road hampering her vision. She switches her headlights to high beam as she navigates the road. With her new job on her mind, she wonders what her first day will be like. She recalls her crazy interview with Beth Jones and the disturbed man she saw cursing out the receptionist in the hospital lobby. The two incidents left her wondering if she made the right call in accepting the position. She decided, after some thought, their peculiar behavior were just mere coincidences.

She despises Monday mornings. Getting up early to be somewhere on time often irritates her nerves. However, this morning, she is hyped. Her stomach is in knots but she is thrilled to start a brand-new job as a clinical social worker. She speeds into the parking lot and parks, right in front of the barely visible East Campus Hospital. The fog so thick only the outline of the building can be seen.

She turns off the ignition and relaxes there for a minute, peering through the thick grey mist and trying to get her mind in gear for the day ahead. Although it is seven thirty in the morning, it's still quite dark outside, with the sun not rising until eight. A stable factor in the Great Northwest. Feeling warm, she checks herself in the mirror. Her forehead damp with perspiration is a sure sign her anxiety is getting the best of her.

She reaches in her handbag and pulls out a tissue. She dabs her face, taking deep breaths and being careful not to mess up her make-up. Within seconds, she calms down and her confidence returns. She opens the door and steps out of the car. The crisp air, feels cool against her face as she struts across the parking lot to the hospital building. Her high heels click hard on the dark pavement as she makes her way to the entrance. Once she arrives, she rings the buzzer but the sliding door doesn't budge. She grips the handle and tries to pry it open with no success. She presses her nose against the cold glass door and peers through the glass. Joyce, sitting at the reception desk with her back to the door, doesn't seem to notice she's there. She knocks hard on the glass but Joyce still doesn't look up. Rachel frowns and knocks harder but the receptionist continues to ignore her.

"The doors don't open until eight o'clock," said a booming raspy voice right behind her. "You need a key to get in after hours." Rachel flinches and then spins around to see who is speaking to her. She locks eyes with a tall slender man, chaining his ten-speed bicycle to a nearby rack.

"Excuse me," she said checking the man out from head to toe. She realizes right away he's the same man she saw riding his bike on the road two weeks ago. "You need a key to get into the building after hours," he repeats again.

"Oh," she said impressed by the man's fit and muscular build. His sparkling deep blue eyes are inviting and his well-groomed sliver gray beard and mustache complimented his blue sweat suit and wool hat.

"Good looking," she thought at first until he broke out into a chess cat grin showing two rows of badly stained teeth. "Are you here for an appointment?" he asks. She clears her throat. "Humph, I'm the new social worker for the admissions unit," she said. "This is my first day. My name is Rachel Thomas."

"Well it's nice to meet you young lady," the man said giving her a sheepish look. "I'm Doctor George Benny!"

"Nice to meet you too," she said looking off to the side, trying not to stare at his yellow teeth. He walks over to her after he secures his bicycle on the rack. "I heard you were coming," the doctor said still grinning like a chess cat. "We definitely need another social worker on the admission unit. Where are you heading?"

"To Beth Jones' office," Rachel said.

"Allow me to accompany you there," the doctor said.

"Why thank you," she said.

Doctor Benny unlocks the sliding glass door and steps into the building with Rachel following behind him. The psychiatrist waves at Joyce as he and Rachel pass the reception desk. Rachel doesn't wave, still sore the receptionist ignored her earlier. It's not long before they arrive at the admissions unit. He unlocks the heavy gray steel door and shoves it open, gesturing for Rachel to enter the unit ahead of him. She struts pass him, stepping onto the unit and he follows, allowing the door to slam behind him. Rachel follows the doctor down the hall to Beth's office and she coughs several times, bothered by the faint odor of stale cigarette smoke lingering in the air.

When they arrive at the supervisor's office, the door is slightly cracked and a trail of cigarette smoke escapes through the crack. Rachel coughs. Doctor Benny knocks on the door, but Beth doesn't acknowledge him. Beth, with her feet propped on the desk, is gobbling down a snicker's candy bar with her eyes tightly closed. Dressed in a lime colored low cut tent dress, granny boots and a matching hat pinned to the side of her head. She looks like a big leprechaun in a horror flick. She smacks and licks her lips savoring every morsel, unaware of the two-people standing at her door. The doctor knocks again and there is no response.

He beckons for Rachel to follow him, taking the liberty to enter Beth's office without asking for permission. Beth opens her eyes. She shoots Doctor Benny a dirty look and then directs her attention on Rachel. "Well, good morning dear," she said leaving Rachel wondering what the cross look was all about. Beth slides her feet off the desk and pops out of her seat. Still holding onto her empty candy wrapper, which she balls up and throws across the room like a basketball into a nearby trash can. She then plops down in her seat and puts her feet up.

Doctor Benny rolls his eyes. "Good Morning," he mutters.

"Good Morning, Beth," said Rachel with her eyes big and looking confused. "I see you came back," Beth teases. "Glad to see you again." "Yes ma'am, I am excited to be here," Rachel said smiling shyly. "Honey, take a seat," Beth said grinning like a chipmunk with a piece of chocolate embedded in two teeth. "Thank you," Rachel said.

She pulls off her coat and settles in a chair across from Beth, dropping her coat in her lap. Doctor Benny hovers by the doorway, leaning against the wall. Rachel, looking like a model in a fashion magazine, is wearing a red Liz Claiborne dress with matching two-inch pumps. For the first time since her arrival, she feels out of place. She is embarrassed by being overdressed compared to her new supervisor and Doctor Benny. "Tomorrow I dress a little more causal," she thinks to herself.

"Comfortable?" Beth asks.

"Yes, thank you," Rachel said. Beth then directs her attention to Doctor Benny, as her big green eyes flash different shades of green through her bifocals, with her fierce gaze.

"Have you heard from Susan Cole?" she asks with her tone blunt. "It's been two weeks since she disappeared from the unit!"

Doctor Benny scowls. "Miss Jones, don't start with me!" he said curling his lips and showing stained yellow teeth again. "I haven't seen or heard from that woman!"

"Uh, huh," Beth said clearing her throat and rolling her eyes. She looks him up and down again, sucking her teeth. "She didn't leave this unit by herself doctor," she said. "I believe she had some help!" "Hell, you are just speculating," he said now irked. "You don't know what the hell you are talking about!" Her green eyes narrow and she glares at him. "The ethics committee is looking into this....." she said trailing off. "The ethics committee can go to hell," Doctor Benny hisses back his face contorted and red. "How dare you speak to me like that!" she scolds him, bolting out of her seat with her hands on her hips. "Do you know how serious this is?!"

Doctor Benny's face turns to stone as he can feel the blood curdling in his veins. He steps inside the office and slams the door. Beth flinches, as he pounds on her desk. The sparkle in his deep blue eyes has disappeared, now replaced with a fiery, steely gaze. Rachel squirms in her seat with her eyes big like saucers.

"Get off my case!" he hisses gritting his yellow teeth. "I have no idea how that woman got off this unit," he said. "So you can tell the ethics committee to go to hell!"

Beth glares at him and he glares back with his face wolfish. He kicks her trash basket and swings the door wide open. The door hits the wall so hard that two screws pop out of the hinges. He storms out of Beth's office. Beth and Rachel stare at the doorway for a few seconds and then Beth reaches for her half-lit cigarette and begins to smoke, taking several drags.

"He's defensive this morning, don't you think?" she said with her voice soft, still staring at the doorway. "He's got something to do with Susan Cole's disappearance," she said nodding her head. "I just know it!" Rachel doesn't say a word, too afraid to move or breathe. She wonders why Beth suspects Doctor Benny in the first place and the volatile dynamics she just witnessed between the two of them scares her to death. She watches Beth chain smoke and flick ashes in and around the ash tray as she collects her thoughts. After a few minutes, the supervisor snuffs out her cigarette and peers over her bifocals with her gaze stern and penetrating. Rachel fidgets in her seat, her stomach in knots, bracing herself for the next explosion. It never comes. Rachel is relieved when the supervisor speaks in a soft tone. "Today, my dear, you are going to hang out with Jamie Lee," Beth said, her voice sweet. "She's assigned to that asshole Doctor Benny but she knows the rules around here and will show you the ropes!"

"Okay," said Rachel forcing a smile and stunned by Beth's choice of words. "This woman is not all there," she thinks to herself. She wonders if she can deal with Beth over the long haul. The thought of it boggles her mind.

"Are you with me?" asked Beth giving her the stink eye and interrupting her thoughts. "Yes ma'am, sorry," said Rachel, her face hot with embarrassment. "Then pay attention," said Beth. "First, I'm going to take you to your office so you can settle in."

"Okay," Rachel said.

"And then, I am going to take you to meet Jamie Lee," she adds. Beth slides out of her seat and wobbles to the door. She beckons for Rachel to follow her. "Let's go," she said opening the door.

"Okay," Rachel murmurs hopping out of her seat. She follows Beth into the hall.

The two social workers make their way down the hall passing oodles of black eyes staring back at them from a sea of thick, white smog. Rachel gags and coughs all the way to the smoke free dining room. She breathes deep, taking in the fresh air as she follows Beth across the room. They run into a thirty-something woman dressed in seventeen century clothing. The young woman curtsies and gives them a big sweet smile.

"Hi, I am Mary, Queen of Scots," the young woman said with her voice squeaky like a mouse. "Madam, what's your name?" Rachel coughs and clears her throat. She tightens her lips to stifle a laugh. "Rachel Thomas, your new social worker," she manages to say. "Pleased to meet you." The young woman breaks out in a grin. "Did you know honey bees hum in the key of "F?" she asked. "No," said Rachel.

"Well they do," the woman said curtseying three times.

"And did you know flies have x-ray vision?" the woman giggles.

"Ellen," Beth said her voice sweet. "Go back to the table and eat your breakfast before its gets cold."

"Sure," Ellen said. She shrugs her shoulders and hurries away, turning once to glance back at the two social workers. Beth leans in close into Rachel's ear, her breath smelling like a mixture of chocolate candy and stale cigarette smoke. Rachel backs up, overwhelmed with the odor. Beth, unfazed, ignores her.

"Ellen dresses like that when she's delusional," she whispers. "Last week she thought she was Marie Antoinette." Rachel chuckles. They watch Ellen struggle with her big puffy dress, knocking several breakfast trays on the floor as she tries to sit down at the dining room table. The two social workers bust out laughing as they continue their trek to Rachel's new office. On the way, they pass Doctor Louis' office and she wonders if he is there. Beth reading her mind offers an explanation. "Doctor Louis is out this morning," she explains. "You will meet him later this afternoon."

"Good," said Rachel feeling uncomfortable again. They walk further down the hall, passing two doors before they finally arrive at Rachel's assigned office and Beth gives her the key. She jams the key in the lock and it clicks opens. She flips on the light and steps inside. The half empty room has a large cherry wood desk with a matching swivel chair. In a nearby corner is a tattered frayed red love sofa. The office has no windows, a detail that surprises her. "I guess I will get used to this," she muses to herself. She flops into the swivel chair and spins around in a circle, looking dreamy and visualizing how she would decorate her new space.

A loud tapping interrupts her thoughts, jerking her back to reality. She swivels her chair around and faces the door. Beth glares at her from the doorway with both hands on her hips. She taps her boot on the floor in a synchronized rhythm. "Are you ready?" she asked, not waiting for an answer. She takes off, marching down the hall like a tin soldier as her lime tent dress swishes back and forth around her knees.

Rachel scrambles out of her seat and locks her handbag inside of her desk. She tosses her coat on the chair and hurries out the door. When she catches up with Beth two minutes later, she slows down and walks alongside her. She mimics the supervisor's soldier-like strut, as the two of them march in silence, all the way to Jamie Lee's office. Although the silence between them is deafening, Rachel welcomes it as her mind wanders. She uses the time to ponder what other surprises are coming her way. In a few minutes, she will soon find out.

Chapter Four

Jamie Lee, her head buried deep in the Seattle Times, sits at her desk with her feet up. Mornings, her favorite time of the day, allows her to reflect from the previous day's events. Dressed in black and wearing ringlets of silver bracelets on her wrists, Jamie is a plain looking woman with salt and peppered hair, styled in a jazzy, short pixie. Her light-brown eyes express a hint of sadness, a reflection of lifelong pain.

Married to a Jewish priest for eleven years with no children, she left him three years ago, after she fell in love with a psychologist named Anne Cleveland. A devout Catholic, Jamie felt guilty about her relationship with Anne, often praying to God and asking for forgiveness. Despite her intense guilt, she refused to give up her lover. Anne is the love of her life, her confidante, a person she couldn't live without. It's not long before Beth and Rachel darken her door way. Jamie drops her newspaper and flashes them a crooked grin.

"Good morning people," she said sliding her feet off the desk and rising from her seat. "Jamie, meet Rachel Thomas, our new social worker," Beth said wobbling over to the desk with Rachel right behind her. "Hi," said Jamie reaching for Rachel's hand. She squeezes her hand hard and Rachel grimaces. "Nice to meet you," she said. "You too," said Rachel, wincing with pain. "Show Miss Thomas the ropes," Beth said. "See to it she gets a picture ID." "We'll do," Jamie said rolling her eyes. "Is there anything else?" "No," said Beth. "Just show her how things are done around here."

"Okay," Jamie said. Beth wobbles out of her office, slamming the door behind her. Jamie makes a face. "That woman gets on my damn nerves," she mutters pointing to the sofa. "Have a seat." "Thank you," said Rachel. She struts over to the sofa and flops down making herself comfortable.

"Now tell me, what's your story?" Jamie asks leaning back in her seat with her hands clasped behind her head.

"Well, I worked for a nursing home part-time after graduating from school last June," Rachel said. "This is my first mental health job."

"Well, well," Jamie said cracking a smile, rocking back and forth. "You definitely will get some good work experience here."

"I hope so," Rachel said surveying her new colleague's office. Scrutinizing every detail and unimpressed with her decorating style. In every corner of the room, there were stacks of newspapers and the walls were white and barren. The place reeked of alcohol and soiled cat litter. Rachel sneezes and rubs her nose hard. She sneezes again.

"Are you alright?" Jamie asked.

"Yeah," Rachel said, with her eyes watery.

She rubs her nose again. "Has a cat been in this office?" she asked.

"Yeah, why?" asked Jamie.

"I'm allergic to cats," Rachel said. Jamie frowns. "That's too bad," she said. "The cat's my pet and he lives here."

"Oh," said Rachel sneezing again but with this sneeze harder than the first. Jamie hands her a box of tissue. "Thank you," said Rachel. She snatches a tissue out of the box and blows her nose.

"Tell me about Beth," she said sniffling, her face red. "How is she as a supervisor?"

"Bitchy and controlling," Jamie said leaning on her desk. "Slamming my door like that is her typical MO. She's so arrogant and rude!"

"How so?" Rachel asked, her curiosity now piqued.

"She likes things her way and she knows every damn thing," Jamie said tapping the desk with her pen. "It's rumored she tried to kill her ex-husband, a psychiatrist, after learning he had an affair with some young scrawny thing in his office."

"Oh, my goodness," said Rachel with her dark brown eyes big as grapefruits. "Yeah, girl, she spent two weeks on a psych unit nursing her wounded ego," Jamie said chuckling.

"Poor lady," Rachel said sniffling and shaking her head.

Jamie ramps up the gossip, thrilled to have a captive audience. "You know, she has a crush on Doctor Louis," she said with her voice low.

"Really?" asked Rachel, leaning forward.

"Yeah girl," Jamie said. "She wears low-cut tent dresses to seduce him, but he pays her no mind," She laughs. "He likes his pussy young. He's married to a woman twenty years his junior," she continued. Rachel gasps and covers her mouth. "Yep," Jamie said ignoring her colleague's reaction. "Doctor Louis likes his pussy young!" Rachel giggles, as she couldn't help herself. "So, what doctor are you assigned to?" she asked, changing the subject. "Doctor Benny," Jamie said. "Beth didn't tell you?" "No, she didn't," Rachel fibs. "What's he like?"

"Well, he's alright, but a bit eccentric," Jamie laughs. "He is passive-aggressive when he gets angry. Did you know one of his patients escaped from the unit two weeks ago?"

"Yes, I heard about the escape on the news," Rachel said looking attentive and interested in what Jamie needs to say on the subject. "I didn't know it was his patient."

"Yep, it is," Jamie said with a whisper. "Her name is Susan Cole. Her escape is proving to be quite a mystery."

"I'll say," Rachel sighs. "Do you have any idea how she escaped?"

"No ma'am," Jamie said shaking her head. "But I'll tell you this... It's rumored they are lovers and Doctor Benny may have helped her escape!"

"Oh my goodness," Rachel said looking intrigued. She now understands why Beth was so rude to the doctor earlier.

Jamie changes the subject. "So, I hear you're working with the Colonel," she said.

"The Colonel?" asked Rachel, raising an eyebrow and looking confused.

"Yeah, Doctor Louis," Jamie said raising her voice.

"Oh," Rachel said. "Why do you call him the Colonel?"

"Because he is," said Jamie. "He's a retired Army Colonel and he runs the admissions unit like a damn boot camp!" Rachel giggles. Then the door rattles off its hinges. "Who is banging on my door like that," Jamie said frowning. "Come in," she hollers. The door swings open and hits the wall with a bang. A disheveled looking man prances in, making an entrance with his long, scraggy, blond hair wild and unruly.

He is dressed in a dingy, white shirt with matching socks peeking out underneath high-watered beige pants. Rachel recognizes him right away and bolts from her seat. She high-tails it across the room and parks herself right behind Jamie Lee. Jamie turns and cuts her eyes at her, but doesn't say anything. Instead she faces the disheveled looking man in front of her and frowns.

"Dude, what is it?" Jamie asked.

"Hiram wants your list of patients for court tomorrow," he growls scratching his butt.

"What?" Jamie asked, with her face contorted.

"Hiram wants to see your list of patients," he demands again.

Jamie, seething, hands him the list. He scans it, wrinkling his brow. "Anything else?" she asked, with her gaze fierce. He holds up the piece of paper with his right index finger and thumb and stares at it. He then drops it as the paper floats in the air until it lands on Jamie's desk.

"The patients on this list are not Hiram's monkeys or his circus," he said flipping his unruly blond locks to one side.

Jamie bolts straight out of her seat. "Damn it, Hiram, stop acting like a nitwit and talking in third person," she said. "You are ridiculous with that! Where are your manners?! Do you see this new employee standing behind me? Introduce yourself!"

Rachel, her eyes big as saucers, locks eyes with Hiram. He gives her a big silly grin. "Hiram apologizes for being so rude, Miss...." "It's Rachel Thomas, sir," she said with her fingers gripped tight on Jamie's chair. "Well, hello Missy," he said. "My name is Hiram Gottschalks. I am the attorney for the poor souls locked up in this hell hole."

Rachel loses it and laughs out loud. She covers her mouth, embarrassed by her outburst. "You can't be serious," she mutters under her breath.

"What? Hiram didn't hear you," he said cocking his head to one side like a jay bird.

Rachel regroups. "Did you say you are an attorney?" she asked.

"Yes missy," he said frowning. "And what's it to you?!"

"Forgive me, I don't mean to offend you," Rachel said shrugging her shoulders while trying hard not to laugh again. "It's a pleasure to meet you Hiram."

"Humph," he said giving her the eye. He then focuses his attention on Jamie again and Rachel sighs with relief. He moves closer to Jamie's desk and pokes his chest out, cocking his head to one side.

"Please forgive me for my rude manners, sweet sugar tits," he said with a smirk. "But you, my little witch is as rude as they come!" Jamie lunges at him. "Get the hell out of my office you weasel of a troll," she said shaking her fist. "I had enough of your shenanigans. Get the hell out!"

"My, aren't we bitchy this morning?" he teases with a wicked gleam in his eye. He wrinkles his nose, sniffing the air like a dog as he backs away. "You smell like a pissy bottle of liquor! Have you been drinking again, Miss Lee?" he sneers. Jamie turns beet red and grabs her coffee cup. She throws it at him and he ducks. The cup sails over his head, hitting the wall with a thud. The cup breaks up in a million pieces all over the floor. "Volatile, aren't we?" he asked, laughing like a hyena and backing toward the door.

Jamie, red-faced, grabs another cup and goes after him.

Hiram bolts out the door, almost falling on his butt as he turns and skips down the hall in rapid speed. She dashes out the door after him and throws the cup straight in his direction, but she misses him again. The cup hits the floor breaking up in chunky pieces. Hiram zigzags down the hall like a jack rabbit, squealing with delight.

"I will kill you, you little shit if you come to my office again," she screams. "Do you hear me you little shit?! I will kill you!"

Hiram, still laughing, sprints down the hall to the exit and then he stops. He spins around and gives Jamie the finger and then he opens the door and runs out.

"You shitty little troll!" she screams breathing heavy. "You stay away from me!" She crouches over with her head between her thighs, taking deep breaths. A second later, she rises and trudges back to her office with her face etched in pain. When she arrives there, she slams the door so hard the room shakes, causing stacks of books to tumble off her desk onto the floor. She stumbles to her chair and falls in it looking very defeated. Rattled by Hiram's insults, she struggles to regain her composure.

"Are you okay?" asked Rachel looking worried.

Jamie doesn't respond. Instead, she stoops over and looks underneath her desk. She grabs her handbag and drops it in her lap. She unzips the bag and pulls out a bottle of Jack Daniels. She unscrews the cap and turns the bottle up to her lips. She sucks down the brown liquor in gulps, stopping once to take a breath and then she finishes off the bottle. "Ahhhhhh," she said wincing and wrinkling her nose. She screws the cap on the bottle and throws it in a nearby trash can. Stunned, Rachel's eyes are so big they run together. Not only is the attorney a maniac but her co-worker may be a full-blown alcoholic.

What kind of place is this? she wonders. Maybe she did make a mistake taking a job here, but it's too late now, she reasons. She's here for the long haul and she must make it work. She shakes her head and trudges over to the sofa and flops down.

She glances at her watch, only to discover time has remained stagnant. It's only eleven o'clock and she is already exhausted from the day's events. She sighs as she gathers her thoughts and wonders how two people as crazy as Hiram and Jamie could ever hold down a job.

"Are you alright sweetie?" asked Jamie, interrupting her thoughts with her eyes glassy.

"Huh, huh," Rachel sighs. "Just a little tired," she said.

"Would you like some coffee?" asked Jamie, leaving her seat to go over to the coffee pot.

"No Thank You," Rachel said. Jamie pours herself another cup of coffee. "What's the deal with Hiram?" Rachel asked. "He seems a little weird!" "He's more than a little weird," Jamie said sipping her coffee and rolling her eyes. She returns to her desk. "That weasel of a troll is out of his damn tree!"

"How so?" Rachel laughs agreeing with her.

"The man is a nut," Jamie said. "He always speaks in third person which really gets on my damn nerves!" "I noticed that," said Rachel. "Why does he do that?"

"Who knows?" asked Jamie. "Two weeks ago he went to a beauty supply store and bought a bunch of wig heads with hats and painted faces on them. He brings them to work and lines them up on top of the reception desk in the lobby."

Rachel giggles. "I saw those wig heads two weeks ago when I came for my interview," she said. "I wondered why they were there. What possessed him to do such a thing?"

"Crazy," she said. "He thought the lobby needed a little sprucing up." Jamie chuckles. "He threatened to sue Joyce if she tried to take them down."

"The first time I saw Hiram, he was having a hissy fit in the lobby," Rachel said recalling the incident. "He knocked the wig heads off the counter and stomped on them," she said. "He scared the holy shit out of me!" Jamie laughs. "I bet he did," she said. "The man is a knucklehead!" "How does he get away with being so crazy?" Rachel asks, very intrigued.

"Who knows? But he's smart despite his craziness," Jamie said.

"Really? How so?" Rachel asks.

"Well, he's a Harvard graduate and a damn good attorney," Jamie reveals. "He graduated at the top of his law class twenty years ago, so people around here tolerate him."

"Oh," said Rachel. "Why is he so dirty? He looks like a homeless person!"

Jamie howls. "The man has money, but he chooses to live like a pauper. Sleeping nights in an old garage of an auto shop down by the beach. He's definitely a piece of work," she said. "I'll say," said Rachel chuckling. "Well, I am hungry," Jamie announces getting up from her seat. "Let's break for lunch and then I will take you to personnel to get your picture ID." "Okay, see you then," Rachel said welcoming the needed break. She hops off the sofa and leaves Jamie's office.

She rehearses the morning's events in her mind as she struts back to her new office. She is amused by the craziness of it all. Once alone in her office, Rachel shuts the door and locks it. Feeling safer, she settles in at her desk and grabs her lunch bag out the drawer. She tears it open and pulls out her peanut butter and jelly sandwich. "Damn, what a morning! This place is too weird," she mutters scooting down in her seat. She then gobbles down her sandwich.

Chapter Five

Later in the afternoon, around one-thirty, Jamie and Rachel head down to personnel. Neither one speaking to the other as they are too enamored with their own thoughts. Rachel flinches when a man's voice booms out of a loud speaker. His abrasive tone jerking her back to reality. "Unit one needs butt control, Unit one needs butt control," he said with his voice vibrating from one end of the hall to the other.

Rachel becomes tickled and snickers to herself. She looks over at Jamie and she maintains a straight face. She contemplates on whether to inquire about the announcement while all the time wondering what this "Butt Control" issue is all about. With her curiosity getting the best of her, she takes a risk and broaches the subject.

"What's this Butt Control?" she asks.

"It's a committee responsible for sweeping cigarette butts off the floor," Jamie finally said cracking a smile.

"Huh?" Rachel asked, surprised by the answer.

"Yeah girl," Jamie chuckles. "Every day the patients throw their cigarette butts on the floor after finishing their smoke breaks," she said. "The charge nurse has to clean up the mess."

"Oh," said Rachel shaking her head.

Jamie continues. "The charge nurse got so tired of cleaning up the mess, he recruited a group of patients and named them the Butt Control Committee," she said. Rachel cracks up laughing. "That's the most ridiculous thing I ever heard," she said. "Well it's the truth," Jamie said.

Soon they arrived at personnel and Jamie bangs her fist on the opened door. "Hey Tran," she yells. "There's somebody I want you to meet." An Asian man with dark round beady eyes peers over the counter. He stands upright. His towering, long and skinny frame is over six feet tall. He nods, beckoning for the women to enter his office. "Ladies, what can I do for you today?" he said with his accent choppy and his dark eyes narrow.

"This is Rachel Thomas, our new social worker," Jamie said throwing her arm around Rachel's shoulders. "She needs a picture ID."

"Okay, okay, okay, stand over there," Tran said pointing to an orange painted wall behind the counter.

Rachel follows his directive and saunters behind the counter. She fixes her hair and leans against the wall flashing Tran a cheesy grin. While Tran fiddles with his camera, a huge ball of black fur leaps over the counter and Rachel screams like a hyena.

"What was that?" she said with her eyes wild, as a rush of adrenalin rips through every nerve in her body. She hops up and down. Jamie scoops the feline intruder into her arms and Rachel screams with her eyes filled with tears. Jamie and Tran burst out laughing. The cat, big like a bobcat, purrs when Jamie caresses him. Her short fingers buried deep into his thick, long fur. The cat's yellow eyes gaze up at her, studying her face and then he buries his massive head deep into her breast. Rachel wipes a tear off her cheek, hot with embarrassment. "This is not funny," she said sniffling. "He's not going to hurt you," Jamie reassures her, still giggling. "His name is Peepers, he's the resident kitty." "The resident kitty my foot," Rachel said, with her voice trembling. "That cat is huge! It needs to be in somebody's zoo!"

"I know," Jamie laughs. "His size can be quite intimidating."

"What type of cat is that?" Rachel shrieks, keeping her distance.

"It's a Russian Siberian cat," Jamie explains. "These cats are usually bigger than the average domestic cat."

"Just keep him away from me," Rachel said. "He's too big for my taste!"

Jamie puts the cat down on the counter. The cat hunches on his hind legs and licks his long thick black fur. His piercing yellow eyes stare straight through Rachel and she stares back hypnotized by his mysterious gaze. Wondering what secrets the cat may be harboring behind those big yellow piercing eyes. Tran snaps his fingers interrupting her thoughts.

"Miss, Miss, Miss, you ready to take the picture?" he asked in a choppy Chinese dialect.

"Yes, I'm ready," she said getting herself together.

"Okay, okay, okay, stand over there," he said pointing to the orange wall again.

She stands in front of the wall and Tran situates the camera. She poses giving him an instant smile and then he snaps the picture. Minutes later, her picture ID is pinned to her dress and she and Jamie leave Tran's office waving good-bye. On the way to Beth's office, Rachel searches for the exotic cat, but much to her surprise, the big cat is nowhere to be found.

"Girl, you got a creepy cat," Rachel said. "He scares the hell out me!"

Jamie laughs. "You'll get use to him," she said. "Everybody does eventually." "How was your day ladies?" Beth asked, as the two social workers darken her doorway.

"Fine," Rachel lies. Jamie, grinning foolishly, chooses not to answer. Beth, not missing a beat, tears into Jamie.

"What are you up to?" she asks her with a fierce look.

"Why do I have to be up to something?" Jamie asked, rolling her eyes. "You are so paranoid."

"Humph," said Beth clearing her throat. She decides to ignore Jamie turning her attention to Rachel instead.

"Doctor Louis called out sick for the rest of the day," she said. "He will be here tomorrow."

"Okay," said Rachel looking disappointed.

"If you like, you can leave early," Beth said. "I don't have anything else planned for you today."

"Thanks," said Rachel, very relieved to hear this. She thanks Jamie for the interesting day and then she heads to her office, walking with a brisk pace. When she finally arrives there, she unlocks the door, grabs her coat and handbag and then she steps out into the hall again locking the door behind her.

She hurries to her car and wonders if she can work in such a crazy, unusual place but she quickly dismisses her doubts, deciding she's up for the challenge. Safe in her car, she turns on the ignition and speeds out of the parking lot. She thinks about her day again and something Beth said crosses her mind. She laughs out loud. "Beth," she said shaking her head. "You are absolutely right. The people here at Salter's Point Regional are off their rockers alright, but they are not the patients. Not even close."

Chapter Six

Six weeks later, it's April and Salter's Point is drenched with bruising heavy rain. The wet weather continues for days on end and the town's residents hibernate only venturing out when they need too. By the end of the month, the rain decimates and the town is alive again with its little league soccer games, bustling restaurants and late night thumping jazz clubs. On a clear sunny day, no matter where you are, Mount Rainer, a snow-capped fourteen-thousand-foot rock of wonder can be seen for miles and miles. The drier weather also brings out the budding of the town's oak trees and soon a sweet fragrance fills the air. It's not long before spring fizzles out and summer rolls in. A welcomed diversion to a long wet season.

Rachel, now settled in her new job, loves the unpredictable nature of it. Never knowing what her day will bring. One thing she's certain for sure. There is no job as challenging and bizarre as this one and coming to work every day in this crazy environment has proven to be quite an adventure.

Although, she was initially assigned to Doctor Louis' team, he has not been around due to a health scare that almost sent him to glory land. Rumor has it the poor doctor suffered a heart attack while having rigorous sex with his young wife, Sierra one evening. For the past several weeks, she has been home nursing him back to health. Two more months will pass before Rachel will meet the infamous doctor.

To cover the doctor's absence, Doctor Beebe, the hospital's medical chief, convinces Doctor Benny to oversee the admissions unit. Beth assigns Rachel to his team while Jamie serves as back-up. It's not long before the three of them become a formidable, cohesive team. As time passes, Rachel and Jamie become tight friends. Every morning at eight-thirty, they meet for coffee while taking turns using each other's offices. They chat up the latest gossip and talk about their patients. Rachel, still green under the collar, admires Jamie's assessment skills and quick wit. Rachel, being a quick study, soon adopts Jamie's clinical talents. Despite her admiration for Jamie, she worries about her excessive drinking. Particularly when she has a fight with Anne.

When she and Anne are on the outs, Jamie's drinking escalates. She comes to work reeking of alcohol, hiding in her office with the door closed and refusing to speak with anyone including her assigned patients. Her volatile relationship with Anne makes her ornery, of course, causing her to lash out at colleagues and wallow in self-pity. When feeling up to a good fight, Rachel sometimes confronts her, hoping to chastise her into seeking help. However, her efforts never work. Instead Jamie just blows her off, insisting she has everything under control. On good days, she and Jamie work well together, often taking turns sitting in on Doctor Benny's counseling sessions and giving their professional opinions and advice. They take turns investigating and gathering information on new admissions, documenting their findings in the medical record and preparing documents for court hearings.

Doctor Benny, appreciative of their expertise, depends on them. Often asking them to accompany him to court to assist him with the testimony. It's not long before they develop a reputation, hospital wide, as competent, experienced social workers.

"What's the matter with you?" asked Rachel one morning, while she and Jamie wait in the conference room for report to start. Jamie sobs with her eyes red and puffy.

"I think Anne is seeing someone," she whines laying her head on the table. "Really? How do you know?" asked Rachel looking surprised. "She came home at six o'clock this morning," she said sniffling. "We had a huge argument and she threatened to leave me. She thinks I am too possessive!"

She bawls. Her shoulders heave up and down in a jerky like rhythm. Rachel slides out of her seat and goes over to her. A faint scent of alcohol hovers over Jamie and Rachel wrinkles her nose. She ignores the smell and gives Jamie a tight hug.

"Listen," Rachel said, with her voice soft. "Maybe you should give Anne some space for a couple days," she said. "Then when you are less emotional and a little calmer, bring up the issue again."

"Okay," Jamie sniffles. "Do you think God is punishing me?"

"What do you mean?" Rachel asked.

"A lot of people would say I'm committing a sin by having a relationship with a woman," she said sobbing.

"I wouldn't worry about what other people think," Rachel said. "But I do think your relationship with Anne causes you a lot of grief and that, my friend is not healthy," she said.

"Yeah, you are right," Jamie said.

"I just think you spend too much time fighting with her," said Rachel.

"You need to evaluate whether you want to continue this relationship. After all, do you really want to be with someone who cheats?"

"No, I guess not," said Jamie wiping tears off her cheeks.

She pokes out her bottom lip and gazes into Rachel's face, with her dark brown eyes sad like a puppy. "But I love her," she said wiping snot from her nostrils.

"I know," Rachel said. "But it's not fun living with someone you can't trust. Being unhappy all of the time and working every day in this crazy ass place can be a little too much."

"Yeah, I guess," Jamie sighs, letting out a small giggle. She struggles to stand.

"Are you alright?" Rachel asked, very concerned.

"I'm okay. Just woozy," Jamie said. "I need to get myself together before the nurses come in for report."

"Yep, you sure do," Rachel said. "They will be here in ten minutes."

Jamie trudges out of the room and heads straight to the bathroom. It's not long before the nurses meander in one by one, taking seats at the conference table. Sally Roberts, the head nurse, struts in like a peacock and grabs a seat at the end of the table. An attractive woman, in her early forties, she's tall and plumb with long auburn red hair pulled high into a thick pony tail. She's dressed in a bright red over-sized blouse with slacks and shoes to match. A vain woman, Sally struts around the hospital like she owns it. Showing off the latest threads and diamond rings her retired general husband has given her.

Despite her occasional bragging and pompous demeanor, Sally is witty, forthright and quite the compassionate nurse.

"Good Morning, my people," she said, with her demeanor playful. "There are some interesting characters to discuss in today's report. Needless to say, the moon was full last night!"

"What do you have?" asked Jamie, prancing into the room looking chipper, with no signs of being previously upset. Rachel wonders if she had a drink while holed up in the bathroom.

"Well, let's see," Sally begins. "Last night, a business man was admitted for dropping his office equipment out of a five-story window. After he did that, he went to his bank and withdrew thousands of dollars and then he gave the money away to people on the street." "Now where was I when he was doing that?" a male nurse teases. "I could have used that money to get my freak on at the strip joint!"

The nurse howls, tickled by his own joke, while his female colleagues give him dirty looks and rolled their eyes. Rachel and Jamie laugh out loud and shake their heads while Sally, looking disgusted, doesn't crack one smile. She ignores the comment and carries on.

"Two schizophrenic men in their early twenties were also admitted last night," she continues. "One thought he was Jesus and almost drowned in the Puget Sound trying to walk on water and the other man complained of hearing female voices telling him to flip every five minutes." "I know he's tired as hell," Rachel said grinning from ear-to-ear. Everyone cracks up laughing, shaking their heads while Sally gives her the stink eye. Rachel scoots down in her seat and twiddles her thumbs while Sally continues with her report.

"Then finally, we have a high school teacher in her early thirties claiming to have multiple personalities," she said. "How many personalities does she have?" one nurse asks with great interest.

"Three." Sally volunteers. "Her family reports she often reverts into three personalities. A four-year old little girl, a professor and a prostitute."

"Now that's a damn combination," Jamie said chuckling.

"Yeah," said Rachel. "The chick is definitely messed up!"

Everyone cracks up. "So what personality is she this morning?" another nurse asks.

"It's my understanding the little lady is dressed like a prostitute today," Sally said. "The principal called the police after receiving reports of her seducing some of her male teenage students during class."

"Now this chick is a trip," Jamie said with a wicked grin on her face. "I bet her interview will be a blast."

Sally cuts her eyes at Jamie. "Ladies, get serious. We need to make sure our ducks are in order before we take these patients to court," she warns. "Hiram will fight us all the way. He doesn't think patients should be committed against their will."

"Oh, please," said Rachel laughing out loud. "Hiram is a nut himself! He should be committed!"

Loud laughter erupts around the room. "You definitely got a point," Sally said finally cracking a smile. "But he's all we got, so we must deal with him and his crazy antics," she said.

"Ugh," Jamie said. "He makes me ill!"

"He's funny to me," Rachel said.

"You would say that," Jamie said rolling her eyes.

Sally rises to her feet. "That's all I have this morning people," she said. "Everyone enjoy your day here at the nut house! This meeting is adjourned!"

Sally heads to the door and several nurses get up and follow her, marching one by one out of the conference room. Soon Rachel and Jamie are alone in the room again. They sit, not talking for a few moments. Both enamored with their thoughts and then Jamie disrupts the deafening silence.

"I am so behind in my paperwork," she said. "Can you handle the interviews with Doctor Benny this morning so I can catch up?"

"Sure," said Rachel taking a deep breath, knowing full well Jamie is lying. "I'll cover for you."

Jamie feels guilty. "Look, let's get lunch, my treat," she said. "Do you want to meet about 12 noon today?"

"Okay, cool," Rachel said sliding out of her seat and heading to the door. "I'll see you at twelve." "Cool Beans," Jamie said. "See you then."

Chapter Seven

Rachel fumes. "How dare she put her work off on me!" she said with her fist clenched as she makes her way down the hall. She turns the corner and heads to Doctor Benny's office.

"I bet she's half lit and brooding about Anne," she said frowning. "It's time to have a chat with that chick about rehab" she mumbles. "Maybe I can get Sally to help me talk her into it."

She sighs deeply and shakes her head. Finally, she reaches Doctor Benny's office and knocks on the door. When she doesn't hear an immediate response, she opens the door and steps inside.

"Good Morning, Doctor Benny," she said closing the door.

The doctor, buried deep in paperwork, is hunkered down at his desk dictating notes into a tape recorder. He glances up at her and breaks into a huge grin.

"What's up Miss Thomas?" he asked clicking off his tape recorder. "I am helping you with the interviews this morning," she said snatching a stress ball off his desk. She squeezes it tight, her face twisted in exaggerated anguish.

Doctor Benny chuckles. "Stressed, aren't we?" he asked. Rachel forces a half smile and squeezes the ball even tighter. The doctor zeros in on her frustration. "Is something wrong?" he asks.

"Jamie and Anne are on the outs again," she blurts out. "She's back in her office, drowning in her sorrows and she had the nerve to ask me to cover for her." "Don't be out of sorts," he said peering over his eyeglasses. "You know Jamie is self-absorbed and a problem drinker!"

"Yeah, but….." "But what?" he asked.

"She's in denial," Rachel said looking bleak, shrugging her shoulders. "She doesn't think she's an alcoholic."

Doctor Benny nods in agreement. "That's typical," he said. "Her drinking will be the death of her one day. Mark my words."

"Oh I hope not," Rachel snaps back, frowning. "She'll come to her senses one day," she said. "I have faith in her."

"Somebody needs to," he said. His face dark, not sold on the idea. He sighs, feeling bad for Rachel. He admires her loyalty to Jamie, but he knows she is wasting her time. He keeps the peace and changes the subject.

"Let's get down to business," he said. "I have reviewed the records on the new admissions and these patients are pretty sick. They need to be committed."

"Okay, which one do you want to see first?" Rachel asks, still squeezing the stress ball.

"How about Lola, alias Mary Peters," he suggests. "She claims to have multiple personalities. She sounds pretty interesting."

"Okay," said Rachel dropping the stress ball in a tray on the doctor's desk. "I'll bring her to your office."

"Great," Doctor Benny said. Rachel heads to the door and walks out leaving the door wide open.

On her way to the patient lounge, a man flipping cart wheels down the hall knocks her against the wall. She shrieks. "Good gracious," she said regaining her balance. The man cart wheels down the hall in a rapid succession until he disappears around the corner. Rachel hugs the wall and catches her breath.

A wave of guilt creeps in her psychic when she recalls the comment she made earlier in report about the man's predicament. She drops her head and trudges down the hall.

When she reaches the patient lounge, she eyes Lola perched on the sofa. She is sucking on a lollipop, her mood somber. Dressed in a low-cut pink blouse, she's wearing a black leather mini skirt and fish net stockings, with matching black stiletto heels. Her dark brown hair is teased wild all over her head and her bright red lipstick and heavy made up dark brown eyes adds drama to her style. She stands when Rachel approaches her.

"Good Morning," Rachel said checking her out.

"Good Morning sweet cakes," Lola said, her tone low and wispy while twirling a lollipop between two fingers. Rachel's face turns to stone.

"The name is Rachel Thomas, not sweet cakes," she said with her voice terse. "I am your social worker today. Doctor Benny and I want to talk to you."

"Sure, R-a-c-h-e-l," Lola said enunciating each syllable in her name.

Rachel rolls her eyes and beckons for Lola to follow her. Lola struts and sways her hips, keeping two steps behind Rachel. Stopping one time to blow a kiss at a group of male patients huddled in a corner. The men whistle and holler as they watch Lola sashay by. Rachel scowls. "Don't tease them like that," she warns. "It sends mixed messages." Lola grins wickedly. "Okay, sweet cakes," she said slurping on her lollipop. "I'll keep that in mind." "Good," Rachel said giving her the eye.

When they finally reached Doctor Benny's office, Rachel opens the door and allows Lola to enter ahead of her. She sashays pass the social worker and flops down on the sofa crossing her shapely legs. She licks her lollipop and plays with her hair wrapping a few strands around her index finger. Rachel shuts the door and pulls up a chair. Doctor Benny leaves his desk and takes a chair across from the two women and then he leans back and crosses his long legs.

"Good Morning Miss Peters," he said. "My name is Doctor Benny."

"Hello handsome," Lola said winking at the doctor. She uncrosses her legs and spreads them wide, exposing her crotch and then she crosses them again. Doctor Benny fidgets in his seat trying to fight off the warm sensation in his crotch. He uncrosses his legs and leans forward giving her direct eye contact. Rachel, very quiet, keeps her eyes fixated on Lola.

"Lola," he said with his voice shaky. "Tell me why you are here today?"

"Are you a trick?" Lola asks ignoring his question.

"No ma'am, I'm not," he said with his voice calm.

She uncrosses her legs and rolls her skirt up to mid-thigh. Beads of water break out on Doctor Benny's forehead and the bulge growing in his crotch threatens to forsake him. He panics and snatches a book off his desk and lays it over his crotch. Rachel shoots him a quizzical look. "What the hell is wrong with him?" she ponders. She keeps one eye on him and the other on Lola. "Feeling hot doctor?" Lola asked, with a sultry smile on her face. He ignores her question, focusing on his question instead. "Do you know why you're here, Miss Peters?" he asks again.

"Huh, huh," she whispers.

"Tell me," said Doctor Benny with one hand pressing down on the book.

"This trick arrested me for messing around with the younger tricks," she said swinging one leg. "He's nothing but an old jealous geezer!"

"A geezer? Who are you talking about?" Doctor Benny asks looking amused, despite the annoyance growing in his pants.

"The principal," Lola said twirling her lollipop around in two fingers. She puckers up her lips and winks at the doctor again. "I told you he's jealous of the younger tricks," she said. "What makes him think I want his ugly butt?! I prefer a good-looking trick like you!"

"Lola, do you realize the tricks you are referring to are teenage boys? Minors per the law," Doctor Benny said still leaning forward in his chair and pressing down on the book.

"You don't say," she whispers recalling the incident. "No wonder the old fart was so upset."

"Miss Peters are you aware you can go to jail for having sex with minors?" the doctor inquires with perspiration rolling down his face. Rachel, quiet as a church mouse, studies the doctor's demeanor. "What is going on with this dude?" she wonders. She shakes her head.

Lola, realizing she's getting to the doctor, spreads her legs wide. She blows him a loud kiss. "You can partake of this any time," she said with her voice breathy. Doctor Benny's erection explodes and the book slides to the floor. Rachel's mouth drops open. Lola applies more pressure.

"Man, I can make you climax better than a good shit in the morning," she moans swinging her open legs back and forth.

"Now, now young lady that's not nice," Doctor Benny stutters showing two rows of big yellow teeth. "You are being very naughty!"

"Naughty indeed," she shoots back batting her eyes. "And you like it, don't you?" she squeals with excitement. Rachel cringes and cuts her eyes at Doctor Benny. She takes over the interview. "Lola, please close your legs and stop the nonsense," she said.

Lola rolls her eyes and closes her legs. Rachel talks fast. "Tell us about your altered ego, Mary Peters," she said re-directing her. "I would like to know more about Mary."

"Mary?" Lola said shrugging her shoulders. "What about her?"

"Tell me about her," Rachel said.

"The woman's a prude," Lola said.

"A prude?" Rachel asked. "What do you mean by that?"

"The bitch doesn't approve of my lifestyle," Lola said glowering. "She hates sex! She's boring as hell!"

"Where is Mary now," Rachel continues to press her.

"Who cares where she is?" Lola snaps back annoyed with the social worker's questions. "Why do you care?"

Rachel searches for an appropriate response, but she's at a loss for words. Lola laughs. "I guess the cat has got your tongue sweet cakes," she said mocking her. Rachel gives her a dirty look. Lola smiles and turns her attention to Doctor Benny. "Hey handsome," Lola said batting her eyes. "Why not kick your nosy side kick out of here so we can get it on," she said. You know you want too! I can tell!"

"Lola, I.......," the doctor trails off, fidgeting in his seat, his hard on now forming a tent in his pants.

Rachel bolts out of her seat. "What's wrong with you?" she said finally getting her zest back. "Are you out of your freaking mind? This interview is over!"

Doctor Benny turns three shades of red and loses his erection. He scoots down in his chair and lowers his head. Rachel gets in Lola's face. "I want you to close your legs right now," she said.

Lola's eyes water. She crosses her legs and begins to cry. Rachel grabs the tissue box off the desk and sticks it in her face. "Take one," she said. Lola snatches a tissue from the box and blows her nose so hard, sounding like a bull horn. Rachel rolls her eyes.

"Doctor Benny and I are taking you to court tomorrow morning," she informs her. "You need hospitalization."

"Why?" Lola whines sounding like a little girl.

"Apparently, you experienced some sort of trauma and you are having a hard time coping," she explains. "You need extensive therapy to help you get better."

"How long will I have to be here?" Lola sobs, tilting her head to one side. She twists a strand of hair around her index finger.

"At least two weeks," Rachel said. "Hiram Gottschalks will stop by your room to see you," she said. "He's an attorney and he will prepare you for court. Do you have any questions, before you go back to the unit?"

"Nooooo," Lola whines, wiping her eyes like a little girl.

"Then you can go," Rachel said opening the door. Lola doesn't budge. She just sits there wiping her eyes. Feeling upset and impulsive, Rachel fights to stay in control.

"If this little hussy doesn't leave this office, "she fumes pursing her lips. "I am going to throw her out."

She snaps her fingers. "Let's go Lola," she said pointing to the door. Lola rises and sashays to the door. She stops in the doorway and faces Rachel, her tears gone. With one hand on her hip, she grins, exposing straight white teeth. "Sweetie," she said her voice throaty. "You need to lighten up and stop being a tight ass! Get you something sweet to suck on!"

Rachel's blood curdles and she ushers Lola out into the hall. "We are done here Miss Peters," she said. "This conversation is over."

"Good bye handsome," Lola yells. "Don't forget about me," she said.

Rachel slams the door. She turns and faces Doctor Benny, her eyes narrowing. He stares into his lap trying to avoid her angry glare, but he can feel it blazing right through him. She blasts him.

"Doctor Benny," she said. "Your behavior was out of line and incomprehensible!"

"I'm sorry," he said looking over the rim of his glasses with watery eyes. "You are right. I allowed the situation to get out of control!"

"You are damn right," She said gritting her teeth. "You were flirtatious with a patient! What possessed you to behave like that?!"

"I don't know," he said. "I guess I got turned on!"

"Turned on?" she asked. "You can't be serious! You're the damn doctor for goodness sakes! You are not supposed to be turned on! What's wrong with you?! He folds his arms across his chest and pokes his bottom lip out like a little kid.

The two of them sit in silence, the room very quiet except for the clock ticking on the wall. After some minutes pass, he musters up courage and breaks the deafening silence. "Listen," he said, his voice low. "Let's not worry your pretty little head about this. There's no harm done and you will never see me do this again. I promise you."

Rachel huffs. "Don't placate me," she said. "Your behavior was out of line, just admit it!"

"I know, I'm sorry," he said. "Please don't tell anyone. It will never happen again, I promise."

She stares at him, her gaze fierce. He gets up and goes to his desk. "Look I promise this won't happen again," he repeats again. "Please don't let this get out. It will ruin me!"

"Okay, I'll keep your little secret for now," she lies, knowing full well she can't wait to tell Jamie the first chance she gets. "It's safe with me."

"Thank you," said Doctor Benny feeling relieved.

Rachel heads to the door. "I need a break," she informs him changing the subject. "Can we do these interviews later?"

"Sure," he said.

"I'll be back in forty-five minutes," she said.

"Take your time," he said welcoming the break. "I'll see you when you get back."

Rachel doesn't respond. She swings the door wide open and leaves his office slamming the door behind her. She heads to her office thinking about Lola's interview. A disturbing question crosses her mind. What if Beth is right about Doctor Benny's role in Susan Cole's disappearance?

His behavior with Lola is disconcerting to say the least, she reasons. "I need to check some things out," she surmises. "I need to talk to someone who knows this man well."

So, she bypasses her office and makes a quick detour to Jamie Lee's office instead. "It's time to get to the bottom of this," she said.

Chapter Eight

Rachel pounds on the door. "Open up Jamie," she said. "I have to talk to you."

"Is that Rachel?" asked Sally, sipping her cup of Starbucks coffee. "It sure sounds like it," Jamie said.

Rachel pounds on the door again. "Open this door right now," she said. "I can hear you! I know you're in there!"

"Just a minute," Jamie hollers sliding out of her chair. She hurries over to the door and swings it open.

"Girl, what's wrong with you?" she asked with her voice sharp. "Have you lost your marbles?!"

"Not quite but if I keep working here, I just might," she snaps back, shoving Jamie to the side as she struts into her office. "Close the door, I have something to tell you!"

Jamie closes the door. "What now?" she sighs, her face twisted. She walks back to her desk and sits down.

"It's about Doctor Benny," Rachel said talking very fast with her hands on both hips. "You guys are not going to believe it!"

"What happened?" Sally asked. "You look upset."

"I am," Rachel said. "I can't get over Doctor Benny! He's a straight up dog!"

Jamie rolls her eyes. "Stop talking in circles," she said. "And tell us what happened!"

"Okay," Rachel said glaring at Jamie. "You don't have to be so nasty!"

"Well you are frustrating the hell out of me," she said looking flustered. "Get on with it!"

"Calm down, ladies, calm down," Sally said waving her hand. She zeros in on Rachel. "Girl, tell us what happened."

Rachel's face darkens. "We interviewed Lola Peters this morning," she said almost whispering.

"Go on," said Sally. She scoots to the edge of her seat and leans forward.

"Doctor Benny flirted with the woman right in front of me," she said. "It was disgusting!"

"You don't say," Jamie said. She giggles while she and Sally exchange knowingly glances.

Rachel doesn't miss a beat. "What was that?" she said.

"What do you mean?" Sally asks.

"That look the two of you gave each other," Rachel said frowning. "Don't play with me!"

"Well I'm not one to spread gossip," Sally said. "But Doctor Benny has a reputation of being flirtatious with the women around here."

"Even with patients?" Rachel said bug-eyed, not believing her ears.

"Yeah," Sally said.

"Well I'll be damn," Rachel said shaking her head in disbelief.

"Let's not get off the subject," Jamie said folding her arms across her chest. "I want to hear what happened."

"Okay," Rachel said. "Lola Peters seduced Doctor Benny and he had a hard on, a big one at that," she said exaggerating a little. "He even told the woman she was naughty!"

Jamie cracks up laughing. "What a dog," she said. "What a dog!"

"This is not funny," Rachel said, her brow furrowing. "His behavior was unethical and you know it! You should be ashamed of yourself for laughing!"

"Now calm down dear," Sally said. "Jamie doesn't mean any harm. We believe you, but we think your reaction to the whole thing is a little hilarious."

"Why?" Rachel asked, folding her arms across her chest. She pokes out her bottom lip. "I fail to see the humor!"

"Lighten up girl," Jamie said. "This is not Doctor Benny's first rodeo at being inappropriate with a female patient."

"What do you mean?" Rachel asked, looking serious.

"I'm going to tell you something, but you have to promise not to tell anyone," Jamie said in a low voice.

"Okay, I promise," Rachel said flopping down on the sofa next to Sally.

"Doctor Benny has been married and divorced eight times," said Jamie.

"Get out here!" Rachel said.

"Yeah, Girl," Jamie said. "His last wife was one of his patients whom he met while living in Texas some years ago."

"You are lying," Rachel said shaking her head in disbelief.

"No, dear I'm not," Jamie said. "He started a sexual relationship with this woman while she was in therapy with him. Someone found out about it and reported him to the licensing board. After spending a month in jail, the judge dismissed the case." Rachel bolts off the sofa and puts her hands on her hips. "How in the hell did that happen?" she said. "Are you telling me this man got away with this crap?!"

"Yep, he sure did," Jamie said grinning.

"How?" said Rachel with a worried look on her face. "How did he get away with this?"

"His wife refused to testify against him," Sally said sighing. "You see, in Texas the law protects spouses who choose not to testify against each other."

"No way," she said. "Well he's one smart, slippery old dog!"

"I agree he's an old dog," Jamie said winking at Sally. "But a smart one, that's a stretch. He's just better at covering up his shit!"

Rachel howls. "Now that's a good one girl," she said slapping her thigh. "That's a good one!"

"Jamie, you are never at a loss for words," Sally said giggling and shaking her head.

"So who else knows about this?" Rachel asks.

"No one, except Anne," Jamie said.

"So, what happened to his crazy wife?" Rachel said flopping back down on the sofa.

"His wife skipped out on him," Jamie said. "She went to the bank and withdrew all of his money and he never heard from her again."

"Serves him right," Rachel said feeling a little better. "I'm glad she took his money! How do you know all of this stuff anyway?"

"Anne told me," Jamie said. "She was his partner in private practice."

"Get out here!" Rachel said.

"The plot thickens," Sally adds laughing out loud.

"So Anne's a psychiatrist to?" Rachel asks.

"No, she's a psychologist," Jamie said. "They were partners for five years."

"Very interesting," Rachel said.

They sit in silence. Thinking, thinking, thinking, the three of them in very deep thought. Jamie reaches for her newspaper and begins to read it.

"Since we are telling secrets," Rachel said finally breaking the silence. "I have something else to tell you guys."

"Aren't you full of news this morning," Jamie said dropping her newspaper on the desk. "What now?"

"Yeah share," Sally said moving her chair closer to the desk.

"On my first day here, Doctor Benny escorted me to Beth's office," she said recalling the incident. "Beth questioned him about Susan Cole's disappearance and he became very angry."

"Really?" Jamie said glancing at Sally again. "Go on."

"I didn't think much about it at the time," she said. "But now, I'm beginning to think there's something to Beth's actualization."

"I see where you're going with this," Jamie said cradling her chin in both hands. "Keep talking."

"Since I have witnessed Doctor Benny's behavior with Lola and have heard your story, I believe Beth may be right!"

"Maybe," Sally said nodding her head in agreement. "However, we don't know for sure. Doctor Beebe is investigating the situation. He hasn't come up with any conclusions yet."

"I know," Rachel said. "But should I tell him about Doctor Benny's behavior today? It might help him with his investigation."

"I think you need to tell someone but not him," Jamie said.

"What do you mean?" Rachel asked, frowning.

"You need to follow the chain of command and tell Beth first," she said.

"Yeah I suppose you are right, "Rachel said hesitating. "I hate this. I don't want to cause trouble for him."

"You have to tell her," Jamie insists. "You can't keep this a secret."

"I know," she said doleful looking. "Will you go with me?" she asks. "Beth really scares me. She's weird."

"Sure," Jamie said laughing. "I wouldn't leave you out to dry. We're a team!"

"You're a gem," Rachel said, with her smile broad and feeling relieved.

She takes a glimpse at her watch and realizes she has used up her break time. She hops off the sofa and runs to the door.

"Oops, I'm late," she announces. "The old dog himself is probably wondering what's happened to me. I got to go!"

"I'll call Joyce and make an appointment with Beth," said Jamie reaching for the phone.

"Great," Rachel said opening the door. "I'll talk to you guys later." She runs out and slams the door behind her.

Chapter Nine

When Rachel returns to Doctor Benny's office, she finds a note taped to the door. She snatches it off the door and reads it. She balls it up and jams it in her pocket and then takes off running. When she reaches the nursing station, she opens the gate and walks in.

"Good Afternoon," she said to the nurse sitting at the counter.

"Hello," said the nurse. Rachel pulls up a chair and plops down.

"Is Doctor Benny here?" she asked.

The nurse points across the room. "He's over there," she said.

Rachel cranes her neck to see over the counter. She finds him stooped down in front of a male patient engaging in conversation. She recognizes the patient. He's the one who knocked her against the wall doing cart wheels in the hall earlier. Now calm and content, he's perched in his seat with his legs folded underneath him, telling the doctor his life story. The urge to flip is no longer there, at least for the moment. His big brown puppy dog eyes look intense as he leans close in the doctor's face speaking to him in a soft whisper.

"Who's that patient with Doctor Benny?" Rachel asked.

"His name is Robbie Banks," the nurse said.

"Thanks," said Rachel.

She pulls Robbie's clinical record from the chart rack and reviews his admission sheet. She searches for a contact number, notices his mother's phone number on the bottom of the page and she calls her.

His mother gives her the run down on Robbie's psychiatric history and she learns Haldol is the drug of choice for relieving his predicament. Although Robbie's mother possesses a wealth of information, she was unable to say why he stopped taking the drug. Rachel dialogues with Robbie's mother for a few more minutes and then she ends the conversation hanging up the phone. She documents the telephone call in Robbie's clinical record while she waits on Doctor Benny.

Soon he wraps up the interview. He stands and makes his way to the nursing station. Robbie hops out of his chair and back flips across the room. Rachel hops up, her eyes big, shaking her head in a violent manner. "No, no, no," she said. "Look out! Oh my goodness!"

Robbie back flips pass a female patient, almost knocking her to the floor. She moves out of his way just in a nick of time. Rachel sighs with relief and sits back down.

"He needs to stay here," Doctor Benny said opening the gate to the nursing station. He saunters in, pulls up a chair and sits down. "He's hearing voices. I'm taking him to court."

"Yeah you need to," Rachel said. "He almost knocked that patient down in the dining room just a few seconds ago!"

"Yeah, I saw that," Doctor Benny said.

"So what do the voices tell him?" she asks.

"Well, he told me the voices only talk to him when he's standing up," he said. "They tell him to flip constantly. He says he's getting tired."

"I bet," Rachel said. "What else did he say?"

"He told me the voices are quiet when he is eating, sleeping or using the toilet," Doctor Benny said chuckling a little.

"Oh, come on," Rachel said laughing out loud.

"I'm just telling you what the man told me," Doctor Benny said flashing his yellow grin. "Did you reach his family?"

"Yes," Rachel said. "His mother reports he takes Haldol. The drug seems to work."

"I already have him on a low dose of the drug," Doctor Benny said. "Maybe he needs an increase. I'll send a new order to the pharmacy."

"Sounds like a plan," said Rachel, reaching for another record.

They settle in at the nursing station for the afternoon reviewing charts and making telephone calls. Suddenly, they hear a heated argument taking place in the dining room. They both stand to see what's going on.

"I don't want that pink pill," Harry said with his face beet red. "Pink is for girls! I'm not taking it!"

"Don't worry about the color Harry," Steve said trying to placate him. "The pill is good for you. It makes the voices go away."

"I don't care," he said. "I'm not taking it. It's poison!"

"It's not poison, Harry," Steve said.

"Yes, it is," said Harry his face red as a cherry. "You can't make me take it!"

"If you don't take it, the doctor must keep you here longer," Steve said.

"The hell he will," Harry said. "I'll take him out."

Harry shakes his wooden cane in the air. "He doesn't know who he's messing with!"

"Give me your cane sir," Steve said with his voice low.

"No," Harry said. "This is my cane!"

"Give me your cane before you hurt somebody with it," Steve said as he steps closer to the patient.

"No," said Harry. "Get your own damn cane!"

"If you don't give it to me, I will have to call security," Steve said as he beckons for Harry to hand him the cane.

Harry glares at Steve, his face puffed out like a blow fish. "You better stay away from me," he said. "I'm warning you!"

"Give me the cane Harry. Right now," Steve said with his face stern.

Within seconds, Harry whops Steve in the face. A deep red gnash splits open above his eyebrow. "Ouch!" Steve said touching his forehead. "Why did you do that?"

"I told you to stay away from me," Harry said. He hits Steve in the face again.

"Damn you," Steve hollers jumping back as blood trickles down his forehead. "Somebody call security!"

"Security? You're calling security on me?" Harry said. "No you're not!"

He beats the nurse down like a dog, hitting him in the head and then switching gears and beating him on the shoulders and arms. Within minutes, Steve jerks the cane out of Harry's hand causing him to fall backwards on the hard floor, landing on his butt.

"You son of bitch!" Harry hollers as he gets off the floor rubbing his butt. "Give me back my cane! It's not yours!"

Out of nowhere, a man with long blond hair, flies like superman while jumping over two dining room tables. Hiram Gottschalks lands on his feet right in front of Steve and sucker punches him in the nose, knocking him straight to the floor. He hops on top of the nurse and slaps him in the face.

"Get off me you big turkey!" Steve yells as he grabs a clump of Hiram's hair twisting strands in his fingers.

"You bully," Hiram yells back as he pries the nurse's fingers from his hair. "How dare you push these patients around," he growls, as a mist of water sprays out of his mouth. He pins the nurse's hands to the floor.

"Stop spitting on me, you son of a bitch!" Steve hollers. "Somebody, call security and get this asshole off me!"

Three husky looking male nurses come to Steve's rescue. They pull Hiram off the badly beaten nurse shoving him to the side. Hiram falls on the floor and rolls over like a dog. He hops back up while one nurse helps Steve off the floor. He wrestles himself free from the nurse and glares at Hiram balling up his fists.

"You want a fight?" Steve asked with his face twisted. "Then be a man and do it the right way," he growls.

"Alright," Hiram said flexing his muscles. "Let's duke then!"

Steve makes a run at Hiram and pushes him to the floor. Hiram slides on his butt and hops up. He sprints toward Steve, his head down like a defensive guard and collides into him, head first. He knocks him straight to the floor. He then hops on top of the nurse and beats him in the head with his fists. Three nurses fall on top of Hiram like football players and wrestle with him rolling from one end of the floor to the other. Steve breaks free from the human pile of sweaty bodies and limps to safety moaning and groaning, feeling every muscle in his body aching. Hiram and the nurses continue their fist fight knocking over tables, chairs and ash trays. Soon a circle of patients whooping and hollering surround Hiram and the nurses.

They clap and jump like a bunch of jack rabbits egging them on. "Fight! Fight! Fight!" they chant repeatedly.

Doctor Benny runs out of the nursing station and forces himself into the fight. In the mist of trying to break up the brawl, he gets punched and knocked to the floor.

"I'm so sorry," Hiram yells as he scrambles over to the doctor. "Are you alright? Hiram didn't mean to hit you!"

"No I'm not," Doctor Benny mutters. He sits up and his head spins. "You jerk!" he said grimacing and rubbing his jaw.

"I said I was sorry," Hiram said. A nurse runs over and jerks Hiram by the hair and drags him across the room. "I'm not finished with you yet," he sneers.

"Let go of me you jack ass!" Hiram said.

He pinches the nurse's hands so hard, the nurse releases the attorney, dropping him on the floor. He takes off running. Hiram flips on his stomach and hops up. He sprints after the nurse, overtaking him and then he body slams the nurse against the wall. "Ouch! That hurts," he said. "What are you trying to do, kill me?"

"That's what you get for pulling Hiram's hair, you jack ass," the attorney said as he backs away from the nurse, flexing his muscles.

"You are crazy," the nurse said gasping for breath. "You almost knocked the wind out of me!"

"Rachel, call security right now," Doctor Benny hollers still rubbing his jaw. He gets up and hobbles to the nursing station.

"I'm trying to. Nobody answers," Rachel said with her ear pinned to the telephone. A patient hops up on the counter, whooping and hollering at the top of his lungs.

"Get down from there!" Rachel screams wildly gesturing for him to get off the counter.

"No," he said. "I want to see the fight. I can see it better from up here!"

"Get down I said," Rachel demands.

The patient hops off and gives her the finger as he sprints across the room like a road runner while whooping and hollering like a hyena. Finally, a security guard answers the phone and Rachel tells him the situation. Within minutes, five men dressed in black fatigues bust through the unit's door. They run down the hall like a stampede of elephants to the patient dining area. One guard grabs Hiram and puts him in a head lock. Another guard hollers into a bull horn.

"Stop fighting and line up against the wall!" he said. The nurses stopped fighting and look at each other. They mutter amongst themselves as they follow the guard's directive. All five nurses line up against the wall like suspects. The patients clap and cheer while some stomp their feet. "Fight over!" they chant. "Fight over!"

"Go back to your rooms," one guard yells. "Someone get these patients back to their rooms... Now! We need to secure the area!"

Two nurses step up to the task and usher the patients to their rooms. "That was a hell of a fight," said one patient heading down the hall to his room. "Yep, it sure was," said another patient giggling her heart out. The guards release Hiram and Steve after they promise to calm down. A fiery red bump emerges on Steve's forehead just above the nasty red gnash on his brow. Hiram, his face red and a little bruised, walks over to the nurse and extends his hand. "Sorry man," he said. "I guess Hiram was a little over the top."

Steve takes Hiram's hand and shakes it. "Apology accepted," he said wincing with pain. "I need you to take me to emergency. My head is killing me!"

"No problem," said Hiram. "That's the least I can do."

"I want you to pay my bill too," he said giving the attorney a crooked grin.

"No problem," Hiram said grinning back.

The two men throw arms around each other and limp down the hall with Hiram rubbing his behind with the other hand. The two men exit the unit. By the time Doctor Benny hobbles back to the nursing station, he's groaning with pain. He pulls up a chair and sits down. He stretches out his long legs and kicks off one of his shoes. "My toe is killing me," he groans. "I think I hit it on one of those tables out there."

"You look terrible," Rachel said hopping out of her seat. "I'll get you something for that nasty shiner on your face," she said.

She goes to the medicine cabinet and returns with cotton balls and a bottle of peroxide. A sharp pain shoots along his jaw line and he grimaces. "I hope my jaw's not broken," he said.

"Let's hope not," Rachel said. She opens the bottle of peroxide and begins treating his wound. "Did this shit really happen?" she asked, looking glazed.

"Yep," Doctor Benny said wincing as Rachel dabs the cut with the peroxide. "This sure has been a hell of a morning," he sighs.

"Yep, you can say that again," Rachel said nodding her head in agreement.

Chapter Ten

The news of Steve and Hiram's infamous brawl spreads like wild fire throughout the hospital, overshadowing the mystery behind Susan Cole's disappearance. It's been two months since Susan disappeared and the hospital's top management still can't figure out how she escaped from a locked unit. Although her disappearance remains a mystery, nothing compares to what is happening right now. Work place violence is a disturbing reality at Salter's Point Regional.

Back on the admissions unit, hunkered down in Rachel's office, she and Doctor Benny were recovering from the morning's fiasco. They spend the afternoon interviewing and evaluating patients in preparation for court. They decide after much discussion to take both Robbie and Lola to court. Hiram, argumentative and confrontational, looks like a red balloon when he learns of their decision. When he fails to sway them his way, after presenting a convincing argument, he stomps out of Rachel's office and slams the door behind him.

Hiram's antics, they know too well. They accept his twisted outlook on life. Acutely aware he's mentally ill but their efforts to encourage him to seek treatment have proven to be a losing battle. So, they put up him and his crazy arguments. They humor him until he becomes so frustrated he pitches a fit and stomps off in a huff. After Hiram and Doctor Benny leave, Rachel picks up the phone and calls her partners in crime, Jamie and Sally.

Less than thirty minutes later, the women roll up in her office with their cups of Starbucks coffee. They fall on the sofa and get comfortable. They gossip about the latest events, including the recent infamous brawl in the hospital dining room. Rachel, excited and animated, acts out Hiram's fight moves while Sally and Jamie are doubled over in hysterics.

"Hiram came out of nowhere and sucker punches Steve right in the face," Rachel said imitating the attorney. "You would have thought he was some sort of superhero or something!"

"The man is a maniac," Jamie giggles. "He needs to be committed!"

"He's seriously ill alright," Sally said sipping her coffee. "He definitely can use some days in the hospital."

"Hell yeah!" Jamie said laughing out loud. "You definitely got that right."

Rachel cracks up. She leans back in her chair holding her stomach. "I wish you guys were there," she said howling. "You had to be there to believe it!"

They laugh out loud, telling each other "Hiram jokes," only to be interrupted by a hard firm knock on the door. The door flies open, hitting the wall with a thud. All three women jump clear out of their seats. A picture falls off the wall onto the floor and the frame breaks up into a million pieces.

"You scared me," Rachel said, her eyes big and wide. "And you ruined my picture!"

Beth shoots Rachel a steely glare. Tapping her foot and looking like an overgrown Easter bunny. She's dressed in a florescent pink low cut tent dress and pink Nikes. "What are you ladies up to?" she asked.

"Can we help you?" Jamie asked looking crossed. Beth ignores her, stepping over the glass as she enters the room. "I repeat, what are you ladies up to?" she asked, her green eyes flashing. "Don't you have work to do?"

"We do," Jamie said rising from the sofa. "But we are taking a break, so do you mind?!"

"Yes I do mind," Beth said giving her the eye. "There is no time for idle breaks when there's work to do!"

Jamie frowns. "Damn," she said as she picks up the broken pieces of glass off the floor. Beth ignores her.

"I have someone here who wants to meet Rachel," Beth said. She turns and edges to the door and pokes her head out. "You can come in now," she said.

A tall woman with long cherry blonde curls sashays into the room. A faint musky scent suddenly fills the air. The woman, with a stethoscope hanging around her neck, is dressed in a long white lab coat. Her bare legs are covered with thick long blonde hair. Her toenails, painted with cracked pink nail polish, peek out from a pair of crusty brown sandals which are too small for her size nine feet. Rachel wrinkles up her nose and stares at the woman. A musky stench soon takes over her office with a vengeance.

"My name is Doctor Grace Hornsby," she said with her eyes pinned on Rachel. She extends her hand, "Glad to meet you."

"You too," Rachel said clasping her hand and trying hard not to breathe. She recoils inwardly turned off by the doctor's wet, clammy handshake.

"Sorry," said the doctor reading her mind. "I didn't dry my hands well after washing them."

"Oh my," Rachel said while wiping her hand on her slacks. She holds her nose and backs away from the doctor as her office was now reeking like a herd of Billy goats.

Doctor Hornsby faces both Jamie and Sally and smiles. Jamie, with a gleam in her eye, wrinkles up her nose. "Feeling ripe this afternoon?" she said. Sally snickers, nudging Jamie's elbow.

"I hope you two don't run this one away," Doctor Hornsby said ignoring Jamie's comment. "Girls, remember what happened to the last social worker we had?"

"Who is she calling a girl?" Jamie asked under her breath. "That stinky ass wench has the nerve to call us girls?!" Sally nudges her again and holds her breath.

"Excuse me," said Doctor Hornsby.

"Oh don't mind her," said Sally waving her hand in the air and running interference. "She talks to herself all of the time."

"You need to get that checked dear," Doctor Hornsby said forcing a smile. Jamie frowns and fans her nose.

"Tell me what happened to the last social worker," Rachel said rubbing her nose and changing the subject. Her eyes were burning from the stench.

"She left after three months on the job. She couldn't take the stress," Doctor Hornsby said.

Beth shoots the doctor a dirty look. "Are you trying to run my new social worker away?" she said glaring at the doctor. She turns to Rachel. "Ignore her. She has a wild, crusty hair up her butt!"

"And a stinky one too," Jamie mutters under her breath. Rachel snickers and slaps her hand over her mouth to keep from laughing and Sally, tight lipped, stares at the ceiling.

"Let's go before you get yourself into trouble," Beth said shoving the doctor out the door. "I'll talk to you ladies later."

She slams the door leaving the three of them alone in a musky office fanning their noses. "Whew, that woman stinks," Rachel said gagging. "Someone needs to introduce her to some serious soap and water! She smells like a Billy goat!"

Sally and Jamie busted out laughing. "She smells like that all the time," Jamie said. "Apparently, she's allergic to bathing."

"Ick," said Rachel. "She needs a shave too. Her hairy legs look like a damn gorilla's!"

"Ha, ha," Sally laughs. "That's funny!"

"Why haven't I seen her around here before?" Rachel asked. "Where does she work?"

"Over in the West Campus Hospital," Jamie said giggling in hysterics. "She does the physicals."

"Whew," Rachel said. "I wouldn't want her touching me smelling like that!"

"Me either," said Sally still fanning her nose.

"But you must admit, Doctor Hornsby is right," Jamie said. "The craziness around here can get to you if you are not careful!"

"Well, I think I'm doing alright," Rachel said poking her chest out. "I have no worries."

"Yeah, yeah, yeah," Jamie teases. "Super is your first name and social worker is your last name. I name you super social worker!"

Rachel throws a wad of paper at Jamie missing her. "You think that's funny?" she asked, cracking a smile.

"Well you certainly act like it sometimes," she said laughing.

"Sally, do you think I act like a super social worker?" she asked, facing the nurse.

"Sometimes," Sally said giggling. "You can be a little over zealous."

"Oh please," Rachel said. "Forget the two of you!"

She reaches in her desk drawer and pulls out her handbag. "Tell me more about Doctor Hornsby," she said changing the subject. "What's her story? I know she's got one!"

"You don't want to know," said Jamie. "Doctor Hornsby has a checkered reputation."

"What do you mean?" Rachel asked, while applying her lipstick.

"The woman's a damn slut!" Jamie said giggling out loud.

"Jamie, don't be so harsh," Sally said frowning. "We don't know that for sure."

"Okay, she's loves sex," Jamie said. "Her hook-ups with the security guards around here are regular gossip. She gets more sex than anyone I know."

"Smelling like that?" said Rachel looking like a dear caught in headlights. She drops her lipstick back in her handbag.

"Yeah girl, she's one hot momma," Jamie said laughing. "The men are too horny to notice the smell! They are just trying to get some and she delivers!"

"Whew," said Rachel shaking her head in disbelief. "How disgusting," she said.

Sally frowns and gives Jamie a dirty look. "Jamie, stop being so mean," she said.

"Okay, but you know I speak the truth, girl," said Jamie rolling her eyes. "Has anyone ever caught her in the act?" Rachel asks, dropping her handbag in the desk drawer.

"Nope," Jamie said flatly. "Well, I'm not surprised," Rachel said shrugging her shoulders. "This place is jacked up with a bunch of crazy knuckle-heads!" Jamie and Sally crack up. "So true, so true," Jamie said.

"Well ladies," Sally said hopping off the sofa. "I have to go. I need to get back to work. I have a lot of paperwork to do before I go home for the day."

"Me too," Rachel said.

"Good luck with that," Jamie said. She stands and follows Sally to the door. "See you in the morning."

"Okay," Rachel said. The two women leave her office and Rachel settles in for a long afternoon.

Later, it was around six thirty in the evening and Rachel had been working hard for the past four hours. She completed her documentation for morning court. Her stomach growls like a lion because she hasn't eaten all day. She glances at the clock and it's six forty-five. "The cafeteria will be closing soon," she realizes. So, she grabs her wallet and rushes out of her office. She steps fast down the hall with her heels clicking hard against the linoleum floor.

She arrives at the cafeteria just in time before it closes for the evening and she buys a big salad and a glass of ice tea. With her dinner in tow, she leaves the cafeteria and begins her short trek back to her office. On the way, she runs into Peepers. The big cat lurches in front of the employee lounge cocking his head to the side and flashing his pearly white fangs. His yellow piercing eyes look fierce as he stares at the closed door.

As she approaches the big cat, she hears growling and moaning coming from behind the door. She stops and listens, soon recognizing John's voice. She puts her salad and ice tea on the floor and then she opens the door, cracking it just a little. She peeks inside.

"OOOO, woman, give it to me," John moans. "That's it, that's it, that's.......it. Damn you feel good! "

Rachel's eyes get big as plates and her mouth drops open. John and Doctor Hornsby are wrapped in each other like a couple of weasels in a wrestling match. Their naked bodies roll back and forth across the floor as the two of them engage in hot heavy intercourse. Rachel gags as the stench in the room is so rabid that she almost throws up. She shuts the door. She leans against the door, taking deep breaths. She flinches, startled by the loud barking now coming from inside the lounge. "I don't remember a dog being in there," she said gazing down at the big cat.

The cat arches his back and every black hair on his body stands up like a sharp needle. His pearly white fangs flash with fierce intensity and his big yellow eyes turn into narrow slits. He hisses, clawing on the door leaving long, deep marks.

The barking gets louder and louder and Rachel wonders if a dog is trapped inside. Maybe she didn't see the poor thing in her brief state of shock. So, she decides to check things out again and with caution opens the door again, cracking it just a little. She holds her breath as she looks inside. She gasps almost peeing on herself when she sees John's red pimpled butt moving up and down like a seesaw between the doctor's thick hairy thighs. "Give it to me, woman," he growls, his face dripping with hot sweat. "Give it all to me!"

Doctor Hornsby holds onto him for dear life sliding back and forth on the floor in sync with his erratic rhythm. Her long, pink polished finger nails are gouged deep in his hairy back. "Woof, woof," she barks. "Take me, take it all," she screams. "Woof, woof, woof," she barks again.

"When you bark like that, it turns me on," he growls. "Bark again," he said. Bark again!"

He slaps her hairy butt two times and she barks. "Woof, woof," she said in a high pitch voice.

Peepers, beside himself, hisses and flashes his sharp fangs as he scratches feverishly at the door. The big cat tries to force his massive head inside but Rachel nudges him away with her foot. John and Doctor Hornsby are so engrossed with each other; they don't notice Rachel and Peepers outside the door. Rachel gags and shuts the door.

"I can't believe this woman is barking like a damn dog," she whispers to herself. "Who does that?"

She kneels and picks up her salad and ice tea. "Come, kitty, kitty, kitty," she said trying to distract Peepers. He lurches at the door hissing and flashing his fangs. "Come kitty, kitty, kitty!"

The cat turns and stares at her with his big yellow eyes intense. He creeps toward her, his stride hesitant. Rachel turns around in the direction of the lobby and steps down the hall, her gait brisk, hoping the cat will follow her. He does, catching up with her by the time she arrives in the lobby, his front paws on top of her heels. She goes over to the sofa and plops down. She takes deep breaths, trying to recover from the shock of it all. Closing her eyes to block out the images in her mind and that rabid smell.

She decides Jamie is right. Grace Hornsby is a slut and a stinky one at that. After all, she saw the woman in action with her very own eyes. She rips the plastic off her salad and begins to eat it. She wonders if John and Doctor Hornsby were having sex the night Susan Cole disappeared. Definitely a possibility, she reasons.

The events surrounding her disappearance has been sketchy at best. At least until now. As she sits in the lobby contemplating these thoughts and enjoying her salad, Peepers hops up on the sofa and cuddles next to her. No longer frightened by his size, she has gotten use to him and his big yellow piercing eyes. She wonders how many evenings the cat has witnessed Doctor Hornsby and John getting it on in the lounge. Convinced the cat harbors secrets behind those mysterious, big eyes of his. One thing she's certain about for sure. She will no longer put off telling Beth what she knows about Doctor Benny. No, not anymore. When she arrives to work in the morning, the first thing she's going to do is stop by Beth's office. "It's time I spill the beans," she said as she finishes her salad.

Chapter Eleven

The very next morning, just before sunrise, the clock located in the East Campus Tower chimes seven times while disturbing a few brown bats hanging along the clock's narrow ledge. The bats take off and search for another place to take up residence. They finally settle in a grove of pine trees next to the hospital parking lot. The nocturnal creatures visit the clock tower every night only to fly back to their cave at sunrise. A hidden, deep, solace underneath Salter's Point Cliff. Although the bats don't bother anybody, the hospital staff complain about the creatures often. Turned off by the little piles of dark brown excrement the creatures deposit on the parking lot in their wake. Daily prepping of the hospital parking lot is a task the maintenance staff despises.

Rachel parks her car underneath a street light and sits there, bopping her head to Madonna's latest hit on the radio. "Borderline," a favorite of hers. She yawns, feeling tired, not getting enough sleep from the night before and anxious about her anticipated meeting with Beth. She worries what will happen to Doctor Benny after she informs Beth of his secret. Feeling guilty about it, although she knows she can't keep his secret forever.

She pushes the guilt out of her mind, deciding instead to groove to the music. Her upper body swaying to the beat and the bass sound thumping through the car speakers. As she grooves to the music, the orange glow of the sun finally peeks over the horizon, rising above the hospital. Its warm rays lighting up the paved parking lot.

The sunrise forces the bats from the grove of pine trees and the creatures high tail it back to the cave underneath Salter's Point cliff, where they will hang out until nightfall.

Rachel glances across the parking lot and notices Doctor Benny walking with a tall man with a big afro and dark sunglasses. The two men were deep in conversation. The man, dressed in an army jacket, blue jeans and black combat boots, piques Rachel's interest by his peculiar dress and style. She checks him out, admiring his smooth swagger as he glides across the parking lot like a panther. His stride long and smooth. "I wonder who that is?" she ponders, making a mental note to find out the first chance she gets.

When the two men finally disappear into the building, she gets out of the car and locks the door. She runs inside the building, waving at Joyce as she hurries pass her desk on the way to her office. Once she arrives there, she unlocks the door and steps inside, moving like lightening to her desk. She locks her handbag in the bottom drawer, takes off her coat and throws it on the sofa. She leaves her office locking the door behind her.

She runs to Jamie Lee's office. She can't wait to tell her about Doctor Hornsby's and John's sexual encounter. Her meeting with Beth for the time being must wait. At least until she has a chance to talk to Jamie. Finally, she reaches her office and bangs on the door.

"Come in," Jamie hollers putting down her newspaper. Rachel opens the door and steps inside shutting the door behind her. She rushes to the sofa and flops down. Her chest heaves up and down trying to catch her breath.

"What's up girl?" Jamie asks, reaching for her coffee cup. "Why are you breathing so hard?"

"I ran all the way here," she said out of breath. "You're not going to believe what I saw last night!"

"Okay, what did you see?" Jamie sighs putting down her coffee cup and folding her arms across her chest.

"I saw John and Doctor Hornsby having sex on the floor in the employee lounge," Rachel said talking very fast.

Jamie screams and throws both hands over her mouth with her eyes round like buttons. "Girl you are lying to me," she said.

"No I'm not!" Rachel said hopping off the sofa. "He was humping her like a dog and she was barking at him!"

"Wait, what?" Jamie said her eyes narrowing. "Repeat that again," she said.

"Doctor Hornsby and John were getting it on in the employee lounge last night," Rachel repeats very excited.

"Yeah I got that part," Jamie said. "What's this about barking? Who was barking?"

"Doctor Hornsby," Rachel said. "The woman barked like a dog the whole time she and John were having sex! It was weird as hell!"

Jamie howls almost falling backwards out of her chair. "I told you the woman's a slut," she said feeling vindicated. "Barking? Now that's precious!"

"No it's disgusting," Rachel said frowning. "Who does that? The woman is weird!"

"That's an understatement," Jamie said still laughing. "This requires a little celebration! This is too good!"

She reaches in her desk drawer and pulls out a bottle of Jack Daniels. Rachel frowns. "Really Jamie?" she said. "A drink? Really?"

"Don't start," Jamie said screwing the cap off the bottle. "I just need a little sip to celebrate. This thing with Doctor Hornsby is too good! Barking?! This is way too much!"

She turns the bottle upright and takes a sip of the brown liquor. "AHHH, that's so good," she said wincing. She screws the cap back on the bottle and puts it in the drawer. "There, I'm straight now."

Rachel rolls her eyes and shakes her head. Jamie's drinking gets on her nerves. She refrains from chastising her and decides to keep the focus on Doctor Hornsby instead.

"Do you think they were having sex the night Susan Cole disappeared?" she asked.

"Girl, you may be on to something," Jamie said clearing her throat. "John definitely was on duty that night and so was Doctor Hornsby! They both said they didn't see anything that night."

"Well there you are," Rachel said flopping back down on the sofa. She folds her arms across her chest. "They didn't see anything because they were in the lounge getting it on."

"I think you got something there," Jamie said again. "It's time we have a talk with Beth!"

"Did you call Joyce yesterday to make an appointment?" Rachel asks.

"Yeah," Jamie said. "She told me Beth's calendar is full for the rest of the week, but we can't let that stop us! We should tell her because she needs to know."

"I agree," said Rachel. "I'm going by her office today. Are you still coming with me?"

"Of course," said Jamie. "I would not miss it for the world! I want to see Beth's face when you tell her this shit! Let's go now!"

"Okay," Rachel said.

The two women rush out of Jamie Lee's office. Seconds later they are in front of Beth's door, only to discover she's not there.

"Let's check with Joyce," Jamie suggests. "I bet she knows where Beth is."

"Okay," said Rachel.

The two women walk to the lobby, their gait brisk, making a detour to the reception area. Joyce, dressed in black from head to toe, sits at her desk typing a report.

"Joyce, have you seen Beth this morning?" Jamie asks leaning over the counter.

"No, and good morning to you too," Joyce frowns, irritated by Jamie's poor manners. She checks out the two social workers and grimaces. "Beth called out. She will be in after lunch."

"Oh," said Jamie grinning foolishly. Her and Rachel exchange knowingly glances.

Joyce gets suspicious. "What's going on with you two?" she asks raising one eyebrow. "You two look like you are up to something!"

"Up to something?" Rachel asked, giggling. "I wouldn't say that." "Joyce, we just need to talk to Beth," Jamie said trying to minimize the situation. "Please tell her to call one of us when she gets in."

"Sure," said Joyce rolling her eyes.

The two social workers giggle as they wave good bye to the receptionist. They head back to their respective offices.

Court has been in session for two hours and it's now one o'clock in the afternoon. The judge, a bald man with a brown mustache, sits at the head of the table with Hiram on his left.

The attorney picks his nose and flicks a booger or two across the table, grossing out Rachel. She frowns and turns her head in disgust while Doctor Benny, unaware of the attorney's gross antics, sits quiet in his seat while reviewing his notes.

The judge has seen every patient except for Robbie Banks. Finally, stabilized on Haldol, Robbie's voices have pretty much disappeared. He sits quiet at the head of the table with his legs folded underneath him looking somber with his brown puppy dog eyes as he checks out everyone in the room. Determined to get Robbie's case dismissed, Hiram, his mood pompous, slides out of his seat and begins his argument. He wiggles his bushy eyebrows and flips his long blond hair away from his face.

"Your honor, this young man is no longer in need of care," he said prancing around the room.

He stands behind Robbie placing his thick hands on his shoulders. "This young man no longer hears voices sir," he said. "He's stabilized on his medication and he's ready to scoot out of here."

"Your honor," Doctor Benny begins, shifting in his seat. "It's true the voices are not as prominent; however, Robbie is not out of the woods yet. I need to monitor him a little longer before I feel comfortable sending him home."

"Your honor," said Hiram, shooting the doctor a dirty look. "Do you see this gentleman? He's not hearing voices! He's as calm as a sleeping baby in a cradle your honor! He's cured! This case needs to be dismissed!"

"Oh, come on," Doctor Benny moans rolling his eyes. "You can't be serious!"

"Order in the court!" the judge shouts. He studies Robbie for moment and then he asks a question.

"Young man," he said. "Can you control these voices long enough to stop doing flips and cart wheels?"

"Sometimes," Robbie said. He stares at the judge with his brown puppy dog eyes and then he tilts his head back and laughs like a hyena. Hiram cringes. The judge's face turns white as snow. He waves for Hiram to return to his seat, which the attorney does, looking defeated.

"Obviously, this young man still has some problems," he said looking grave. "I agree with the doctor. He needs to remain in the hospital."

"But your honor," Hiram said. "He hasn't done any flips or cart wheels for the past two days. He's getting so much better......."

Robbie hops out of his seat and climbs on top of the table. He performs two back flips right in front of the judge stopping short of landing in his lap. The judge scoots his chair away from the table just in a nick of time, his face white as a sheet.

"Oh my," he said. "This man is out of control!"

"Dude, get off the table," Hiram shouts wildly flagging him down. He grabs his arm and jerks him off the table.

"Sit down," Hiram said, his face red and cross. Robbie falls in the chair and folds his legs underneath him. He pokes out his bottom lip and stares down into his lap.

"I am so sorry," Hiram apologizes. "This was not expected."

"I'll bet," Doctor Benny smirks, feeling vindicated.

"Mister Gottschalks, I do not think this young man is ready to leave this hospital," the judge said with his face stern. He scoots back to the table and reaches for his gavel. He pounds it hard on the table.

"Robbie Banks," he said. "You will remain in this hospital for fourteen days with no exceptions. This is my final ruling!"

"Thank you, your honor," said Doctor Benny, grinning like a chess cat.

Hiram glares at the doctor. The judge rises from his seat. "This court is adjourned," he said. He tosses the gavel on the table and marches out of the room.

Looking defeated, Hiram remains silent, refusing to speak. He slides out of his chair and beckons for Robbie to follow him. Robbie unfolds his legs and hops out of his chair. He winks at Doctor Benny and then he performs a series of back flips around the room. Hiram's face turns to stone. "Dude, will you stop that?" he growls. "Don't you think you have embarrassed Hiram enough?"

"Sorry man," Robbie said.

"Let's go," said Hiram. He opens the door and Robbie back flips out the room.

"I told you to stop that," Hiram said running after him.

Rachel laughs out loud. "Well, we won that one," she said.

"Yes, we did," Doctor Benny said feeling triumphant. "I love it when we whip Hiram's butt!"

"Here, here," Rachel cheers glancing at her watch. She hops up from her seat and rushes to the door.

"Where are you going?" he asked.

"I have to see Beth," she said. "I'll talk to you later."

Before he can ask another question, Rachel is gone. "I wonder what she's up to," he said looking suspicious. He gathers up his notes and heads to the door. "It's probably nothing," he said. However, he was wrong. In twenty-four hours his whole world will fall apart.

Chapter Twelve

On the way to Beth's office, Rachel runs into Jamie. The two women walk together, planning their strategy as they make their way down the hall.

"Let me start the conversation," Rachel said. "Then you can jump in if I leave something out."

"Okay," Jamie said.

"I hope she listens and doesn't give us a hard time," Rachel said.

"Don't worry, she won't," Jamie said. "She hates Doctor Benny."

It's not long before they reach Beth's office. Cigarette smoke seeps through her slightly ajar door. Jamie shoves it open and pokes her head inside. "Beth," she said. "We need to talk."

"What do you want?" Beth asked, with burning eyes, taking a drag off her cigarette.

"We have something to tell you," Jamie said. "Can we come in?"

"Bring your behinds in here and have a seat," Beth said blowing a puff of smoke into air.

Rachel follows Jamie into the office and closes the door behind them. The two social workers shove empty juice bottles and soda cans out of two chairs and then they sit down. As soon as Rachel's butt hits the seat, she feels something wet. She tries to shift her body weight, but she is unable to move. She frowns.

"Are you alright over there," Beth asks.

"Yes, I'm okay," Rachel lies.

"What the hell do you ladies want?" Beth asked, with her big green eyes flashing different shades of green through her bifocals. "I got work to do."

"I have something to tell you," Rachel said with her eyes wild.

Jamie gets up and pats her butt. "What's this wet, sticky stuff?" she curses under her breath. She shakes her head and sits back down. Rachel glances Jamie's way hoping to get her attention but Jamie, preoccupied with her seat doesn't see her. Instead she shifts her body weight back and forth mumbling and cursing to herself. Rachel tries to get up again but is unsuccessful.

"I'm waiting," Beth said looking indifferent. Rachel ignores the damp sensation she feels on her butt and begins her story.

"Yesterday, Doctor Benny and I interviewed Lola Peters," she said.

"Yesss," said Beth taking another drag off her cigarette. Two big puffs of smoke, one right after another, float out of her mouth into the stale air. "Go on," she said.

"She made a play for Doctor Benny and he responded in an unprofessional manner," Rachel said.

"Huh, huh," Beth said leaning forward on her desk, with her green eyes narrowing. She puts her cigarette out.

"He told her she was being naughty," Rachel said trailing off. "And I noticed he had………"

"Honey, stop muttering and speak up," said Beth now glaring at her.

"Okay, okay," Rachel said with her heart racing. She hesitates for a moment trying to get her bearings.

"I'm waiting," Beth said, with her eyes peeled on the nervous social worker.

"Okay, okay," Rachel said. She takes a deep breath and continues the story. "Lola spreads her legs wide open and shows her crotch," she said as her voice drifted off. "I noticed Doctor Benny had, had......."

Beth pounds on the desk. "Will you speak up," she said. "You are boring the hell out of me!"

Rachel's eyes water. "He had a hard on while he was interviewing her," she said raising her voice.

Jamie snickers. Beth springs out of her seat. "Girl, what the hell are you trying to say?" she asked, with her big green eyes looking bigger than ever.

"Beth, come on," Jamie said mocking her. "Are you deaf? The man had a damn hard on, an erection, for goodness sakes!"

"Oh be quiet!" Beth said giving Jamie the eye. She faces Rachel again, her gaze fierce. "Are you sure about this?" she asks.

"Yes," Rachel said, her cheeks rosy red.

"Did you confront the horny devil?" Beth asks.

"Yes, I did," Rachel said suddenly feeling hot. "But he blew me off."

"What do you mean he blew you off?" Beth asked in a high pitch voice.

"He minimized the situation and he apologized," Rachel said with her stomach in knots. She tries to get up again, but she can't. Her behind is now glued to the seat.

"That horny devil," Beth murmurs. She falls in her seat and reaches in her drawer for her purse.

"We thought you needed to know," Jamie said softly. "You know how he acts around female patients, especially the attractive ones!"

"Damn him," Beth said.

The three women sit in silence, alone in their thoughts. Beth retrieves another cigarette out of her purse, lights it and begins to smoke. She whistles and puckers her lips, sending big puffs of grey smoke into the air.

"You know, I saw that rascal getting awful cozy with Susan Cole during her time here. More than any other patient," Beth said breaking the silence. "I thought something may be going on between them."

"Yeah, I thought that too," said Jamie. "He was quite flirtatious with her," she added.

"You said the man had a hard on?" Beth asked, checking to see if she heard Rachel correctly.

"Yes, ma'am, he certainly did," she said.

Beth takes her notepad out of her desk drawer and begins scribbling on it, stopping once to take a drag on her cigarette. The two social workers exchange looks and Rachel signals for Jamie to tell her side of the story. Jamie hesitates and gathers her thoughts and then she turns her attention to Beth. Rachel braces for the explosion.

"There's something else I need to add," Jamie said in a low voice.

"Yessssss," Beth said, looking up at Jamie, as she stops writing on her notepad.

"A friend of mine told me Doctor Benny's last wife was a patient he treated in private practice when he lived in Texas," Jamie said.

Beth's eyes turn into marbles. She rises from her seat like an inflated balloon, only to sit back down again.

She takes a drag from her cigarette sucking in the tobacco flavor and then gradually releases a puff of grey smoke into the air. The puff of smoke creeps pass Rachel's nostril drowning her senses, causing her to cough. Jamie, unfazed by the smoke, presses on with her story.

"The woman was depressed when she came to him for treatment," Jamie said. "Within a month, the two of them were in a full-blown affair."

"What a dog," Beth mumbles looking disgusted. "Then what happened?"

"His staff found out about the affair and reported him to the medical licensing board," Jamie said. "He spent a few days in jail and then he was released. Three months later the case was dismissed for lack of evidence."

Rachel coughs again. "Are you alright over there?" Beth asks.

"I think I'm allergic to cigarette smoke," she said gasping for air.

"Well, why didn't you say something dear?" Beth said with her voice sweet. She puts out her cigarette.

"Thank you," Rachel said coughing again. "I appreciate that."

Beth nods. "No problem," she said. Rachel coughs and studies her supervisor's face, searching for cues to determine what she's thinking.

She wonders how the information will be used against the doctor, knowing full well, it will not be pretty.

"Why was the case dismissed?" Beth asks getting back on the subject.

"Apparently, it was dismissed because he and the patient got married and she refused to testify against him," Jamie said.

102

"That dirty dog," said Beth in a high pitch voice. She picks up the telephone receiver and dials a number. "Doctor Beebe needs to know about this!"

"Wait, wait, there's more," Jamie said gesturing for her to place the phone on its receiver.

"Okay, I'm listening," said Beth hanging up the phone. Jamie nods at Rachel signaling her to give the rest of the story.

"Last night," Rachel said still coughing. "I heard moaning and groaning in the employee lounge."

"Okay, go on," Beth said.

"The door was closed so I opened it to see what was going on," she said hesitating for a moment.

"Huh, huh," said Beth. "Go on."

"Doctor Hornsby and John were on the floor having sex," she said almost whispering.

"What?" Beth said almost shouting. "What the hell did you say?!"

"Doctor Hornsby and John were having sex in the employee lounge last night," Rachel said raising her voice an octave. "And Doctor Hornsby was barking!"

When Beth bolts out of her seat, her pink hat topples off her head. "Who was barking?" she asked, her eyes wild with excitement.

"Doctor Hornsby," Rachel said. "I guess she was turned on."

Beth screams. "I knew it, I knew it, and I knew it," she said. "I knew there was something strange about that woman! Barking? Who barks during sex?"

"She does," both social workers responded in unison. The three women crack up.

"I knew Doctor Hornsby and John was an item," Beth said still chuckling. "The barking is what gets me," she said.

"Me too," Jamie said giggling. "So you knew about their relationship?" she asked.

"Of course," said Beth, feeling vindicated. "For the past year I heard rumors about them having sex during work hours. The evening nurses complained about it a lot."

"What did they say?" Jamie asked, poking for more information.

"The nurses complained Doctor Hornsby would disappear and not answer any pages when they needed orders," she said. "Then she would show up hours later looking disheveled and ripe claiming she never received any pages."

"It's been going on for months," she added.

"Well I'll be damned," said Jamie. She gets up and pats her butt again and then she flops back down.

"Beth, I have a theory," Rachel said.

"What's that?" asked Beth retrieving her hat from the floor.

"Is it possible that no one saw Susan leave the unit because John left his post to be with Doctor Hornsby?" asked Rachel.

"Yeah, it's possible," Beth said falling in her chair. She puts her hat back on. "Someone definitely assisted her off the unit," she said. "This information you gave me confirms my suspicion. It's all making sense now."

"Are you going to tell Doctor Beebe?" asked Jamie.

"I most definitely am," Beth said bolting out of her seat again. "Thank you ladies for this information. You can leave now," she said waving at them in a dismissive manner. "If you find out anything else, let me know."

"Yes, ma'am," both social workers responded in unison. When Rachel forces herself up, she hears a loud rip.

She spins around and glances down at her chair. A large piece of pants material is stuck on the seat. Her face turns ruby red when she touches her butt and feels her underwear.

"Oh no," she said. "I have a big hole in my pants."

"How did that happen?" Jamie asked.

"I don't know," Rachel said almost in tears. "There is something sticky on the seat and it got on my pants!"

Jamie pats her butt again. "My pants are sticky too," she said frowning. She looks over at Beth. "What's in these chairs making our butts sticky and wet?" she demands.

"What do you mean?" Beth asked, grinning like a big chipmunk.

Jamie glares at her. "You think this is funny?" she asked. "Our butts are sticky and wet! What's in these damn chairs?" she demands again.

"Calm down," Beth said. "I probably spilled some juice or soda on those chairs by accident," she said grinning from ear-to-ear. "I'm really sorry about that. It's nothing worse than a wet sticky ass!"

Rachel and Jamie exchange twisted looks and then they laugh out loud. "Beth, you are a nut! You realize that?" Jamie said shaking her head.

"It takes one to know one, "Beth said cracking a smile.

"Bye Beth," Jamie said. "I got to do something about these wet pants."

"Me too," Rachel said as she hurries through the door, leaving it wide open. She presses a sheet of notebook paper against her butt as she hurries down the hall with Jamie close behind her.

Beth cracks up and closes the door. "That's some funny shit," she muses. She goes to her desk and snatches the phone off its receiver. She dials Doctor Beebe's number. She can't wait to tell him the latest news on his most prized psychiatrist. The great Doctor George Benny. Her distaste for him is palpable. She can't stand the man and his sneaky ways.

Determined to bring him down, she gravels for a moment feeling triumph. Pleased she finally has information to end not only his medical career but his employment at Salter's Point Regional Hospital. A wicked grin spreads across her face when she hears Doctor Beebe's voice on the other end of the line. "Good Afternoon Carl," she said in her sweetest voice. "I have some interesting news to share with you."

Chapter Thirteen

Doctor Beebe slams the phone on its receiver and frowns. Beth just called requesting an emergency meeting, a request he was reluctant to grant. As far as he's concerned, he has enough on his plate, with the disappearance of Susan Cole and the brawl on the admissions unit. Now Doctor Benny, his long-time colleague and friend, seems to have a history of inappropriate behavior with female patients. He dislikes Beth and he hates her nosey ways and over the top demeanor. He finds it unpleasant to deal with her at times, but underneath her abrasive manner is a sense of forth rightness and professional integrity which he admires. If she said something wasn't right, it usually wasn't.

He broods as he rolls his wheelchair over to the coffee pot. He pours himself a cup of Starbucks coffee and sits there. His mind is all over the place, thinking about everything at once. He sighs, taking a deep breath at the enormity of it all. His mind boggled with pure exhaustion. He wishes every little negative thing he's facing would just go away but he knows this is wishful thinking. He slumps down in his chair and sips on his coffee. Contemplating, waiting on Beth and wondering what other dilemma he will soon have to tackle. It will not be long before he finds out and when he does, it will throw him for a loop.

Downstairs on the ground floor, back in the nursing office, Rachel and Jamie are taking turns blow drying their pants. They tell Sally about their meeting with Beth. She is in hysterics, with tears streaming down her face, unable to stop giggling.

"Oh my," she said with her face wet. "I'm glad you were able to free yourself from the chair."

"Me too," said Rachel looking crossed. "The whole thing is so embarrassing!"

"Let's hope the liquid came from those soda cans and not some patient who peed in those chairs," Jamie said, grimacing and handing the blow dryer to Rachel.

"Whew," Rachel said with her eyes big. "I hope not!"

"Well, I don't smell any pee," Jamie said, sniffing her pants.

"Thank goodness!" Sally laughs. She snatches a tissue from the Kleenex box on the desk and wipes her face. "So did you tell Beth everything?"

"Yeah," Jamie said flopping down in a chair. "The woman was in rare form as usual. I think she's going to tell Doctor Beebe."

"Whoa," Sally said clapping her hands with excitement. "I can't wait for this to hit the fan!"

"Mm-hm," Jamie said folding her arms across her chest. She scoots down in her chair and checks out Rachel. Her mouth flies open.

"Girl, you took off your pants?" she shrieks. "What the hell?!"

Rachel, in her underwear, is perched on the sofa inspecting the hole in her pants. "Does anyone here have a needle and thread?" she asks.

"Sure do," Sally said. "I have one right here in this drawer."

Sally reaches in her desk drawer and pulls out a needle and thread and hands it to her. Rachel takes it and begins to repair her pants.

"Tell Sally what you saw last night," Jamie said.

"Tell me, tell me," Sally said clapping her hands like a little school girl, with her eyes big with anticipation.

"I saw Doctor Hornsby and John having sex in the employee's lounge last night," Rachel said with her voice low, almost whispering.

"Get outta here!" Sally hollers, covering her mouth with one hand.

"Yes I did, yes I did, yes I did," Rachel sings, nodding her head.

"Girrrl, that's some mess there," Sally said.

The three women bust out with laughter. A patient opens the door and sticks his head in. "Ladies," he said. "You are disturbing the peace! Please lower your voices! I can't hear the little girls singing opera in my head!"

He closes the door and the three women howl even louder. Sally hyperventilates, taking deep breaths. "Did you tell Beth what you saw?" she asks.

"Yep," Rachel said. "She told us the nurses often complained to her about them having sex during work hours."

"You are kidding me," Sally said, batting her eyes like a peacock.

"That's what she told us," Jamie said.

"You know this will hit the fan soon," Sally warns.

"Yeah, you got that right," the two social workers chimed in together. Rachel slides into her pants. "Thanks for the needle and thread," she said handing the items back to Sally. "You're a life saver!"

"Glad to help," Sally said giggling. A soft knock is heard at the door. "Come in," Sally hollers.

The door opens and three nurses, all the same height, march in one right after the other with their gait robot-like. They all take a seat on the sofa, sitting side by side and crossing their legs. "Let's get this meeting rolling," one nurse said, with her eyes peeled on Sally. "I have a lot of work to do!"

"Okay," Sally said.

She gives Rachel and Jamie the nod and the two social workers hop off the sofa. "I'm sorry ladies," she said.

"No problem," Rachel said heading to the door. "We will talk later."

"Bye," said Jamie as she follows her colleague out the door. Once out in the hall, the two social workers giggled, giving each other high fives as they make their way back to their offices.

Meanwhile, Beth Jones marches across the lobby like a tin soldier, with her high heels clicking hard on the floor, while covering a lot of ground as she makes her way to Doctor Beebe's office. When she makes a swift turn around the corner, her pink hat topples off her head again. She stops for a moment and snatches it off the floor and then she throws it back on her head. She tilts it to the side and continues with her journey.

When she reaches the doctor's office, she finds his door propped open. She stands in the doorway, tapping her foot, watching him tinkered with a cross word puzzle. Doctor Beebe, a peculiar looking character, is bald with dark brown bushy eyebrows hanging over his oval shaped brown eyes. His thick white handle bar mustache covers his whole upper lip. He's dressed in a candy-striped shirt with a black bow tie with slacks and shoes to match.

He's disabled, as he is paraplegic. A condition he inherited from a massive stroke he suffered two years ago. Despite his disability, he gets around the hospital quite well in his electric wheelchair. Often speeding in the halls like lightning and always in a hurry. His role as the medical chief of East Campus Hospital is often challenging to him. Especially when dealing with his subordinates and their crazy personalities.

Keenly aware of Beth's presence in the doorway and engrossed in his crossword puzzle, he doesn't look up when he beckons her to enter his office. She meanders in and shuts the door. She wobbles to the table and stands there tapping her foot.

"I see you Beth," he said frowning. He finally looks at her. "Stop being a nuisance and tell me about this nonsense you are talking about."

"I have information on Doctor Benny that you might want to investigate," Beth said with her voice firm.

"So what is it?" he asked.

"I found out Doctor Benny had a sexual relationship with a patient he was treating in private practice back in Texas," Beth said.

"Oh," said Doctor Beebe. "Go on," he said.

"He got in trouble about it and was reported to the Medical Licensing Board there," she said. "He spent time in jail for a few days and then he went to court. The case was dismissed because he married the patient and she refused to testify against him."

He stops working on his puzzle. "Who told you this?" he asks.

"One of my social workers," Beth said.

"That's hearsay," he said grimacing and shaking his head hoping the information is not true.

Beth groans. "Hearsay? Come on," she said. "Miss Jones, I need facts not hearsay," he said with his thick bushy eye brows running together. "Doctor Benny's background checked out clean when we hired him a year ago. I can't discipline the man on hearsay!"

"Carl, I understand your concern," Beth said. "But you only contacted the medical licensing board here in Washington State to clear him. His private practice was in Texas."

"Okay, okay," Doctor Beebe said getting frustrated. "Why are you so up in arms about this? Has he tried to have sex with any of our female patients here?"

"Not to my knowledge," Beth said. "But this is my suspicion."

Doctor Beebe rolls his eyes. "Go on," he said.

Beth bends over and places her elbows on the table. Her tent-like dress sticks straight out from behind her exposing the blue spider veins running up and down her thighs and her knee-high stockings. She sways back and forth laying out her suspicions.

"I believe he had something going on with Susan Cole and he helped her escape," she said.

"Beth, really?" said Doctor Beebe his brow furrowing. "That may be your suspicion, but you have no concrete evidence he did such a thing!"

"Yes, you are right," she said peering over her bifocals. "But there's something not right with him and I urge you to investigate the man's background a little more."

"Don't you think your request is a little outrageous?" Doctor Beebe asked, raising his voice.

Beth glares at him. "No, I don't," she said. "Another social worker on my staff observed him flirting with Lola Peters yesterday! She said his behavior was quite unethical!" "Okay, okay, I'll check it out," Doctor Beebe said looking flabbergasted. "Is there anything else or are you finished?"

"There's one more thing," she said gloating.

Doctor Beebe groans. "What?" he asked. He massages his temples and closes his eyes.

"One of my social workers witnessed Doctor Hornsby and John having sex in the employee lounge last night," she said grinning

"Who are these damn social workers who are reporting this stuff?" he asked. He glares at her. "And how is this related to Doctor Benny?"

"I prefer to keep their names confidential," Beth said. "But to answer your question. Consider this, John told us he did not see anything the night Susan Cole disappeared, remember?"

"Yes, I do," Doctor Beebe recalls. "So what are you getting at?"

"The reason why he didn't see anything is because he was back in the employee lounge getting it on with that stinky slut, Doctor Hornsby," she said.

"And by the way, she barks like a dog during sex," Beth added, as she laughs like a hyena.

Doctor Beebe looks confused. "She...she does what?!" he stammers.

"Never mind, "Beth said giving him a dismissive wave. She marches to the door and swings it open. She turns and faces the medical chief one last time.

"Carl, you need to investigate Doctor George Benny," she said. "You just might be surprised on what you may learn."

She wobbles out of his office and slams the door behind her. Doctor Beebe, red-faced and mad as hell, broods as he contemplates the steps to take next. He can't stand Beth. She knows how to get under his skin. He just doesn't believe his colleague, his long-time friend, could behave in such an unethical manner. He knows if he doesn't check into the matter, Beth will nag him to death until he does.

He sits there thinking how he should proceed. After much thought, he thinks of something. Maybe his old friend James Cole can help him. After all, he's a retired detective. So, he picks up the telephone and dials his number. As he listens to the phone ring, Beth's accusations against Doctor Benny creeps across his mind. He frowns, disturbed by the whole scenario. He hopes James can help him figure it out. When he finally hears his old friend's voice on the other end of the phone, he clears his throat. "Hey man, I need to talk to you right away," he said. "I have a problem I need to discuss with you."

Chapter Fourteen

Later that afternoon, Susan Cole, lounging in a nightie with her blond hair pulled up in a ponytail, is stretched out on the sofa. She is eating a bag of popcorn. Engrossed in her favorite daytime soap opera "General Hospital," she has gotten very comfortable in Doctor Benny's modest home, which is a few blocks from downtown Salter's Point. She feels like a queen with her every need met, lacking nothing and very appreciative of the doctor's generosity. She doesn't remember any man, not even her own father, ever showing her such kindness.

As an only child, her father, an alcoholic, sexually abused her. Her self-serving drug addicted mother, aware of the abuse, failed to protect her leaving her to fend for herself. As soon as she graduated from high school, she left home and found work as a waitress to make ends meet. Occasionally she would shack up with undesirable men when short on money in return for sex.

One lover, her boss, fired her after his live-in girlfriend caught them in bed together. His girlfriend beat her to a pulp and she ended up in ICU for over two weeks after the beating. Too embarrassed to press charges, she left town as soon as she was released from the hospital.

It wasn't long before she found another lover, moving in with him after he agreed to take care of her. He left a year later upsetting her so much she ingested a handful of Tylenol, attempting to kill herself.

Her failed suicide attempt landed her in the hospital again where she was stabilized just enough to be transferred to Salter's Point Regional. When she first laid eyes on Doctor Benny, she fell for him right away. She adored his bedside manner and loved his kind demeanor. It wasn't long before he showed feelings for her, often seducing her and engaging her in sex during her therapy sessions. Her daily romantic episodes with the doctor were the highlight of her day and she was thrilled when he asked her to move in with him. They planned her escape for several weeks, finally executing their plan in the wee hours one morning and escaping without being detected.

Now she spends her days watching game shows and soap operas on television while he is away at work. On occasion, she checks the news for any stories on her escape, very aware everyone is looking for her. Despite her love for Doctor Benny, she often feels like a prisoner, stuck in the house and never going out or showing her face. So, day after day she remains under the radar content for now. However, as time goes by, her prolonged seclusion will finally get the best of her.

The very next morning, the admissions unit is in full swing and buzzing with lots of excitement. Just barely at work, and only in her office for a few short minutes, Rachel hears laughter in the nursing station. She leaves her office to see what's going on. She struts down the hall running into huddles of nurses laughing and conversing with one another. When she arrives at the nursing station, Jamie, Sally and several nurses are already there. They are standing in a circle reading and passing around a piece of paper while screaming with laughter.

"What in the hell is going on here?" Rachel asked, looking wide-eyed. "What's so funny?!"

"Doctor Beebe sent this memo to the staff this morning," Jamie said giggling. She hands Rachel the memo. "You got to read it! It's so damn funny!"

Rachel snatches the memo from Jamie's hand and reads it. A few seconds later she's howls with laughter. The memo reads:

To: East Campus Hospital Staff

From: Dr. Carl Beebe

Subject: Unprofessional Conduct

It has come to my attention some staff in this hospital are having unorthodox sex in the employee lounge during work hours. Under no circumstances will there be any unorthodox sex in the employee lounge or in the office of said person during on-call or working hours. Please see your supervisor if you have any further questions concerning this matter... Thank you.

"What does he mean by unorthodox sex?" Rachel screams with her face wet.

"Who knows?" Jamie asked, chuckling. "But I do think this memo deserves a written response!"

Sally at ear shot, over hears Jamie's suggestion. "Listen up," she said raising her voice. "Jamie thinks we should respond to this memo!"

Several nurses shout, cheer and stomp their feet urging Jamie to write Doctor Beebe a response. She fudges, holding her head in her hands, cursing under her breath. Finally, she shows her face, as a wicked grin emerges. "Okay I'll do it," she said. Sally claps her hands. "Wonderful," she said with her smile broad. She steps onto a stool. "Everybody, please be quiet," she said waving her hands. "I need to say something."

117

Almost everyone settles down except for a couple of nurses giggling in a corner. Sally cuts her eyes at the nurses, but she doesn't acknowledge them. Instead she addresses the crowd. "Jamie has agreed to type up a response to Doctor Beebe's memo," she said. "Everybody will sign it and I will put it in his mailbox. Does everyone agree with this plan?"

"Yesssss!" everyone shouts in unison.

"Good," Sally said. "Then let's get this done."

Sally hops off the stool and Jamie sits down at the typewriter. Sally, Rachel and several nurses peer over her shoulder making comments as they help her construct the memo. Within minutes, the memo is written and the final document is done. It reads:

To: Dr. Carl Beebe

From: East Campus Hospital Staff

Subject: Unorthodox Sex

We the staff at East Campus Hospital are responding to the memo you sent us this morning. We would like to know if one can have unorthodox sex in the office or employee lounge on his/her OFF hours. In addition, can you clarify for us, on what you mean by unorthodox sex? Furthermore, since you do not approve of unorthodox sex, do we have your approval to have ORTHODOX sex in the office or employee lounge during on-call and working hours? We appreciate a prompt response. Our professional work depends on it... Thank you.

After checking the memo for errors, Sally passes it around until every staff person has signed it. "Okay, I'm off," she said waving the memo in the air. "I'll be right back.

Everyone claps when Sally struts like a peacock to the exit, waving the memo in the air.

When she arrives there, she turns and faces the crowd and bows. She unlocks the door and exits. Everyone cracks up laughing.

As the rest of the day progresses, the news of Doctor Beebe's memo circulates through the hospital like wild fire, threatening to tarnish his reputation. No one, not one person, bothered to inquire about the names of the employees who were having sex in the employee lounge. The five people who knew never divulged those names and to this very day their identities remain a secret.

Meanwhile, parked at a booth inside Sully's Bar and Grill, Doctor Beebe nurses a coke while waiting for his buddy James Cole to show. The two of them were meeting for lunch to discuss the detective's latest findings. A devout health nut, Doctor Beebe chose the popular restaurant because of its variety of salads and healthy drinks. He fidgets in his wheelchair, anxious to hear what James needs to say. The detective informed him earlier he found some interesting information on both Doctor Benny and Susan Cole.

He looks up from his drink. His brown eyes scan the lobby and soon his eyes rest on James Cole. His tall stature darkening the doorway. He waves at the detective and James waves back heading to the table. The waitress sees James and bounces over to him. "Can I help you?" she asked.

"Yes," he said. "I'm meeting someone for lunch.

He points at Doctor Beebe. "He's sitting right over there."

"Oh," said the waitress. "Allow me to escort you."

"Thank you," he said.

James follows the waitress to Doctor Beebe's table. "How are you doing my friend?" James asked as he grins when he reaches the table. He reaches across the table and gives the doctor a firm hand shake.

"Good to see you man," said Doctor Beebe with his smile broad.

"You too," James said.

He slides in the booth. The waitress gives the two men lunch menus and takes their drink orders. She leaves the table. James, a tall slender man, has a thick head of curly black hair and blue eyes. He's quite handsome, looking dapper in his doubled breasted Perry Ellis black suit and his shiny Allen Edmonds black loafers. Doctor Beebe checks him out.

"Looking good man," he said.

"I do okay for myself," James grins.

"I'll say," said Doctor Beebe. "So, what did you find my friend?"

"Well," he said, retrieving a document out of his briefcase. "Your friend Doctor Benny is an interesting character."

"How so?" asked Doctor Beebe putting on his eye glasses.

"Read this," James said.

He hands the document to the doctor. James waits a few minutes before speaking, giving the doctor time to read it. Doctor Beebe frowns and tosses the document on the table.

"You don't look happy," James said.

"I'm not," he said.

"I told you he's a character," James said.

"I see," Doctor Beebe said. "Tell me more."

"It seems your boy was sexually involved with two of his female patients during their treatment at his private practice," James said.

"This is so troubling," Doctor Beebe said shaking his head.

"Yeah, I know," James said. He continues with his findings. "I found out he married one of his patients and the other one discontinued treatment and left town."

"This is so bad," Doctor Beebe grimaces.

"Yes, it is," James said. "There's more."

"Go on," said Doctor Beebe.

"His partner, Anne Cleveland, reported him to the authorities and he was arrested and put in jail," James said. "He hired himself a good attorney and his case was dismissed on a technicality."

"How so?" asked Doctor Beebe.

"You see, his wife refused to testify against him," James said.

"I was hoping you had a better report than this," Doctor Beebe said, looking bleak. The meeting with Beth crosses his mind. "The old girl was right," he mutters.

"What?" James asked.

Oh, nothing," Doctor Beebe said with his face grave. The waitress returns and places their drinks on the table and then she takes their lunch order and leaves again. The detective continues with his report.

"Susan Cole has lived and worked in several places for the past few years. She is a waitress by trade and has no criminal history," said James. "But…….."

"But what?" Doctor Beebe asked with a vacant stare.

James pauses for a moment, taking a sip of water.

"She spent some time in ICU in California a few years ago after being brutalized by her boss' girlfriend, who discovered her in bed with him."

"Boy she has led a checkered lifestyle, hasn't she?" said Doctor Beebe raising an eyebrow.

"It seems that way," James said.

"Do you know her boss' name," Doctor Beebe asks.

James reaches for his report on the table and flips through it. "Yeah, his name is Ray Cooper," he said flatly.

"Hmmm," said Doctor Beebe shaking his head.

"Also I found out Susan had a baby out of wedlock five years ago and gave it up for adoption," James added.

"Interesting," said Doctor Beebe.

The two men eat in silence, alone in their thoughts. Finally, after a few minutes, Doctor Beebe breaks the silence. "This is the deal James," he said. "We suspect one of our own is responsible for Susan's disappearance," he said. "My social worker supervisor believes it may be Doctor Benny."

"Well, I can see why she believes that," James said sipping his drink.

"Me too," Doctor Beebe said. "She told me he gave Susan a lot of attention, even as far as flirting with her when she was a patient on the unit."

"Interesting," James said. "How do you plan to proceed?"

"I would like you to follow him for a couple days," Doctor Beebe said. "I need to find out if he's with Susan Cole."

"Okay," said James. "Do you have any pictures of these two people?"

"Yes," Doctor Beebe. He reaches in his coat pocket and pulls out two pictures. "Here is a picture of Susan Cole and here is Benny's picture," he said.

"Quite an attractive blonde," James said arching one eyebrow. "What's Benny's home address?"

"I'll write it down for you," Doctor Beebe said.

He snatches a napkin out of its dispenser and scribbles Doctor Benny's address on it. He hands the napkin to the detective. James tucks the pictures and napkin in his suit coat pocket. "Give me twenty-four hours and I will have something for you," he said.

"We'll do," Doctor Beebe said with a slight smile on his face.

The waitress brings the two men their lunch order placing it on the table. After checking to see if they needed anything else, she leaves the table again.

"So what's your charge going to be?" asked Doctor Beebe.

"No charge sir," James said with a big smile. "This one is on me!"

"Thank you," said Doctor Beebe. He reaches over the table and shakes the detective's hand. The two men spend the rest of the afternoon catching up with one another. No longer feeling sympathy for his old friend, Doctor Benny, he's determined to get to the bottom of Susan Cole's disappearance once and for all. He has help now and if James proves Doctor Benny is involved with her disappearance, he will personally see to it the man never practices medicine again.

Chapter Fifteen

"Do you think Doctor Beebe will respond to the memo?" Rachel asked as she and Jamie stand in line to pay for lunch.

"Probably not," Jamie chuckles. "He doesn't do well with confrontation."

After the two social workers pay for their lunch, they walk over to a table in the corner of the cafeteria and sit down. They begin to eat their meal.

"Does Anne know about your meeting with Beth?" asked Rachel, taking a bite of her salad.

"Yes, but she wasn't happy about it," Jamie said frowning. She reaches for her glass of tea and takes a sip.

"Well, what did she say?" asked Rachel.

"She just told me she didn't want her name connected to Doctor Benny's problems," Jamie said. "I assured her, her name was never mentioned in my conversation with Beth."

"I know, I was there," Rachel said. "So, you are safe."

"Good," Jamie said feeling relieved.

"So, how are things with you and Anne anyway?" asked Rachel being nosy.

"Things have gotten a little better," Jamie said proceeding with caution. "We talked a little about our problems, but I still get the feeling she's seeing someone." "How so?" asked Rachel, looking concerned.

"She comes home late from work and never offers me an explanation," Jamie reports looking pitiful. "If I ask her why she's late, it starts an argument."

"Oh," said Rachel deciding not to inquire any further and not in the mood to listen to Jamie's relationship woes. The two women eat in silence and Jamie, still feeling down, starts up the conversation again. This time venting anger.

"Anne thinks I drink too much," she interjects frowning. "She thinks I should go to alcohol treatment."

"Really?" Rachel asked. "How do you feel about that?"

"Pissed," Jamie said. "She drinks too," she said taking the spotlight off herself. "She has a lot of nerve!"

"Maybe you both need treatment," Rachel said trying to be diplomatic. "You two seem to enable each other."

Jamie makes a face and changes the subject. "Sally, Anne and I are meeting at Sully's tomorrow evening for dinner," she said. "Why don't you join us?"

"Sure, why not?" Rachel said forcing a smile. "It's time I meet the infamous Anne Cleveland anyway," she said.

Jamie grins. "Very funny," she said.

"What time is dinner?" Rachel asks finishing up her lunch.

"Five-thirty," said Jamie rising from the table.

"Okay, I'll be there," Rachel said getting up from the table. The women exit the cafeteria leaving their trays on the table. They head down the hall soon separating in different directions to go to their offices.

"See you tomorrow evening," Rachel said.

"We'll do", said Jamie.

Friday mornings are usually busy and hectic. Social workers and nurses are running around trying to tie up loose ends as they prepare patients for discharge. There are telephone calls to families being made, referrals for aftercare are being arranged, prescriptions are being filled and bus fare arrangements are being approved for those patients who need a ride home. By the end of the day, most of the staff is exhausted and extremely worn out.

Arriving to work later than his usual time of seven o'clock, Doctor Beebe stops by the mail room to retrieve his mail. As he sorts through his messages, he runs across a memo addressed to him. His face turns to stone when he reviews the memo.

"Damn them!" he curses. He crumples up the memo and throws it in a nearby trash can. "I'm not responding to that shit!" he grimaces.

He searches for a notepad and pen and finds the items on a nearby counter. He snatches up the items and rolls out of the mail room. He speeds like a cheetah down the hall to Doctor Benny's office. On the way, he notices staff snickering and rolling their eyes at him as he flies through the hall. He ignores them, keeping his nose high as he speeds to his colleague's office. When he arrives there, he knocks on the door one time and then he opens the door and rolls inside. Doctor Benny, looking like an deer caught in headlights, is surprised to see him. "Good Morning Carl," he said smiling sheepishly. "What's up?"

"I thought I would stop in and have a little chat with you," said Doctor Beebe situating his wheelchair in front of the doctor's desk.

"Oh, is something wrong?" Doctor Benny asked, twisting up his face. He gets up and closes the door and then he returns to his desk and sits down.

"Well, I have something to discuss, if you don't mind," Doctor Beebe said shifting in his seat, feeling uncomfortable.

Doctor Benny soon realizes this is not a friendly visit. He leans back in his chair, folding his arms across his chest and glares at the medical chief and braces himself.

"You are aware the ethics committee has been investigating the Susan Cole case?" Doctor Beebe asked trailing off.

"Mm-hm, yes I'm aware," Doctor Benny said, with his blue eyes fierce and ice cold.

"The committee investigates all aspects of the case including the doctor's background," Doctor Beebe explains.

"Yeah, so?" said Doctor Benny.

"When we hired you a year ago, we only checked the medical licensing board here in this state. We did not check the board in Texas," Doctor Beebe said.

"And your point?" asked Doctor Benny.

Doctor Beebe fidgets in his seat. Pimples of sweat pop out on his forehead as he continues. "The point I am trying to make is the committee asked me to contact the Texas Licensing Board," he fibs. "And when I did, I found some disturbing information which I need you to clarify."

"What does Susan Cole's disappearance have to do with my background?" Doctor Benny asked, getting defensive. "You think I have something to do with her disappearance, don't you?"

"Well I'm not going to say that's the case," said Doctor Beebe. "The ethics committee is still doing their investigation and no decision has been made yet."

"Then answer my question. What does my background have to do with Susan Cole's disappearance?" asked Doctor Benny, with his face dark.

"Not sure yet," said Doctor Beebe. "I have information from the Texas Licensing Board about you I haven't shared with the committee yet."

"Why?" asked Doctor Benny.

"I wanted to give you the opportunity to explain," Doctor Beebe said.

"Shoot then," Doctor Benny said feeling a bit calmer. "What do you have?"

"I understand you had an improper relationship with two of your female patients you had in private practice back in Texas a few years ago," Doctor Beebe said.

Doctor Benny's face turns very grey. Doctor Beebe looks down in his lap and scribbles on his note pad. He then gives Doctor Benny a vacant look and asks another question.

"Can you tell me what, what.... Happened?" Doctor Beebe asked, stammering a little. "I need to hear your side of the story."

"My side of the story?" Doctor Benny asked, with a smirk on his face.

"Yes," Doctor Beebe said.

"Okay, I admit I had a relationship with one of my patients who later became my wife," Doctor Benny said talking very fast. "However, I'm not aware of having a relationship with anyone else in my practice."

"Did your relationship with your wife start while you were treating her?" Doctor Beebe asks jotting down notes.

"No," Doctor Benny lied. "I transferred her to another doctor before our affair begun."

"I also understand your partner......... Let's see," he pauses glancing at his notes again.

"Your partner, Anne Cleveland I believe, reported you to the board and you spent time in jail for these alleged improper relationships. Were you already married when you went to jail?"

"Yes, we had been married for over a year," Doctor Benny said now irked by the intrusion. "Look, I was cleared of all charges! What's your angle here, Carl?"

"The whole thing just seems........." Doctor Beebe drifts off losing his train of thought and then he flinches when Doctor Benny bolts out of his chair without warning.

"It seems like what?" he asked with his face wolfish. "Carl, where are you going with this?"

Doctor Beebe slams his notepad in his lap. "Where were you the night Susan Cole left this unit?" he asked, getting loud.

"I was at home!" Doctor Benny yells back.

"At home what time?" Doctor Beebe yells.

There's a knock on the door. A nurse with curly red hair and hazel eyes opens the door and sticks her head in. "Is everything alright in here?" she asks.

"Yes!" both doctors holler in unison. They glare at the nurse.

"You don't have to yell," the nurse said looking offended. She rolls her eyes and closes the door leaving the two men to continue with their arguing.

"Carl, do you really think I have something to do with Susan's disappearance? Really, man?" asked Doctor Benny, looking very crossed.

"I really hope you don't," said Doctor Beebe. "But I am charged to investigate this matter and I wish you wouldn't take this so personally."

"How am I supposed to take it?" Doctor Benny asked. "You obviously think I'm guilty, otherwise you wouldn't question me like this!"

"Oh, stop being a wuss and calm down!" Doctor Beebe yells. "No one has accused you of anything yet! The investigation is not over!"

Doctor Benny pounds on the desk causing Doctor Beebe to jerk backwards. "I'm not a wuss," he said feeling victimized. He falls in his chair and the two men fall silent.

The little black clock ticking on the desk and Doctor Beebe's scribbling is the only noise heard in the room. After a while, the medical chief looks up from his notepad and breaks the silence.

"Well, I think I'm done here," he said. "I will let you know the outcome of this investigation."

"You do that," Doctor Benny said with his eyes ice cold.

He hops out of his chair and rushes to the door. He opens it wide so the medical chief can exit his office. He turns and glares at the medical chief, with his mood tense. Doctor Beebe rolls out the door shaking his head. As soon as his wheelchair clears the doorway, Doctor Benny slams the door so hard the frame rattles. Sadness comes over Doctor Beebe's face as he rolls down the hall to his office. "Man, I hate this," he said. "That was rough!"

Doctor Benny, seething with rage, returns to his desk and flops down in his chair. "How dare, he delve into my past like that," he grumbles. "It's none of his damn business what I did in Texas!"

With his secret out, he realizes it's time to make a move. He decides he and Susan should leave town. So, he reaches in his desk drawer and pulls out the yellow pages.

He flips to the airline section and thumbs through the pages until he finds the telephone number to Delta Airlines. He dials the airline's number and a woman answers the phone.

"Delta Airlines," she said. "Can I help you?"

Doctor Benny clears his throat. "I need two tickets to Europe as soon as possible," he said.

Chapter Sixteen

It's five-thirty, Friday evening. Rachel, the first one to arrive at Sully's Bar and Grill, lingers in the lobby casing the area for a place to sit. The bar, dim and alluring, reeks of strong tobacco and it's crowded. A common occurrence on Friday evenings. As the evening wears on, upbeat jazz music thumps loud in the distant background. Men huddle together at the bar, puffing on cigars and enjoying a drink. Soon a blanket of thick gray smog hovers above them in the atmosphere.

Across the room, men and women are packed like sardines around tables grooving to the music, with their heads bopping like big ping pong balls on a string. Some of the patrons lean close to one another, speaking in hush whispers while others just sit alone, nursing their drinks and staring into space. Engrossed in their thoughts.

Rachel eyes a seat near the non-smoking section of the bar and saunters over. She hops on a bar stool and notices the waitress bouncing back and forth between customers serving drinks. Minutes pass before she finally flags her down and the waitress comes running over. "Hi There," she said. "What can I get for you?"

"A glass of Red Merlot," Rachel said.

"Coming right up," said the waitress.

"Thank you," said Rachel.

The waitress bounces off to the kitchen and Rachel shifts her body weight on the stool and faces the door.

She surveys the area and notices an attractive blonde sitting in the shadows at the far end of the bar. She is quiet, mysterious and sipping on a glass of white wine. "I have seen that woman before," she said. "She looks familiar."

She tries to recall where she has seen the woman before, but is unable to do so. For a moment, Rachel locks eyes with the woman but she looks away fixating on her glass of wine, determined not to engage. Rachel checks her out for a few more seconds and then events from the past week invade her thoughts distracting her. While she ruminates about the past week, the waitress returns and places a glass of merlot on the counter. She pays the waitress and then she sips on the wine savoring the light fruity flavor. "Very smooth," she said looking pleased.

It's not long before Sally, Jamie and Anne stroll into the restaurant laughing and teasing one another, with their voices loud and cackling. Rachel waves. "Over here!" she hollers with the music drowning out her voice. The three women see her and make their way to the bar marching in a single line like a band of soldiers.

"Hi girl," said Jamie reaching the bar first. "This is my girlfriend, Anne Cleveland."

"How are you?" Rachel asked. "I have heard a lot about you."

"Really?" Anne asked with her smile tapered. "I heard a lot about you too."

"Good things, I hope," said Rachel.

"Don't worry, nothing bad," Anne said smiling.

Sally hops on a bar stool. "Ladies I need a drink pronto," she said waving at the bartender.

"Me too," Jamie said leaning on the counter.

Rachel laughs. "You two are a trip," she said.

The bartender comes over and the women order a drink while Rachel checks out the infamous Anne Cleveland. She is a little taller than Jamie and plump. Anne has light brown eyes, a pouty mouth and a short page boy haircut. She's dressed in black, wearing a wool sweater and boot cut jeans with matching flats. She crosses her thick legs and checks out the scene around her. Soon the waitress brings out their drinks and Jamie requests a booth by the window. The waitress honors the request, seating the women in a booth by a window across from the stage. Once seated, the waitress gives them each a menu and leaves the table.

"How are you getting along at the funny farm?" Anne finally asked, looking demure.

"I am getting along fine," Rachel said forcing a smile. "It took a little time to get used to, but I'm adjusting."

Anne chuckles. "I bet," she said.

"So, does anyone know if Doctor Beebe saw the memo?" asked Jamie, changing the subject.

"No," Sally laughs. "Doctor Beebe hates to be confronted. He probably will ignore it."

"What memo are you guys talking about?" Anne asked.

The women tell Anne about the memo and she laughs out loud, tickled by the whole story. They chat and share the events of their day until the waitress interrupts them to take their dinner orders. After they place their orders, the women gossip about everyone from Beth Jones to Doctor Louis. Suddenly Jamie springs out of her seat. "Speaking of the devil! It's Doctor Louis and his wife," she said flagging them down.

A tall older man and a woman half his age are standing in the lobby waiting to be seated. He waves back and heads to their table.

"Rachel, you finally get to meet the Colonel," she said grinning like a chess cat.

"It's about time," Rachel said checking him out as he approaches the table. An imposing figure, he's tall and robust. A man in his early sixties with dark brown eyes and deep crevices in his face. His receding hairline is covered with a ratty toupee and he is wearing a blue sports jacket over a pair of gray slacks and black Allen Edmond loafers. Finally, they reach the table.

"Good Evening, Ladies," he roars, with a crooked grin.

"Hi Doctor Louis," all four ladies respond in unison as they check out his wife from head-to-toe.

"This is my wife, Sierra," he said wrapping his arm around her waist and looking proud.

"Nice to meet you ladies," Sierra said smiling with her voice raspy. A tall, petite woman, she has long auburn curly hair hanging past her shoulders and deep-set hazel green eyes.

"Glad to meet you," the women said as they try not to look at each other, fearful their expressions will betray them. Jamie taps the doctor on his arm.

"Doctor Louis, this is Rachel Thomas, our new social worker," she said pointing at Rachel.

"Well, how are you young lady?" he roars giving her a warm smile. "I hear you are doing a good job," he said. "Glad to have you on board!"

Rachel's cheeks turn red. "Thank you sir," she said. "I'm glad I finally got to meet you."

"Me too," Doctor Louis said.

He averts his attention to Anne. "Haven't seen you around lately," he growls. "Are you still working on West Campus?"

"Yes," Anne said. "I keep a low profile these days."

"Sometimes it's safer that way," he said laughing. Anne nods.

"When will you be back at work?" Sally asked, interrupting.

"Monday," Doctor Louis said.

The four women exchange glances surprised by the news. Doctor Louis lets out a deep, roaring laugh. "Ha, Ha, Ha," he said. "I guess no one told you I was coming back so soon!"

"Nope," Jamie said. "Not one soul."

"Go figure," said Sally shaking her head.

"Well you know now," he said.

The waitress returns to the table. "Your table is ready sir," she said.

"Thank you," he said. "Well ladies, have a nice evening."

"You too," said all four women.

Doctor Louis and his wife follow the waitress to a table across the room. As soon as he sits down, the women cut loose.

"That woman is young enough to be his daughter," Rachel said rolling her eyes. "The man is robbing the cradle! He should be ashamed of himself!"

"I know," Jamie said. "I bet she gives him a real work out, if you know what I mean!"

"Yeah, that's why his old ass had a heart attack and almost died," Anne said.

The women crack up. Soon the waitress returns, bringing them their dinner orders. Jamie orders another drink and the waitress takes the order and leaves the table.

Anne gives her a dirty look and Jamie sticks her tongue out at her. "Lighten up," she said. "It's Friday."

Anne rolls her eyes and shakes her head. "Let's eat," she sighs trying to keep the peace. The women follow her lead and for fifteen minutes they eat without saying a word to each other. Finally, Rachel breaks the silence. "How long have those two been married?" she asked.

"Who?" Jamie asked, sipping on her drink.

"Doctor Louis and his wife silly," Rachel said giggling.

"Two years," Sally interjects. "He adores that woman!"

"Does he have any children?" Rachel asks.

"No, and she doesn't either," Sally said. "He can be nice when he wants to but sometimes he can be a real tyrant!"

"Really?" Rachel asked.

"Yes ma'am," she said chuckling. "We don't call him the colonel for nothing, my dear."

"I can handle him," Rachel said.

"Yeah right," Jamie said. The women laugh.

As the evening progresses and Karaoke hour approaches, more patrons pack the restaurant. Jamie, who by this time is on her ninth drink, climbs on stage and snatches the mike. She sings "Purple Rain" with Prince's hit record with her voice shrill and out of tune. At one point, she screams into the mike and everyone boos her. Doctor Louis, huddled with his wife at a nearby table, frowns and shakes his head.

When she finally finishes the song, she stumbles off the stage and falls on her butt. Laughter breaks out around the room, while Anne and Rachel rush to her side. Anne, with a pained look on her face, helps Jamie to her feet with Rachel's assistance. "I think it's time to take you home," she said.

"I don't want to go home," Jamie wails jerking from Anne's grasp. "I'm having fun here!"

"You are embarrassing yourself," Anne hisses in her ear as she and Rachel drag her back to the table.

"I don't care," said Jamie falling in her seat. She sees the waitress and signals for her to come to the table. The waitress rushes over.

"Can I get you something?" she asked.

"Bring me another drink honey," said Jamie with her speech slurred.

Anne's temper flares. "You are not getting another drink! I'm taking you home!"

"I said I want another drink," Jamie said bristling.

"Do not bring her another drink," Anne said glaring at the waitress. "Please just bring me the bill," she said.

"Okay," said the waitress backing away. "No problem."

"Rachel, let's take Jamie to the car while Anne takes care of the bill," said Sally.

"Okay," Rachel said. When the waitress returns with the bill, Jamie gets loud and pesters the woman to bring her another drink.

"Get me a drink, you wench," she yells.

The waitress scoffs. "Excuse me," she said. "What did you call me?"

Rachel intervenes. "Please don't take it personally," she said. "She's really drunk and this is not really her."

"You guys have your hands full," the waitress said frowning.

"Yes we do," said Rachel. She faces Anne. "Take Jamie home," she said. "I'll take care of the bill."

"You are a doll," Anne said.

Sally and Anne each take Jamie by one arm and begin ushering her to the door. She screams profanities at them while several of the restaurant's patrons, including Doctor Louis and his wife, stare her down with disgust. Once outside, Anne jerks Jamie toward her and gets right up in her face.

"You are embarrassing me," she said. "You should be ashamed of yourself!" "Oh please," Jamie said pushing her away. "How dare you chastise me?" "Come on," Anne said pulling her by the arm. "Let's go home." Jamie looks over at Sally, her eyes glassy. "Are you coming home with us baby doll?" she asked.

"Yes," said Sally taking Jamie's other arm. "It's time for you to go."

The two women drag Jamie to the car. Rachel, still inside the restaurant, goes over to the bar and settles the bill. While waiting for her change, the blonde in the corner at the bar catches her eye again. The blonde's vacant stare is fixated on the crowd while she nurses her drink occasionally taking a sip. Rachel wonders if she is waiting for someone. After all, it's late. Close to ten-thirty in the evening. "That woman sure looks familiar," Rachel said racking her brain again.

She tries to make eye contact, but the woman doesn't look in her direction. "Maybe I'll introduce myself on the way out," she said. "I know we have met before."

She snaps her fingers signaling for the bartender to bring her change. He returns with her change a few minutes later and when she looks over at the corner bar again, the blonde is no longer there. "Now that's weird," she said looking around. She grabs her handbag and struts to the exit.

She stops before walking out the door and turns around. She surveys the restaurant trying to relocate the blonde again but she doesn't see her.

She shrugs her shoulders. "I guess she left," she said. Disappointed, she throws her handbag over her shoulder and struts out the restaurant.

Ten minutes later, the blonde woman returns to the bar. She makes eye contact with the bartender as she slips on her coat. He acknowledges her and comes over her way. "Ma'am would you like something else?" he asked.

"No," she said. "Just bring me the bill."

"Okay," said the bartender.

He makes out the bill and brings it to her. She scans it and reaches in her purse, pulling out a fifty-dollar bill. As she settles the bill, the bartender leans over the counter. "Madam is there anything else I can get you before you leave tonight?"

"No," Susan Cole said. "You have a nice evening."

Chapter Seventeen

Susan Cole shivers while she waits for the city bus, as the night breeze is strong and chilly. She buttons her coat and folds her arms across her chest, savoring the last few minutes of her freedom before she returns home to her lover. She dreads facing him and the thought of it makes her cringe. However, fear of his anger is secondary compared to the daily isolation she has endured for the past few weeks.

Sometimes she argues with him about her self-imposed prison and he feels guilty knowing full well the isolation is killing her. He deflects his guilt by reminding her he could end up in prison and she will be out in the streets with no place to stay. Susan, grateful for the doctor's generosity, always backs down and accepts her predicament all for the sake of love and self-preservation.

Doctor Benny finalizes his airline reservations and hangs up the phone. He leans back in his chair and wonders if he can sneak Susan out of the country without being discovered. When he made the decision to sneak her off the unit and bring her home with him, he thought the events surrounding her disappearance would just go away. However, as time progressed his calculation proved to be wrong... Dead wrong. He tries justifying his decision by convincing himself that she too desired the relationship as much as he did. He ignores the glaring fact he has defied all professional ethics by violating her personal rights.

141

Now recent developments have caused him to regret his decision. Feeling a strong sense of urgency to do something to thwart off disaster. With the threat of jail looming over his head, it's just a matter of time before Doctor Beebe figures out his role in Susan Cole's disappearance. Once he does, Doctor Beebe will come after him with a swift vengeance. He glances at the clock and realizes its past ten-thirty. "My girl must be worried," he said. "I better get home."

He gathers up his things and rushes out of his office. When he walks in the door at ten fifty-five and discovers Susan not there, it throws him for a loop. He paces back and forth like a caged animal, stopping periodically to stare out the living room window. His mind all over the place wondering where she is this time of night. As the evening progresses, he contemplates going out to look for her, but soon kills the idea, not sure where to start. "She could be anywhere," he said as he paces back and forth.

He wrestles with his thoughts with his emotions all over the place. Vacillating from anger one minute to worry the next minute. He stops for a moment and presses his nose against the glass window. Gazing out into the dark night, waiting for her return. "Susan where are you?" he whispers. "Where in the hell are you?"

A few blocks down the street, Susan steps off the bus and hurries down the cobblestone sidewalk, with her demeanor in high alert. The moon, full and bright, casts its shadow on the sidewalk and the narrow street in front of her snakes through the quaint upscale neighborhood. She struts, with her gait brisk, glancing behind her every ten seconds to make sure no one is following her. When she realizes she is five minutes away from Doctor Benny's house, she quickens her pace.

Soon she passes a blue ford parked underneath a street light across the road. As she passes the car, fear consumes her when she notices a man hunched down in the driver's seat, with his dark eyes fixated on her. Her adrenalin kicks in and she breaks into a light jog and then a sprint. Running so fast she almost crashes into the gate of Doctor Benny's home. She stops just in time and shoves the gate back then she runs straight to the porch. Hopping over two stairs until she finally reaches the front door. She searches her handbag for her key only to jerk back when Doctor Benny swings the door open startling her. He glares at her with his clear blue eyes laced with rage.

"Where in the hell have you been woman?" he barks. He jerks her inside and slams the door.

"You are hurting me," she said. "You are hurting my arm!"

She tries to pull away but his grip is too tight. "Let go of me," she said tears welling in her eyes.

"Where have you been?" he asked again.

"I had to get out of here! I was getting cabin fever," Susan said.

"Do you realize people are still looking for you?" he asked. "What the hell are you thinking?!

"I needed to get away," she repeats again. "I got tired of being in this house all day!"

Rivers of tears run down her cheeks. "I'm sorry," she said. He lets go of her and she slips out of her coat throwing it on the floor. She runs over to the sofa and flops down. She sits there rocking back and forth, wringing her hands and sobbing.

"George, I am so sorry," she weeps. "I just needed a change of scenery. It won't happen again."

A wave of guilt comes over him. He trudges over to the sofa and sits next to her. He hugs her, kissing the tears off her cheeks.

"I'm sorry for yelling," he whispers. "I was just worried about you."

"I know," Susan said sniffling. "I didn't mean to worry you."

She hugs him back and kisses him on the lips. He gives her a hard kiss back and pushes her down on the sofa. He raises her skirt moving it up over her hips and then he slides one hand between her thighs. He grabs her crotch and she moans, her sex dripping wet. He pulls on her panties and she wiggles her hips helping him until her panties drop to her ankles. She kicks them off on the floor.

She reaches for his belt and unfastens it and then she zips down his pants. He rises from the sofa and his pants and belt drop to the floor. He kicks them off and falls back on the sofa. He unbuttons her blouse and slips it over her shoulders. Her inviting bare breasts beckon him and he kisses each one. Greedily taking each nipple into his mouth and sucking on it like a hungry babe.

As they begin to make love, a man snaps pictures of the two of them through a window. Wrapped up like a couple of octopuses, her legs snug around his hips and he in between her thighs. His hot sex thrusts into her sex like a sledge hammer. His rhythm jerky and rough. She moans as he keeps up the rough intensity until they both reach a welcomed climax and they collapse with his body resting on top of hers.

They lay there, embracing one another and breathing heavy with their eyes closed, while enjoying the synchronized rhythm of their breathing. The man on the porch snaps one more picture and then he runs down the stairs.

Doctor Benny sits up. "Did you hear that?" he asked, moving off her. He sits on the edge of the sofa and stares at the door for a moment and then slips on his pants.

"Hear what?" Susan asked, rising halfway up on the sofa. She wraps her arms around his waist and pulls him back to her. "Where are you going?" she asked.

"I heard something on the porch," he said pulling away from her and reaching for his shirt.

"You are hearing things," she said. "You are so paranoid."

"I guess I am," he said relaxing a little. He turns to face her and grins, showing two rows of stained yellow teeth. "I have something to tell you," he said.

"What?" Susan asked, while picking her panties off the floor.

"I have decided to take time off from work," he said standing up.

"Oh," she said. "Why?"

"I need a break," he said.

"How come?" asked Susan.

"Tired and drained," he fibs.

"How long are you going to be off?" she asked.

"I don't know yet," he said. "But I thought it would be nice for you and me to take a little trip."

"Where to?" she asked, slipping on her panties.

"To France," he said. "I bought airline tickets this afternoon."

"France?" she asked with her eyes big. "Did you say France?"

"I sure did," he said grinning.

"Oh how exciting," she said.

She hops off the sofa and claps her hands like a little girl. "I have never been to France before," she said. "When are we leaving?"

"Next Tuesday," Doctor Benny said.

"Oh I can't wait," Susan said.

She jumps on him and wraps her arms and legs around him. Kissing his face as he holds her up and he spins in a circle, with his movement fast and swift.

"You are going to love it over there," he said. "I just know it!"

"Put me down," she said giggling, with her face flushed. "You are making me dizzy!"

He puts her down and she sways a little. "Are you alright?" he asked.

"I'm fine," Susan said grabbing her clothes off the floor. "I'm going upstairs to find my passport and pack," she said. "I can't wait!"

"Honey we are not leaving until next Tuesday," he chuckles. "You don't have to pack right now!"

"I know," she said grinning. "But I want to. I have a lot to pack."

She turns and runs upstairs. He throws on his shirt. Pleased his plan, for now, seems to be working out. He glides over to the window and looks out, while squinting to see across the street.

His heart beats fast like a drum when he notices a man with a dark hat in a ford parked underneath a street light with his eyes peeled on his house. "Who in the hell is that?" he wonders.

He leaves the window, opens the front door and stands in the doorway. The man rolls up his car window, turns on his headlights and pulls away from the curb. He guns the accelerator and disappears down the road.

Doctor Benny shakes his head and goes back inside. He shuts the door and lingers there with sweat dripping down his face. "Something is wrong," he said looking worried. "I got to get out of here."

"George," Susan yells from upstairs interrupting his thoughts.

"What?" he groans.

"I need to show you something," she said.

"I'll be right there," he said. He locks the door and runs upstairs.

James Cole speeds down the road in deep thought, surprised to learn Susan Cole is living with the doctor on her own volition and is happy and content. Although he is glad he solved the mystery of her disappearance, obtaining an arrest warrant on the doctor may be a difficult task. One that wasn't his burden to bear. However, if his friend Carl Beebe needed help with obtaining the warrant, he will be there to offer his assistance.

His eyelids droop as he merges on the freeway in route home. He turns up the radio to stay awake and he ruminates about the many things on his to do list in the morning, including calling his old friend, Carl Beebe. He shakes his head looking worried. "All hell is about to break loose soon," he mutters. "And it's not going to be pretty."

Over on the other side of town, Sally and Anne help Jamie out of the car. The two women hold her as they drag her up the driveway to her house and she jerks away stumbling backwards as she falls on her butt.

"Damn it," she said. "I think I hurt my booty!"

She sits on the sidewalk with her legs spread apart grimacing and moaning.

Anne and Sally stand over her with their arms folded across their chest, glaring down at her. "What the hell are you two looking at," she said. "You wenches help me up!"

"You are getting on my last nerve!" Anne said with her face red. "I'm so tired of your shit!"

"Oh put a sock in it," Jamie said grinning like a little kid.

Anne ignores her. She and Sally help her up to a standing position and then they walk her up the stairs and into the house. Once inside, Jamie stumbles again. The two women grab her and literally drag her to the bedroom, sitting her on the bed. When they let go of her, she sways to one side and falls over.

"I am so worn out," Jamie said with her speech slurred. She rolls over on her back and giggles.

"No, you are drunk," Anne said, her face twisted like a prune. "Sally and I are going to help you undress so you can sleep this shit off!"

"You bitches leave me alone," Jamie said giggling and punching the air. Sally tries to smooth things over.

"Jamie, you will feel more comfortable, if you take off your clothes and get in your pajamas," she said. "Then you can get back in the bed and sleep off your hangover."

"Hangover? I don't have a damn hangover," Jamie shouts. She rolls to her side and sits up. She snatches off her coat and throws it at Sally.

"Jamie, that is rude," Sally frowns losing her temper. "We are just trying to help you."

"The hell you are," Jamie said. She bends over to untie her sneakers and almost tumbles over.

"We got you," said Sally as the two women break her fall, grabbing her just in time.

Jamie giggles. "Sally your head looks like a big watermelon," she said with her eyes glassy. "What happened to you?"

"I don't know what you mean," said Sally, looking puzzled. "Let's get you undressed."

"Okay," Jamie said. "But you need to see a doctor about that watermelon head!"

Anne lets out a small giggle, despite her anger. Sally, not amused, rolls her eyes. The two women strip Jamie down to her underwear and then help her into pajamas. They assist her back to bed and cover her with a blanket. It's not long before Jamie drifts off to asleep, snoring like a young cub. Exhausted, Anne and Sally leave the room and make their way to the kitchen. When they arrive there, Sally parks herself at the table while Anne goes over to the cabinet.

"I am going to make a pot of coffee," Anne said taking the coffee pot out of the cabinet. "Would you like a cup before you go home?"

"Sure," Sally said exhaling. "A cup of coffee sounds good."

Anne prepares the coffee and then joins Sally at the table. The two women sit in silence, listening to the coffee brew and Jamie's faint snoring down the hall. After a while, Sally breaks the silence.

"I have never seen Jamie like this before," she said almost whispering. "She's really drunk! I'm worried about her."

"Sally, I live with this shit every day," Anne said looking irritated. "She's an alcoholic! The woman drinks nonstop!"

"How long has this been going on?" asked Sally, floored by Anne's revelation.

"At least for the past two years," Anne said. "Frankly, I'm just tired of dealing with it."

"Have you talked to her about getting help?" asked Sally.

"Yes, several times," Anne said taking a deep breath. "But she refuses."

Anne slides out of her chair and goes over to the counter. "The coffee is ready," she murmurs.

"Great," said Sally. Anne pours two cups of coffee and returns to the table. She gives Sally her coffee and then she sits back down. The two women, quiet as church mice, sip their coffee while deep in thought. Sally looks over at Anne and clears her throat. "Look, we need to do an intervention with Jamie," she said. "If we explain to her how her drinking affects us, maybe she'll get some help."

"I really don't think it's going to work," Anne said. "But I am willing to try once you set something up."

"Okay," said Sally. "I'll get a meeting scheduled next week."

She finishes her coffee and then slides out of her seat. "It's time for me to go," she said. "My husband is probably wondering where I am."

"Yeah, it's late," Anne said.

Sally grabs her handbag and struts to the front door with Anne on her heels. Anne opens the front door for her. "Take care of her," Sally said strutting out the door.

"Don't worry, I will," Anne said.

"See you later," Sally said. "It's been interesting!"

"Yes it has," Anne said. "Be careful driving home," she hollers after her.

She watches Sally walk to her car and once she's safe inside the vehicle, Anne goes into the house and closes the door. She returns to the kitchen and pours herself another cup of coffee. She leans against the counter sipping on her brew, thinking about Jamie's behavior at Sully's. She entertains leaving her again, tired of dealing with the stress of it all. For the past few weeks she has thought about walking out, especially after she met a man named Ray Cooper at a party two months ago.

Ray was handsome, with dark brown eyes, a nicely groomed mustache and a short brown afro. Ray left California four months ago and moved to Tacoma to take a job at Microsoft. A month later, he meets Anne at a party and the two of them hooked up. Meeting at Sully's after work every evening for the past two months. Enamored with each other, they soon learn they have a lot in common.

One evening, under the influence of too much alcohol, Ray spilled the beans about his last relationship. It ended when his live-in girlfriend almost killed him, after she found him in bed with another woman. Feeling guilty and unwilling to see her go to jail for his infidelity, he dropped the charges and she moved out, never to be heard from again.

Intrigued by his openness, Anne shares her thoughts about her relationship with Jamie and her desire to end it. Feeling sorry for her, he in turn suggests she come live with him. An offer she found very tempting at first. However, she turned him down, very concerned about Jamie's emotional health and her ability to withstand a break-up.

But tonight, things have changed and she feels different. Jamie's drinking has gotten the best of her and she no longer wants to put up with it. "It's time to move out," she said.

She goes to her bedroom and stops at the door. Jamie, knocked out, is still snoring like a young bear. She cracks open the door and peeks inside. She hesitates a minute and then she opens the door a little wider. Just enough to wiggle her way inside. She waits a couple more minutes and then she tiptoes to the closet, being careful not to make a sound. She slides the door open and grabs her suitcase and while she's at it, she snatches a few clothes off hangers. She stuffs the clothes in her suitcase and then tiptoes to the dresser. She tugs at the drawer and it whines when she finally opens it.

The snoring stops and Jamie flips over on her back. Anne freezes in place and stares at her while holding her breath with her eyes big as saucers. Within seconds, Jamie is snoring again and she sighs, relieved she didn't wake her. She gathers her underwear and a few other items and then she creeps back to her suitcase. She tosses the items in the case and zips it up. Finally packed, she leaves the room closing the door behind her. She hurries to the living room and drops the suitcase by the front door. She makes a detour to the kitchen and snatches the phone off its receiver. She dials a number and it rings on the other end for three minutes and then a man answers.

"Hello," he said.

"Ray," she said.

"Hey babe, what's up?" he asked. "Is something wrong?"

"Sorry to call so late," Anne said. "But is your offer still open? I have to get out of here!"

"Sure babe," he said.

"Well, I'm coming over tonight," she said smiling from ear-to-ear. "Okay babe," he said. "Look forward to seeing you."

She hangs up the phone and searches for a notepad and pen. She finds the items on the counter and writes Jamie a note and leaves it on the table. She returns to the bedroom again and stands there listening to Jamie snore as she reminisces about the good times they had together. Tears well in her eyes and a tear rolls down her cheek. She closes the door and heads to the hall closet and grabs her coat. She slips it on and picks up her suitcase. Then she turns off the lights and walks out the door.

Chapter Eighteen

Saturday morning and barely awake, Jamie squints trying to see the clock on the nightstand. It's eleven-thirty in the morning. She yawns and stretches and then she sits up and swings her legs over to the side of the bed. She rubs her forehead, making a twisted face, as her head throbs with pain. "Anne!" she hollers. After a couple of minutes go by with no response, she hollers again. "Anne, do you hear me?!"

She listens for a response but the house is silent. She slides out of the bed and shuffles across the room into the bathroom. She opens the medicine cabinet and searches for some aspirin. "Damn!" she curses finding none there. She slams the door and shuffles out of the bathroom to the closet in her bedroom. She slides the door to one side and takes out her robe and slippers and puts them on. She leaves her room and heads down the hall to the kitchen.

Her slippers swish softly on the wood floor as she walks. Her head throbs with pain, which makes her very dizzy. She stops for a moment and leans on the wall, steadying herself and then she continues to the kitchen. When she arrives there, she flips on the light and she feels dizzy again. She staggers over to the table, pulls out a chair and flops down. "This is some hangover," she sighs holding her head in her hands. She sits there for a minute and then she's up again, staggering to the counter. She searches for aspirin opening every cabinet door until she finally finds some in the last cabinet by the refrigerator.

She grabs the medication and hurries to the sink. She grabs a glass out of the dish rack and turns on the spigot filling the glass with water. She sways back and forth slumping over the sink, dizzy again. She regains her balance and turns off the water. She staggers back to the table and flops down in a chair. She opens the bottle of aspirin shaking out six pills into her hand, popping each pill one by one into her mouth. She gulps down the water and coughs clearing her throat. Her head spins forcing her to slump over on the table. "Where in the hell is Anne," she said rubbing her temples and closing her eyes.

She tries to recall the evening's events, with her mind foggy and then she remembers Anne helping her to bed and being angry at her. She shudders at the thought of it, feeling a twinge of guilt. She opens her eyes and her heart pounds like a drum when she notices a folded note on the table. She reaches for the note and unfolds it. Big tears well in her eyes as she reads every gripping, devastating word.

"Dear Jamie,

I am leaving you. I can't take your drinking anymore. I am staying with a friend. I will stop by later in the week to get the rest of my things. I wish you the best. Love, Anne."

She crumbles up the note and throws it across the table. She weeps, rocking back and forth in her seat with her arms folded across her stomach. She gets up and scurries back to her bedroom. When she makes it there, she climbs into bed and scoots down in the middle of the bed, pulling the comforter over her head. She cries herself to sleep.

Doctor Beebe slams the phone on the receiver. "I hate this," he said falling back in his wheelchair. He gazes at the ceiling, looking somber. The news of Susan Cole's whereabouts is no longer a mystery and now he's faced with filing legal charges against his long-time colleague. Although he doubted George Benny's innocence, deep down inside, he hoped for another result. Now he has no choice. After all, the hospital's reputation is at stake. He ponders breaking the news to his staff, but decided after some thought, it's too early to do so. Preferring to wait until the warrant is filed instead.

When he solicited James Cole's assistance in filing the warrant, the detective, sensing the doctor's frustration, agreed to accompany him to Salter's Point Police Department Monday morning. Relieved he has support and back up, Doctor Beebe puts the matter out of his mind and pulls out his crossword puzzle. He arranges the pieces and begins working on it, hoping by the end of the day on Monday, the whole disturbing situation will finally come to an end.

Chapter Nineteen

Monday morning is bright, windy and cold and fall is here to stay. The sun hovers high over Salter's Point Regional and the cold whistling wind tosses twigs, paper and pine needle shrubs all over the hospital parking lot. Doctor Michael Louis speeds into the parking lot and parks his Mercedes in front of the hospital. He pulls down the sun visor and checks himself out in the mirror. He pats down the sprigs of hair on his ratty brown toupee and smooths out his mustache. He enjoyed being off and spending time with his young wife Sierra but now it's time to return to the crazy daily grind of Salter's Point Regional.

He shoves the sun visor back in place and steps out of his Mercedes. The strong wind slams him against the car and it takes all his physical strength to finally close the car door, as he uses both hands to slam the door shut. He wraps his coat around his body and begins his journey to the hospital entrance, fighting the wind and pushing against it as he makes his way across the parking lot.

The wind blows so hard, it lifts the toupee off his head, blowing it across the parking lot like a balloon. The wind lifts it up into the air and then drops it on the ground. He runs after it, only to be out run by a black crow that swoops down and snatches the toupee off the ground. "Damn bird!" he curses, shaking his fist in the air. The bird descends up into the crisp blue sky with the hairy rug in his beak. It lands in a pine tree nearby and drops the hairy rug in a nest of twigs.

The bird honks and scopes the doctor out while its head twitches from side to side. Doctor Louis frowns. "Oh shut the hell up," he said as he heads back to his Mercedes. The violent wind knocks him back and forth across the parking lot like a tennis ball and when he finally makes it to his car he unlocks the door and forces it open. He leans inside and the wind slams the door hard against his behind, knocking him head first inside of the car.

"Damn it," he said. "I just can't get a break this morning!"

He climbs in and closes the door. He opens the glove compartment and pulls out his black wool hat. He puts it on, pulling it snug over his ears and then he steps out of his Mercedes again. He fights with the wind for a few seconds, trying to close the door. For a moment, the wind dies down and he slams it almost falling on his butt. He regains his balance and locks the door.

He starts again, making his way across the parking lot to the hospital entrance. When he reaches the building, he taps the button and the door slides to one side. He walks in and hikes through the reception area scowling.

"Good Morning Doctor Louis," said Joyce.

"Humph," he grumbles.

Joyce shakes her head. "The grumpy old colonel is back," she whispers.

He stops by the mail room and retrieves his messages and then he hikes to his office. When he arrives there, he fiddles with his keys, trying to find the one for his door. When he finds it, he forces it into the lock. Rachel hears him in her office next door and slides out of her chair.

She opens her door and sticks her head out.

"Good Morning, Doctor Louis," she said, her tone cheerful.

"Good Morning," he growls refusing to look her way. He unlocks the door and steps inside his office, slamming the door so hard the frame rattles.

Rachel flinches. "What a grouch," she said. "I hope he's not going to be like that all day."

She sighs, shaking her head and then she ducks back into her office and closes the door. As soon as she sits down at her desk, there's a knock on her door. Sally opens the door and sticks her head in.

"Good Morning, dear," she said. "Can I come in?"

"Sure! Have a seat," Rachel said beckoning for her to come inside. Sally struts in and closes the door. She flops down in the nearest chair.

"How was your weekend?" asked Rachel.

"Oh, fine," Sally said smiling. "Doctor Benny is out sick this morning, so Doctor Everett James will be covering today. Have you met him?"

"No," said Rachel. "I know about him, but never met him. What does he look like?"

"Oooh," said Sally, her eyes getting big. "He's easy on the eyes and a hell of a hunk!"

"Huh, huh," Rachel said chuckling. "How is he to work with Sally?"

"He's okay," she said. "He can be a perfectionist at times, but he's okay."

"I hope he's not a grouch, like Doctor Louis," Rachel sighs looking pensive with her elbows on the desk and her chin in one hand.

"Oh did something happen?" Sally asked, raising one eye brow.

"Doctor Louis is in a bad mood this morning," she said. "He sure is grouchy!"

"Already?" asked Sally looking surprised. "He just got back!"

Rachel shrugs her shoulders and laughs. "I know," she said.

"That man is something else," Sally said looking down in her lap. "You better get used to his moods."

"Yeah, I guess so," Rachel sighs. She changes the subject. "Have you seen Jamie this morning?" she asks.

"She called out sick too," said Sally. "I hope she's alright. I'm worried about her."

"Yeah, I am too," Rachel said. "Maybe I will stop by her house later and check on her."

"Good idea," Sally said smiling with approval. "Anne and I talked last Friday. We are going to do an intervention with Jamie," she said. "Are you in?!"

"Hell yeah," Rachel said with her face brightening. "Just let me know when," she said.

"We'll do," said Sally, as she slides out of her chair. "Well, it's time for report. Are you coming?"

"Most definitely," Rachel said. She hops out of her seat and follows Sally out the door.

Nursing and social work staff gather in the big conference room for the Monday morning report. Doctor Louis, still wearing his wool hat, sits at the head of the table scowling. Waiting for everyone to settle down so he can begin the report. Rachel notices a thick tension in the room. There is not as much laughter among staff, like in previous morning reports, she recalls.

She quickly determines Doctor Louis' presence is the reason for the staff's somber mood. Soon a tall man with a big afro, wearing an army jacket, jeans and combat boots strolls in and parks himself at the table. He appears mysterious in his dark sunglasses and Rachel wonders why he's wearing them at all. She studies his face, checking out his high cheek bones and flawless dark smooth complexion. "Mmmm.... What a hunk?" she concludes.

"Good Morning," said Doctor Louis with his voice booming as he glances around the table. "I know everyone is glad to see me back!" Light laughter breaks out around the table and the man with the afro smiles. "For those of you who are wondering who this gentleman is on my left," said Doctor Louis turning to face the man. "This is Doctor Everett James. He's covering for Doctor Benny today."

"So this is Doctor James," Rachel surmises. "Sally is right. The man is not only a hunk but sexy too." She remembers where she first saw him. He was the man she saw the other day walking with Doctor Benny across the hospital parking lot. She continues to check him out, amused by his dark sunglasses. Hoping he would take them off so she can see his eyes. When he finally speaks, his deep voice resonates throughout the room. "Good morning, everyone," he said, with his smile bright and showing perfectly straight white teeth. "I will be covering for Doctor Benny for a couple of days. There is no reason for you to change your routine on my account. So just carry on."

"So he's flexible," Rachel muses. She keeps her attention on Doctor Louis as he begins report, trying not to look the handsome doctor's way. Doctor Louis reviews the list of admissions, giving extensive details on each new patient, with the list daunting. One patient hears Chinese voices although he, himself is not Chinese. Another patient reports his brain is infiltrated by aliens. Still another patient, homeless and living on the streets, was picked up by police for mooning pedestrians as they pass him on the sidewalk.

As Doctor Louis finishes up report, Rachel gets the feeling she's being watched. She glances across the table and catches Doctor James checking her out. He smiles at her and she looks away. She keeps her eyes peeled on Doctor Louis until report is over. When she gets up to leave, he stops her. "Miss Thomas," he said.

"Yes sir, she said.

"Let's meet in my office at ten thirty to interview the new patients."

"Okay," Rachel said. "I'll be there."

Rachel bounces out of the room and makes her way to the nursing station. She goes through the gate and parks herself at the counter, giving the dining area a once over. Several patients pace back and forth, smoking cigarettes. The smoke is so heavy it engulfs the entire area. She coughs repeatedly trying to catch her breath and then she springs out of her seat and gathers up some charts. "I had enough of this smoke!" she said.

She heads to the gate and a deep voice booms from behind her, causing her to jump an inch off the floor. "I'm sorry," he said. "I didn't mean to startle you."

She turns to face him. It's Doctor James, with his smile flawless. "I assume you're leaving because of the cigarette smoke," he said.

"Yes, yes, I am," she stutters, feeling embarrassed. "It's....... It's very nauseating."

"I know," he said taking off his sunglasses. "My name is Everett James. I don't believe we officially met."

Her heart flips-flops in her chest, stunned by his mesmerizing, sexy dark brown eyes. "It's... It's Rachel Thomas," she stammers.

"Glad to meet you Miss Thomas," he said. "Look forward to working with such a lovely lady."

Her heart skips two beats, pleased by his compliment but nervous as a firefly. The man captivates her. Her attraction to him has taken her by surprise. A problem if she's not careful. She decides to act elusive. "Glad to meet you too," she said coolly, not cracking a smile. She makes a U-turn and leaves the nursing station. "I need to keep my distance from him," she whispers. "I can get into some serious trouble with that man."

She chuckles to herself at the thought of it as she heads to Doctor's Louis' office. She shows up there as planned exactly at ten thirty. She meanders into his office and sits in a chair close to his desk. Sally is already there and their first patient, Bobby Lewis, is perched in a chair across from the doctor's desk.

Bobby inspects the room, his mood quiet. He's a short man with icy blue eyes and his blonde hair is tied back in a ponytail. He's dressed in denim clothing soiled with black dirt and a whiff of musk radiates around him. Rachel and Sally glance at each other and wrinkle up their noses while Doctor Louis, ignoring the odor all together, reviews Bobby's chart. After a few minutes, he begins the interview.

"My name is Doctor Louis," he said introducing himself. "And these lovely ladies are Rachel Thomas, your social worker and Sally Dobbins, your nurse," he said.

Bobby nods at the two women but he doesn't say a word. "Tell the ladies your name, son," said Doctor Louis glaring at him.

"Bobby Lewis," he said still casing the room.

"Where are you from?" asked Doctor Louis.

"New York," Bobby said.

"How long have you been here in Washington State?" Doctor Louis asked, glancing down at the chart again.

"A week, "he said staring at the floor.

"What made you decide to move to this state?" asked Doctor Louis.

"Oh, I just needed a change of scenery," he flippantly said.

Rachel fidgets in her seat, as a queasy feeling comes over her. "Something is not right with this dude," she thinks to herself.

"So you came all the way across country for a change in scenery?" asked Doctor Louis, scrutinizing him. "So tell me, how did you get here?"

"I hitchhiked," he said.

"Oh, you did?" Doctor Louis asked, falling back in his chair. "So how did you end up here in this hospital?"

"I guess the people in the streets didn't like me mooning them," he said with a grin. He stares at the doctor with his blue eyes icy.

"In reading your chart, you told the admissions nurse you have never been treated for a mental illness," said Doctor Louis. "Is that true?"

"Yep," Bobby said.

"Have you ever experience hearing voices, feeling suicidal or anxious or having racing thoughts?" Doctor Louis asks.

"Nope," Bobby said, with his voice flat, staring at the doctor.

"Have you ever been in jail before?" asked Doctor Louis as he studies Bobby's face.

Bobby hesitates and then he looks away. "Nope," he said.

"Bobby, are you in trouble with the law?" asked Doctor Louis, getting suspicious.

"Nope," said Bobby still refusing to look the doctor in the eye. He squirms in his seat and clasps his hands together. His icy blue eyes now fixated on the clock hanging on the wall.

"So you hitch-hiked across country for a change of scenery?" Doctor Louis asked. "You expect us to believe that garbage?" he asked.

Bobby glares at the doctor for a minute. "I don't care if you believe me or not," he said. "Who cares what you think anyway?!"

"You are running from something," said Doctor Louis chuckling. "Your story doesn't make any sense!"

Bobby falls back in his chair and folds his arms. He avoids the doctor's gaze and stares at the wall. Rachel and Sally jot down notes.

"I ask you again," said Doctor Louis, leaning forward, his eyes peeled on Bobby. "Who are you running from? Who are you trying to get away from?"

"Nobody," Bobby said fidgeting in his seat.

"Well, I don't believe you," Doctor Louis quips.

"I don't care," Bobby said.

"Alright then," said Doctor Louis. "I don't have any more questions. You can go back to the unit."

"Good," Bobby said. He hops out of his seat and heads to the door. He opens it and then turns to face everyone. "How long will I be here?" he asks.

"Don't know yet," said Doctor Louis. "We will let you know."

"Right," Bobby said. He walks out and slams the door.

"Asshole," Doctor Louis grumbles under his breath. Rachel studies the doctor's face.

"What do you think is going on with him?" she asks.

"I think he's running from the law," Doctor Louis said. "Call the Sheriff's office and make sure there is no outstanding warrant out on this asshole," he said.

"I'll get right on it," Rachel said rising from her chair.

"Yeah, hurry up," Sally said still jotting down notes. "His attitude sucks!"

Rachel giggles and dashes out the door. She goes into her office and flops down at her desk. She dials the number to the Salter's Point Police Department. An officer answers on the third ring and Rachel tells him the information she needs. Five minutes later she hangs up and Jamie crosses her mind. She picks up the phone again and dials her number. The phone rings several times but there is no answer. Surprised, she reluctantly leaves a message on the answering machine and then hangs up the phone.

As soon as the phone hits the receiver, it rings and she answers it. Her mouth drops open when the officer gives her the run down on Bobby Lewis. After he finishes, she thanks him and hangs up the phone. She bolts out of her seat, runs next door and pounds on the door.

"Come in," Doctor Louis hollers.

Rachel opens the door and goes inside. "Doctor Louis," she said panting. "Bobby Lewis alias Johnny Peters is an escaped felon from New York's federal prison. He is a convicted serial killer and the FBI is looking for him!"

"Well, I'll be damned," said Doctor Louis feeling vindicated.

"There's more," Rachel informs him taking a breath.

"Go on," he said leaning back in his chair and clasping his hands together behind his head.

"He has a life sentence with no chance of parole. He murdered fifteen prostitutes several years ago," she said. "Apparently, a guard at the prison helped him escape!"

"You don't say," said Doctor Louis, not surprised to hear this information. "So when are the police coming to get the little twerp?"

"The FBI is on their way as we speak," Rachel informs him.

"Good," said Doctor Louis with a crooked grin.

"Should we call security to keep an eye on him?" she asks.

"Yes," said Doctor Louis. "But don't tip him off. Be discreet."

"Okay," said Rachel. She leaves his office and goes next door to call security. Once security is notified, she leaves her office again and rushes to the nursing station. She finds a chair and plops down. She scans the patient dining area and soon finds Bobby Lewis parked at a table across the room. He seems content, with no care in the world, in deep conversation with two of his male counterparts. "He's in for a rude awakening," she said smiling to herself.

Thirty minutes later, out of nowhere, tall men in black suits wearing dark sunglasses converge on the nursing station and dining area like a swarm of bees. The men surveying the area and looking for their prize prisoner. Aware he's been discovered; Bobby Lewis makes a mad dash to the exit. One FBI agent runs in front of him intercepting his path while another agent hops on top of him and wrestles him to the floor. The men handcuff him and roll him over face down and then they jerk him up and carry him down the corridor like a slaughtered hog. Patients in the area cheer and whistle as they watch the FBI carry Bobby Lewis face down off the unit.

To restore order, the nurses escort patients to their rooms and other areas on the unit. Rachel returns to her office and Jamie crosses her mind again. She dials her number and the phone rings and rings but there is no answer. She hangs up and sits there worrying about Jamie. "I wonder where she is," she said shaking her head. "I hope she's alright."

Chapter Twenty

Late in the afternoon, exhausted after working hard for four straight hours, Rachel wraps things up ending her day. She attempts to call Jamie again, but the telephone just rings and rings. Disappointed, she hangs up the phone, grabs her handbag and then she struts out of her office. She hurries down the hall to the heavy steel door and unlocks it, stepping out into the lobby. She releases the door and it slams, the frame shaking like an earthquake. "That door needs some work," she said as she makes her way into the reception area. She waves at Joyce as she passes through the area.

"See you tomorrow," she hollers.

"Have a nice evening," said Joyce barely looking up.

"You too," Rachel said.

She taps the button on the wall and the door slides open. Once outside, she embraces the warm air. The temperature, being seventy-five degrees, is an unusual occurrence this time of year. She glances at her watch and it's five thirty. She hurries across the parking lot and takes her keys out of her handbag. When she reaches her Toyota, she unlocks the door and hops in. She turns on the ignition and backs out, turning left out of the parking lot.

Her stomach growls and she realizes she hasn't eaten all day. When she finally reaches the hospital gate, the guard, still dressed like Darth Vader, waves her through. She steps on the accelerator and speeds through turning right onto the main thorough fare. She speeds down the road at sixty miles per hour heading straight to Sully's.

It's not long before she's in front of Sully's parking her car. She checks her wallet and there is no money. She panics, searching her handbag, looking in every nook and cranny and finally finding a crumpled up ten-dollar bill. It was hidden in a side pocket of her handbag. "Thank the Lord," she sighs tucking the bill inside her wallet. She steps out of her Toyota, slams the door and then she goes inside.

Once inside the restaurant, she meanders to the bar, giving it a good once over and then she stops. Every muscle in her stomach tightens and her hunger pains are replaced with a hot stinging rage gripping her, drowning her and taking over her very soul.

Anne Cleveland, in a lip lock with Rachel's ex-fiancé, is making out with him at the bar. The two of them so into it that they don't see her coming. It was three years ago when she last saw Ray Cooper. She tried to shoot the man after she caught him cheating on her. She winces with pain when she recalls the incident. That horrible night and the rage she felt, when she came home late one evening and found him in bed with a woman who had long blonde hair. She watched in horror, as the two of them made love. He on top of her, humping her like a dog. The woman's moaning and hollering, to this day, still sickens her and she remembers throwing up right there in the doorway.

And before she knew it, she had taken Ray's gun out of the cabinet and checked it for bullets. With the gun fully loaded, she tiptoes back to the bedroom and lingers in the doorway for minutes on end. She watches them make love as everything in her is about to explode with her blind rage. The only single thought in her head at the time was to blow their behinds out of the water.

She aims the gun holding her breath. The blonde moans and hollers as Ray repeatedly thrusts himself inside of her.

She engages the trigger. The gun pops like a loud fire cracker and the bullet travels pass him, missing him all together. The bullet ricochets against the wall leaving a nail size hole in its wake.

"Oh shit!" he hollers scampering off the woman. He searches the room like a scared rabbit, startled by the loud crackling sound. The blonde screams and covers herself with a sheet. Her face rosy pink.

"It's Rachel," he said. He grabs a pillow and places it over his private area.

"Who's Rachel?" asked the blonde, sitting up in the middle of the bed looking like a deer caught in headlights.

"That's right honey, it's me," she said with her voice cold and calm. She points the gun at the pillow and cocks the trigger again.

He trembles, shaking his head. "No Rachel no," he said. "You don't want to do this!"

"You cheating son of a bitch!" she said advancing toward him. "I'm going to put a cap in your ass!"

"Susan, run," he said. "Run for your life!"

Susan hops off the bed and heads straight to the door. She runs out of the room screaming like a banshee. "You better run you little slut," Rachel said now distracted and heading to the door. "I'm coming after you!" She runs after Susan, her stride swift and long, catching up with her in a matter of seconds and then snatching her by the hair. She jerks her around and then throws her hard on the floor. "I'm going to whip your butt," she said. "You have no business in my bed or in my house, you little slut!"

Rachel pistol whips her and she screams. Fiery red welts pop up on her skin and she scampers across the floor like a little squirrel, wincing in pain. Rachel keeps up the assault with a vengeance, her rage out of control.

"You are killing me," she screams. "Ray, help me! She's killing me!"

"Help your damn self!" said Rachel. She kicks the woman in the shins, striking her repeatedly and then she kicks her in the back and shoulders. "You have no business in my bed you little slut! Ray is not your man and this is not your home!"

"I didn't know…...." Susan squeaks guarding her face with her hands.

"I don't care!" Rachel screams. "You have no business here!"

"Ray, help me," Susan screams trying to get up and then slipping and falling on her butt. "She's trying to kill me!"

"You bet I am," Rachel hisses with her face contorted with rage. Ray, half dressed, runs over to Rachel and shoves her on the floor. He falls on top of her and the two of them wrestle and engage in a fist fight. Susan scrambles across the floor to the sofa and climbs up in it, curling up in a fetal position. She bawls like a baby. Rachel socks Ray dead in the face and he hesitates for a moment, with his head woozy from the impact. A big red knot pops on his forehead and he fights to regain his senses. He then musters up some physical strength and overtakes her. Rolling on top of her so she can't move and then he snatches the gun out of her hand and shoves it across the floor.

"You asshole!" she said. "I hate you!"

"Rachel calm down," he said changing position and pinning her arms hard to the floor.

"Stop it you son of a bitch," she said with her eyes wild with rage.

"I'm not letting you up until you calm down," Ray said, his face dripping wet.

"I hate you," she said. "I hate you!"

"Calm down," he said.

"No!" Rachel said with her face beet red, as she tries to wiggle out from under his grasp. "How dare you bring that slut into our home and our bed!"

"Let me explain," he said.

"There's nothing to explain! Just get off me," she said. "You are hurting me!"

"Do you promise to calm down?" he asked.

Rachel gives up momentarily and lies there. Glaring at him with tears in her eyes. "I promise," she said, barely opening her mouth. She turns away from him.

Okay," he said.

He moves off her. She sits up and cases the room. Her dark brown eyes dart back and forth like an animal on the hunt looking for prey. She sees Susan lying in a fetal position, trembling on the sofa and Rachel bolts off the floor and lunges at her. "Get her out of here," she screams, slipping and falling on the floor. "Get that whore out of here right now!"

"Okay, give me a minute," Ray said coming to her aid. He helps Rachel to her feet and she groans. She stands there massaging the left side of her hip. "You have one minute to get her out of here," she said wincing with pain. "Otherwise, I'm going to beat her to a pulp!"

"Can I finish getting dressed first?" he asks with his face flustered and his eyes watery. "Hurry up," Rachel said. "I can't stand the sight of her!" Susan shakes, unable to control her movements, she wails with pain.

"Oh shut up," said Rachel. "You don't hurt that bad!"

Susan's wailing reverts to a small whimper and Ray leaves the room. He returns five minutes later fully dressed with Susan's clothes in tow.

"Here," he said tossing her clothes to her. "Get dressed so we can go."

Susan begins dressing and the doorbell rings. A second later there is brutal pounding on the door. "IT'S THE POLICE, OPEN THE DOOR!"

"Oh hell," said Rachel. "The police? That's all we need."

"Damn," Ray said. "This is not good."

"All of this is your fault," she said flashing him the evil eye. She flops in the nearest chair across from Susan and fumes with her dark eyes watching her every move.

"OPEN THIS DOOR NOW!" said the police officer pounding on the door. Ray rushes to the door and opens it. Two burly looking police officers, dressed in dark blue uniforms, stare back at him with one hand on their holsters.

"We received complaints of gun shots coming from this apartment," he said with his voice gruff.

Rachel bolts from her seat. "I tried to put a cap in his ass for cheating on me but I missed," she said pointing at Ray with her dark brown eyes wild.

"Is that your weapon?" the officer asked, forcing his way pass Ray to the gun on the floor.

"Yes," Rachel said. "Alright ma'am, we have to take you in," he said snatching the gun and handing it to his partner.

"Fine," said Rachel. She heads straight to the door. "You don't have to handcuff me," she said. "I need to get hell out of here anyway before I kill somebody!"

The officer follows her. "Alright then," he said. On the way to the door, he notices Susan and frowns. "Wait little lady," he said. Rachel stops in the doorway. "What happened to her?" he asks.

"I whipped her butt," said Rachel, her voice calm and cool. "She broke in my home and threatened me. I had to protect myself!"

"Stop lying," Ray said. The officer puts his hand up cutting Ray off.

"Call an ambulance," the officer said. "This woman needs medical attention."

"Okay," Ray said heading to the phone. He gives Rachel a dirty look and calls 911. The officer grabs Rachel by the elbow and ushers her into the hall. "Ma'am you are coming with me," he said.

"Glad too," Rachel said sticking her tongue out at Ray. The officers escort her down the hall to the elevator. She holds her head high while several tenants gathering in the hall whisper with one another. Ray runs out into the hall.

"Babe, don't you worry," he said feeling guilty. "I'm coming down there to get you out!"

She flips him a bird as the elevator door closes leaving him standing there with his mouth open. He returns to his apartment looking dejected. Susan, now dressed, rocks back and forth on the sofa as she cries again.

He sits next to her and hugs her shoulders. "She's gone," he said with his tone soft. "She's not going to hurt you anymore. She's gone."

She bawls even harder. Soon there is banging on the door. Ray springs off the sofa and answers the door.

"Where is she, "said one ambulance attendant rushing pass Ray.

"Over there," Ray said pointing to the sofa. The attendants rush over and throw a blanket around Susan's shoulders. "Are you alright ma'am?" asked one attendant viewing the welts on her arms.

"Noooo," she sobs.

"What happened?" the other attendant asks. Susan mumbles some unrecognizable words and sobs.

"Ma'am, we are taking you to the hospital," he said.

Susan doesn't resist. The attendants lift her up and put her on a gurney, covering her with another blanket. Minutes later she's in the ambulance on her way to San Francisco General, alone and without Ray.

The next morning, as promised, Ray bails Rachel out of jail and drops the assault charges. She returns to their apartment, packs her things and moves out, never speaking to him again.

As for Susan Cole, she remained in the hospital for over two weeks spending most of the time in ICU. Ray never visited her the whole time she was there, dropping her like a hot potato and never seeing her again. When she finally recovered enough to leave the hospital, she decided to cut her losses and not press charges. Heart broken, she quit her job, moved out of her apartment and then she left town.

"Ma'am are you okay?" asked the waitress.

Rachel flinches. The waitress' shrill voice jolts her back to reality. "Yes," she said. "Why do you ask?"

"You looked like you were a million miles away," she said.

"I was," Rachel said frowning.

"Do you want a table?" the waitress asks.

"Yes, no, I mean no," Rachel said. "I'll order something at the bar."

"Okay," said the waitress. "Suit yourself."

With her heart pounding wild against her chest, she approaches the bar, while taking small steps. When she arrives there, she leans against the counter, standing a foot away from them. Anne notices her and slides off Ray's lap. "Hi Rachel," she said with her face beet red. "Here to get a drink?"

"Maybe," Rachel said giving Anne the evil eye.

Ray pivots on his bar stool and his face drops as his brown eyes grow big as grapefruits. "Rachel," he said squeaking like a little mouse. "What are you doing here?"

"I should be asking you that same question," she coolly said with her face straight as an arrow.

"You know her?" Anne asked with her eyes big and looking like an owl.

"Yes he does," Rachel said frowning. "And?"

Ray hops off the stool. He is beside himself. "You live here?" he asked with his heart beating fast like a drum.

"Yep," said Rachel. She glares at Anne. "You are a cheating witch," she said.

"I beg your pardon?" Anne asked, cutting her eyes.

"You heard me," said Rachel giving her a dirty look.

"Look, I don't want any trouble here," Ray said putting his hands up. "I'm just out having a drink with a friend." "A friend?" asked Anne, flashing him an evil look. "Now I'm your friend suddenly?"

Rachel laughs out loud. "Oh, he's got you thinking you are it on a stick," she said. "Girl, he's playing you."

"What are you talking about?" Anne asked.

"You don't know him like I do," Rachel said.

"Oh really?" Anne snaps back.

"Girl, I know him better than you hope to," she said feeling cocky.

"How so?" Anne asked while rolling her eyes.

"Let me enlighten you," Rachel said. "Ray and I were once engaged to get married. We used to live together."

Anne groans and cuts her eyes at Ray. "So Rachel is the woman you told me about a few weeks ago?" she asked. "I don't believe this!"

"Believe it," Rachel smarts off.

Anne sways to the side feeling light headed. She shuts her eyes and leans against the bar.

"Are you alright?" Ray asks, making no effort to assist her.

"I'm fine," Anne snaps back opening her eyes and hopping on the bar stool. "It will pass."

"Okay," said Ray.

Rachel taps him on the arm. "So what did you tell her about me?" she asked with her eyes burning.

"It doesn't matter," Ray said.

"It does matter," Rachel said gritting her teeth. "You have no business talking to this wench about me at all!"

Anne bolts off the bar stool. "Stop calling me names!" she said getting her mojo back. "Face it, you and Ray are over!"

"I know you aren't talking to me like that you big slut!" Rachel said. "Stay out of this if you know what's good for you!"

"I see why you and Ray are not together," she said trying to agitate Rachel. "You are such a b…….."

"Watch it!" Rachel hisses with her face dark.

Anne backs off. "Why are you pestering him?" she asked. "What has he done to you?"

"Well let me tell you," she said. "This asshole you are so enamored with is a cheat and a scoundrel!"

Ray frowns and throws his hands up in the air. "Why are you dogging me out like this?" he asked. "She doesn't need to know our business like that!"

"Oh yes she does!" Rachel said throwing her head back and laughing out loud. "She needs to know what kind of chump she's dealing with!"

Anne grimaces. "Rachel, I'm not interested in………"

"Shut up," Rachel said stopping her cold. "I told you to stay out of this!"

"Anne, come over here by me," he said reaching for her. She moves closer to him and inserts her arm into his.

"Oh, how sweet the two of you look," Rachel said getting sarcastic. "Girl, he can't protect you!"

"Are you threatening her?" Ray asks with his brow furrowing.

Rachel laughs. "What do you think?" she asked.

The bartender emerges from behind the bar. "Ma'am, would you like to order something?" he asked, looking worried.

"I certainly do," Rachel said. "Bring me a cold glass of water with plenty of lemons."

"Coming right up," said the bartender. He dashes off disappearing into the kitchen. Ray fidgets in his seat, looking flustered and unsure of what to do next. He glances at Anne and then back at Rachel trying to figure out what the two of them are going to say and do next. The two women stare each other down.

"Look ladies, you are making me feel uncomfortable here," he finally said. "Let's have a drink, call a truce and forget this ever happened."

"Oh come on," Rachel said. "You can't be serious!"

He glares at her. Anne, quiet as a church mouse, hangs onto him like a little kid. "Woman what do you want then?" he asked, looking irritated.

"I want you to answer some questions," she smarts off.

He groans. "Okay, ask away," he said.

"How long have you been in Salter's Point?" she asked.

"Four months," he reluctantly volunteers. "I work for Microsoft."

"Really?" Rachel asked, with her eyes fixated on Anne. Glaring at her with haughty distain. "That's interesting!"

"Where is this going?" Anne asked, taking a deep breath and now getting inpatient.

Rachel's blood curdles as she fights off the urge to grab Anne by the hair and beat the crap out of her. "I told you to stay out of this," she finally said under her breath.

"Look Rachel," he said. "Let's not have any more animosity between us. The past is the past."

"No it's not," said Rachel. "You are nothing but a two-timing dog!" "Come on, girl," he said. "You should be over this by now! It's been three years! Why are you acting like this?"

"I'm not over it," she said with her face red and her eyes watery. "I'll never get over it!"

"I'm sorry," he said. "But it's over and you have to move on!"

"You are right, I do," she said coming back to her senses.

"I'm glad you agree," he said flippantly. "Now please go. I want to get back to what I was doing!"

Rachel steams. "Oh really?" she asked, placing one hand on her hip. "We'll see about that!"

Ray tenses up. The bartender returns to the bar and places a glass of water with ice and lemons on the counter. Rachel reaches for the glass and takes a sip. They stare each other down, the two of them in a fiery intimidating trance. She places her glass on the counter, her blood still boiling. "How long have you been seeing this whore here?" she asked.

"Who are you calling a whore," said Anne balling up her fists.

"Oh, you are going to hit me now?" Rachel asked. "I dare you!" "I will if I have to," Anne said her face red. "You have no right to call me a whore!"

"LADIES! LADIES! LADIES!" Ray shouted. "Would you please calm down?"

Rachel laughs out loud. "Really Ray?" she asked. "Calm down? really?"

"You are rude," he said chastising her. "You have no right to treat her that way! Anne has done nothing to you." "She's done enough," Rachel said. "Anne is a slut just like the woman I found you in bed with years ago!"

Ray pounds his fist hard on the counter. "Stop drudging up the past," he said. "I don't want to keep talking about this!" "Okay then," Rachel said gritting her teeth. "Then take this!"

She throws the glass of water in his face and he lunges forward with his face and shirt dripping with water. "Woman, what's wrong with you?"

"Nothing," she said laughing like a hyena. "I feel a hell of lot better." She puts the empty glass on the counter and leaves the bar, turning around once to flip him a bird. She struts out the door. Anne, at her wits end, runs after her while Ray searches for something to wipe himself off.

"Come back here," he hollers after her. "She's dangerous!"

Anne doesn't hear him. She's already outside searching the parking lot for Rachel. She soon spots her backing her car out of a parking space and she runs over, waving for her to stop. Rachel stops the car and rolls the window down.

"What the hell do you want? You two-timing whore," she said with burning eyes.

"Listen, I didn't know you and Ray were together once," Anne said. "You can't hold this against me! I didn't know!"

"Oh, I don't hold anything against you slut, but Jamie will," Rachel said putting the car in gear.

"Please don't tell her," Anne pleads. "It will break her heart!"

"Break her heart?" Rachel asked, with her face twisted. "You should be ashamed of yourself, cheating on Jamie like that," she said.

"I know," Anne said. "But don't tell her. I'll tell her when the time is right!"

Rachel explodes. "Bitch, you got two seconds to get the hell out of my way before I run your ass over!" she said.

"You wouldn't dare," Anne said.

"I'm warning you," she said. "Get the hell out of the way!"

Rachel jerks the car forward forcing Anne to hop on the curb. She screams. "What are you doing?" she asked. "Are you crazy?!"

"Huh, huh," Rachel said sticking her head out the window laughing. She lunges the car forward again, driving the front end of the car up on the curb. Anne, white as a sheet, jumps several feet out of the way. She runs into the restaurant, with her hands up in the air, hollering like a banshee. Rachel, enjoying every minute of it, cracks up.

"She won't mess with me again," she said chuckling. She puts the car in reverse and screeches out of the parking lot. She turns left and speeds down the road like a bat out of hell, with her thoughts all over the place. Jamie was right about Anne all along. The woman is seeing someone alright. Her ex, Ray Cooper. What an irony, she muses. One day she will tell Jamie about her little incident at Sully's, but not tonight. She has her own personal demons to contend with for now.

Never in her wildest dreams did she ever think she would run into Ray Cooper again. She now despises him. The sight of him reminds her of too many hurt feelings, a rawness she thought she would never feel again. Now a nervous wreck, she takes long deep breaths, trying to calm down. She searches for a jazz station on the radio and soon finds one.

She falls back in her seat and listens to the smooth tempo of the music, the genre soothing to her soul. She glances at the clock on the dashboard and it's now six-thirty in the evening. "It's time to find out what's going on with Jamie," she said. So, she steps on the gas and speeds down the road like a bat out of hell.

Chapter Twenty-One

It's late Monday evening and the courthouse is packed with town residents taking advantage of the court's extended hours. People are everywhere, either attending court hearings or standing in line to apply for licenses or pay fines. A woman in a wedding dress sprints across the lobby like a bolt of lightning. Frantic and late for her own wedding ceremony. In a nearby corner in the lobby, a little boy screams like a hyena. His mother hugs him and he soon quiets down laying his little head on her shoulder.

Doctor Beebe and James Cole are seated in the waiting area of the courtroom. They are patiently waiting for a copy of the warrant they filed on George Benny earlier that morning. It took a lot of convincing but the judge finally signed the warrant despite the flimsy, but obvious evidence. Doctor Beebe, looking haggard from not getting enough sleep from the night before, broods over how to tell his staff the disturbing news. Not sure how or where to start. He never thought he would ever face such a task of firing one of his colleagues or one of his own.

Finally, the clerk comes out of the courtroom. Short, dumpy with straight red hair parted in the middle. The clerk, dressed in a knit black pants suit, struts over to the two men carrying a sheet of paper. Her red spike heels click hard on the wood floor. She checks them out, her hazel eyes intense, and her smile frozen.

"Here's your copy," she said handing Doctor Beebe a copy of the arrest warrant. "However, the arrest must wait until the morning. It's too late to arrest him now."

"Damn," Doctor Beebe said looking disappointed. "I hope he's home tomorrow," he said.

"I'm sorry," said the clerk. "But that's the best we can do."

She gives him the document and hurries back into the courtroom. Doctor Beebe shakes his head and rolls up his copy of the arrest warrant and sticks it in his coat pocket. "I'll be glad when this thing is over," he said. "This whole thing is so exhausting!"

"Yeah, it is," said James nodding his head. "How do you plan to break the news to your staff?" he asked.

"I have been thinking about that," he said. "It's been on my mind all day. The situation is so delicate."

"You don't have a lot of time my friend," James warns. "The media will be all over this one after the arrest tomorrow!"

"I know, I know," Doctor Beebe mutters, feeling flustered.

"Let's go to Sully's for a drink," James said. "You need a break."

"Good idea," said Doctor Beebe. "I'll meet you there."

"Okay," said James heading to his car.

It's seven o'clock by the time Rachel parks in Jamie Lee's driveway. She leaves her vehicle and runs to the front door. She rings the doorbell, hesitating after each ring and listening for any sound or movement. After several rings, Jamie swings the door open. Her light brown eyes are blood shot and smeared with dried black mascara. Her salt and peppered hair sticks straight up like a porcupine's. "Damn it girl, why are you ringing my doorbell like that?" she asked loudly, standing there barefoot in wrinkled polka dot pajamas.

"You look like a big raccoon," Rachel said chuckling. "Hello to you too," Jamie said glaring at her. "What the hell do you want?!" "I was worried about you," Rachel said, ignoring her frosty mood.

"Why?" Jamie snaps back. "You see I'm fine!"

"Aren't you going to invite me in?" Rachel asked.

"Oh hell, suit yourself," said Jamie. She walks away leaving her standing in the doorway. Rachel steps inside and shuts the door behind her.

"Excuse the mess," Jamie said pushing papers and books off the couch onto the floor. "I wasn't expecting company!"

Rachel ignores Jamie's sarcasm and situates herself on the couch. Jamie plops down in a chair across from her. "So what's up?" she asked, looking irritated. "Why, the visit?"

"I'm worried about you," Rachel said again still ignoring her friend's frosty attitude. "Sally is worried about you too."

"Oh, whoopee," Jamie said with a smirk. "Your concern is so moving! Don't you see I'm still fuckin' kicking it?!"

"Oh, stop it," Rachel said cracking a smile. "You look a damn mess!"

Jamie forces a smile. She can't help herself. She massages her temples. "Girl, I had a hell of a hangover this weekend," she admits.

"I'm not surprised," Rachel said half smiling. "You were drunk as a skunk," she added.

"Yeah I guess I was," she said.

"Are you feeling better?" asked Rachel.

"Feeling marvelous," Jamie said being sarcastic again.

"I don't believe you," Rachel shot back, as she studies Jamie's face. "Have you been crying? What's up?"

"Crying?" Jamie asked. "Yes crying," Rachel said with her eyes peeled on Jamie. "Something is going on!"

Jamie tears up. "Anne left me," she finally said. "She left a note telling me she's moved out!"

Rachel's face turns to stone. A wave of rage overcomes her. She now wishes she had run Anne over when she had the chance. Although, realistically, she would never do such a thing. It sure felt good to scare the hell out of her because she certainly deserved it. She feels sorry for Jamie. She knows what it's like to be cheated on. She wants to tell Jamie about Anne and Ray but doesn't have the heart to do so. Besides, if she told her, Jamie would drink herself into a stupor and she wasn't ready to deal with the aftermath of that. So, she decides to focus on the note instead.

"What did the note say?" she asked.

"Just a minute, I'll get it," Jamie said. She hops up and goes into the kitchen. A few seconds later, she returns with the note, handing it to Rachel. She unfolds the note and reads it with her face turning red hot as she struggles to remain calm.

"What a bitch," she mutters under her breath. "Do you know who this person is she's involved with?" "No," Jamie whispers.

Rachel is furious. She's thinking, thinking, thinking and taking deep breaths trying to tap down the anger smoldering inside. She folds the note and hands it back to Jamie.

"Girl, I know you don't want to hear this, but you need to leave Anne alone," she said. "Your relationship is over."

"I...I...I know," Jamie sobs falling in a chair.

Rachel leaves her seat and searches for a box of tissue. She finds one on the end table and brings it to Jamie.

"Thank you," she said taking a tissue out of the box. She dabs her eyes while Rachel paces back and forth. "That woman is not worth it," Rachel rants. "She doesn't deserve you! The nerve of her to leave you a note like that! How rude?!"

Jamie nods her head. "Girl you need to get revenge," Rachel continues. "Make her suffer!"

"How?" asked Jamie, her eyes filled with tears.

"Simple, "said Rachel. "Hunt her down like a rabid dog and whip her behind!"

Jamie stops crying. "Girl, you are nuttier than I realized," she said forcing a small laugh. "You are right though. She deserves a beat down."

"You damn right she does," said Rachel with her hands on her hips.

"Seriously, if you were me, what would you do?" Jamie asks.

"I just told you. I would whip her butt and never speak to her again," Rachel said.

"You are harsh," said Jamie. "Remind me not to get on your bad side."

Rachel sighs. "I do have a bit of a temper," she said.

"Yeah, I can see that," Jamie said. "Have you ever been cheated on before?"

Rachel's face turns red hot again because she is caught off guard by Jamie's question. She hesitates to answer at first, searching for the right words. However, her reaction doesn't get pass Jamie. "Did I hit a nerve?" she asked.

"As a matter of fact you did," Rachel said. "That very thing you just asked happened to me a while ago."

"Tell me about it," Jamie said. She sits straight up in her chair, eager to hear her friend's story. Rachel takes a moment to sort out her thoughts and then she begins.

"I was engaged to marry," she said.

"Huh, huh," Jamie said, her eyes fixated on her friend.

"One night, I came home late and found my fiancé in bed with another woman," Rachel said recalling the painful memory.

"Get out of here," said Jamie with her eyes big. "What did you do?"

"I pistol whipped her naked behind," Rachel said in a high pitch voice.

"You what?" Jamie asked, dropping her bottom jaw.

"I pistol whipped her behind," Rachel repeats with her face serious.

Jamie cracks up. "You actually whipped the woman?" asked Jamie.

"I sure did," Rachel said nodding her head.

"What did your fiancé do?" Jamie asked.

"He wrestled me to the ground and snatched the gun out of my hand," she said.

"So what happened next?" Jamie asked.

"The neighbors called the police," Rachel said. "The woman went to the hospital and I spent the night in jail."

"Then my two-timing fiancé bailed me out the next day dropping the charges," she further added. "I left him after that."

"What a story," Jamie said. "Why didn't you beat him? He needed an ass whipping himself!"

"I punched him in the face," Rachel said raising her voice. "He had a big knot on his knuckle-head!"

"Besides he deserved it," she said feeling vindicated. "And so did that stupid woman!" "Oh, I agree," Jamie said. "You get no argument out of me," she said laughing.

"What's the heifer's name anyway?" Jamie asks.

Rachel laughs. "Girl I don't remember," She said. "I was so upset her name didn't register."

"That's understandable," said Jamie. The two women giggle and Jamie suddenly feels better.

"My goodness," she said sliding out of her seat. "My manners are so poor! Can I get you something to drink?"

"Actually, I'm hungry," Rachel said. "What do you have to eat?"

"What would you like?" Jamie asks heading to the kitchen with Rachel on her heels.

"How about a grilled cheese sandwich?" Rachel asked.

"Grilled cheese sandwich, coming up," Jamie said grinning.

They go into the kitchen and Rachel parks herself at the table, while Jamie prepares grilled cheese sandwiches for them both. Rachel thinks about Ray and Anne, wondering what they are up to and still sore about her little encounter with them. She wants to tell Jamie about it but she can't because she doesn't want to upset her. She worries about Jamie, wondering if she could survive such a loss, once she finds out about Anne's relationship with Ray.

She tries to shake off her negative thinking but she knows betrayal all too well. Even the most sensible person can head over the edge when faced with such devastation. However, she is grateful she survived, despite her out of control actions. It took some time, but she found a way to cope with her hurt feelings eventually.

"It's done," said Jamie interrupting her thoughts. She places the grill cheese sandwich in front of her.

"Nice," said Rachel. She bites into the sandwich and chews, savoring the cheesy, buttery flavor. "Mmmmm, this is so good," she said.

"Glad you like it," said Jamie looking pleased. The two women gobble down their sandwiches and settle in for a long visit.

Meanwhile, Anne lies in bed deep in thought, waiting for Ray to finish his shower. The incident at Sully's shook her up and she wonders if Ray is over Rachel. He refused to talk about it on the way home irking her to no end. For the first time in their short relationship, she feels disconnected from him.

He finally comes out of the bathroom after forty-five short minutes wearing his wool plaid pajamas. He swaggers over to the bed and flops down with his back to her. He ignores her, combing out his thick wet afro, with his mood indifferent. The deafening silence annoys her and after a few minutes, she breaks it.

"Ray, darling," she said. "I think I should talk to Rachel. I think I'm going to give her a call to smooth things over."

"Leave Rachel alone," Ray bluntly said. "She's not going to talk to you."

"I need to talk to her," Anne insists. "I don't want her telling Jamie about us."

"Then you tell Jamie and forget about Rachel," Ray said looking very serious.

"But I am afraid Rachel may......" Ray cuts her off.

"I told you to leave Rachel alone!" he said facing her with burning eyes. "Keep her out of it! Deal with Jamie on your own!"

"Why are you so angry at me?" Anne asked, getting frustrated. "I'm just trying to do the right thing here!" "Why can't you leave well enough alone and let things work themselves out?" Ray asked, raising his voice again. "I don't want any more run-ins with my ex! Tonight, was enough!"

"Why are you so afraid of her?" Anne asked.

He doesn't answer. He's not ready to tell her the whole story behind his break-up with Rachel, who was the love of his life. He faults himself for his failed relationship with her. He understands her anger and if he could change the past he would, but he can't. Messing around with Susan Cole was a mistake. A mistake he will regret for the rest of his life.

"Ray, are you going to answer my question?" Anne asks interrupting his thoughts.

"I'm not afraid of her," Ray said. "We had a bad break-up over something I did and apparently, she hasn't gotten over it."

"You just cheated on her," Anne bluntly said.

"Look, this is not your business," Ray said chastising her. "I do not want to talk about it. I prefer to leave it in the past."

"But Ray," she insists. "I just want to….."

"Let's get some sleep," he said cutting her off again. "I'm tired. I need rest. I have a busy day tomorrow."

He slides into bed and turns off the light. He turns his back to her and pulls the blanket over his head. Anne, now pissed, scoots down in the bed and pouts. She now knows for sure her new lover has feelings for his ex, which disturbs her. She wonders if she made a drastic mistake moving in with him so soon.

The last thing she wants is to live with a man who is in love with someone else. As she finds a comfortable spot in the bed next to him, she decides to call out sick the next morning. The time has come, she reasons, to find a place to live. It's time for her to be on her own.

Chapter Twenty-Two

It's Tuesday morning. Downstairs on the ground floor, in a shoe box sized office, Doctor Beebe is conducting a secret meeting with Doctor Louis and Beth Jones. He is giving them the latest on the Susan Cole saga. Doctor Beebe coughs repeatedly as cigarette smoke accumulates in the tight office, making his eyes red and irritated.

Doctor Louis and Beth Jones, both preoccupied, puff on their cancer sticks. It looked like the two of them are in competition with one another, on who can blow out the biggest puff of cigarette smoke into the stuffy, tight atmosphere. Every two minutes a whiff of smoke drifts past Doctor Beebe's face and he feels miserable. He gasps for breath, suffocating from the smoky assault. Finally, after a five-minute coughing spell, he's had enough.

"Put out those damn cigarettes!" he said choking and raising his voice. "You are killing me! I can't breathe!"

"You don't have to yell," Doctor Louis growls.

"Get rid of those things," he said.

"Okay, okay," Beth said with a cigarette hanging from her lips. She gets up and ashes drop on the floor as she heads over to the supply closet. She opens the closet door and takes out an ashtray, bringing it back to the table. She snuffs her cigarette out and shoves the ashtray over to Doctor Louis and then she parks herself at the table. Doctor Louis reaches for the ashtray and puts his cigarette out and then he gets up and strolls over to the window. He opens the blinds and peeks out the window. Red cardinals flittering from one tree to the next capture his eye.

"Fascinating," he said. "These little critters are so fascinating."

"The things people get excited over," Beth smirks rolling her eyes. He ignores her and faces Doctor Beebe, taking his attention off the little creatures for a few moments. "What time will George Benny be arrested?" he asked.

"Anytime now," Doctor Beebe said still coughing. "Its eight-thirty and I should be getting a call soon."

"Is he home?" he asks gazing out the window again.

"He's home," Doctor Beebe said. "He called out sick this morning."

"That means nothing," said Doctor Louis, arching one eye brow and still preoccupied with the red cardinals. "You better hope he's there by the time the police arrive."

Doctor Beebe twists his face up, annoyed with Doctor Louis' sarcasm. Instead of confronting him about it, he changes the subject. "We need to schedule a staff meeting," he said. "Staff should know about George Benny's impending termination."

"Yeah, Yeah, Yeah," said Doctor Louis. "But first, I want a word with that spineless bottom feeder once he's arrested. I have a few questions to ask him," he said.

"What is it you want to know that you don't know already?" Doctor Beebe asked, looking exasperated.

"How he got away with it," he flatly said.

Beth interjects. "I can tell you"....... Doctor Beebe gives her the cut throat signal and she stops talking in mid-sentence. He does not want Doctor Louis to know about Doctor Hornsby's little sex heist with John the night Susan Cole disappeared. If he knew, he would go ballistic and Doctor Beebe just wasn't up for a fight.

Beth, tight lipped, acknowledges his cue.

However, her imposed silence doesn't escape Doctor Louis who pounces on her.

"Did you say something?" he asked.

"Oh never mind," she said cutting her eyes at Doctor Beebe.

"What's going on between you two?" he asked, not missing a beat.

"Oh, nothing," said Beth.

He knows she's lying so he presses her. "But you were going to say something," he said looking suspicious.

"Oh, I was going to suggest we schedule the staff meeting tomorrow morning at ten o' clock," she fudges.

"Okay," Doctor Louis said. He looks at Doctor Beebe and then at Beth who is whistling and looking up at the ceiling. He shakes his head and strolls back to the table. He pulls out a chair and sits down. "Carl is that a good time for you?" he asked.

"That's fine with me," Doctor Beebe sighs, relieved he dodged a bullet.

"I'll tell Joyce to put a memo in everybody's box," Beth said, scooting her chair from the table. She bolts up and wobbles to the door.

"Thank you," said Doctor Beebe. "Don't forget to reserve the conference room."

"I won't," Beth mumbles as she wobbles out of the room.

Rachel overslept and is late for work. She is tired from staying up with Jamie the night before. She speeds into the parking lot and parks her Toyota five feet from the hospital entrance. She checks her make up in the mirror and applies her lipstick. It's not long before a red fiat speeds into the parking lot and comes to a screeching halt.

"I guess I'm not the only one running late," she chuckles straining her neck to see who it is.

The door to the fiat flies open and out steps Doctor Everett James with his afro bigger than life. He's dressed in his usual bizarre attire, including dark sunglasses on the bridge of his nose. He swaggers across the parking lot to the hospital entrance, leaving the door to his fiat flung open. Rachel checks him out until he disappears into the building. She waits a few minutes before she leaves her Toyota trying to determine if he plans to return to his car but he never does.

"Scatter brain," she said shaking her head. She leaves her car and struts over to the fiat and slams the door. Then she hurries into the building. Once settled in her office, she makes a few phone calls and an hour later she's heading to the nursing station. Her heart flips somersaults when she walks into the nursing station and lays eyes on Doctor James. He's parked at the counter, quiet as a church mouse, reviewing charts and writing orders. She edges over to him, her heart thumping hard in her chest.

"Good Morning, Doctor James," she said.

"Good Morning to you, Miss Thomas," he said smiling, with his dark brown eyes sultry.

"Damn, he's fine," she thinks to herself. She melts, looking away trying to avoid his sultry gaze.

"Did you know you left your car door wide open?" she asked, glancing down at the floor.

"Oh, I did?" he asked, chuckling. "I have a lot on my mind this morning."

"I see," said Rachel.

He checks her out, looking her up and down, as he grins showing perfectly straight white teeth. "I must say, you look very pretty this morning," he said.

Rachel blushes. "Thank you," she said looking pass him.

"You're welcome," he said still grinning.

"I secured your car for you," she said trying to re-direct him.

"Thank you, Miss Lady," he said. "I appreciate you looking out for me."

"You're welcome," Rachel said, now giving him direct eye contact. "I like your car. It's cute!"

"Thank you," he said. "That car has been with me a long time. Maybe I can take you for a spin sometime."

"Mm-hm," said Rachel. She goes over to the counter and sits down. Her hand trembles out of control when she pulls a record out of the chart rack.

"You know I don't bite," he chuckles noticing her discomfort.

"Who said you did?" Rachel asked, giggling nervously.

"Let's get to know each other better," he said. "After all, we will be working together. How about dinner sometime?"

"Uh, no, I don't think so," Rachel quickly said. "I do not mix business with pleasure, doctor!"

He gives her a wicked grin. "Trying to play hard to get, I see," he said.

"No, I just don't believe in dating work colleagues," she snaps back, with a stone-cold look of confidence.

"Mm, hmm," he said winking at her. "You are a smart young lady!"

Her heart skips two beats, very flattered by his compliments but wary of his intentions. She yearns to learn more about him, but she hesitates, very intimidated by his forwardness.

Despite her discomfort, she continues to engage him in a conversation. She can't help herself, attracted to his dark brown eyes and mysterious aura.

"Doctor James, "she said. "I have a question to ask you."

"Shoot," he said.

"Are you married?" she blurts out.

"No, I'm single," he said. "What about you, Miss Thomas? What's your status?"

"I'm asking the questions here, doctor," Rachel boldly snaps back. "But if you must know, "I'm single as well."

"Feisty, I see, "Doctor James said. He stares at her, his gaze very intense. Her heart flutters and she looks away feeling embarrassed.

"I don't mean to make you feel uncomfortable," he said recognizing her discomfort again. "I like your assertiveness and I like a woman who speaks her mind."

"Mm-hm," she said. She knows he's lying. What man likes a woman who speaks her mind all the time? she ponders. After a couple of minutes pass, she's feeling brave again. She asks him another question.

"Why do you dress like that?" she asked. The words come out before she even thinks about it. "Are you dressing for war?" she chuckles under her breath.

He lets out a hearty laugh. "No," he said. "I use to belong to the Black Panther Party and I find this style comfortable."

"Oh," said Rachel.

"You don't like the way I dress, pretty lady?" he asked.

"Well, it's different," she said being brutally honest.

"So, if I dress more to your standards," he teases. "Would you consider going to dinner with me?"

Rachel's heart thumps harder in her chest. The man has a tantalizing effect on her and his smooth demeanor turns her on; however, she manages to put him off.

"Let's keeps things professional," she snaps back. "I just met you," she said.

"Very well then," he said backing down.

Rachel slides out of her chair. "I have a lot work to do today," she said looking serious. "See you around."

She takes off, leaving him in the nursing station. "You have a productive day Miss Thomas," he hollers after her.

She doesn't answer. Doctor James remains on her mind all the way to her office. She can't help it because she's attracted to him. He's handsome, sexy, tall, dangerous and definitely her type. A romance with him is out of the question. Especially at work. By the time she reaches her office, she has mapped out a strategy to keep the handsome doctor at a distance. "I'm not going anywhere near him," she convinces herself. "That way I won't get myself into trouble."

Doctor Beebe jerks forward when the phone rings. "Damn that phone is loud," he said.

"Maybe it's the police chief," said Doctor Louis.

"I hope so," said Doctor Beebe picking up the phone.

"Hello, this is Doctor Beebe," he said. He listens for a moment and then he breaks out in a big grin. He hangs up the phone.

"You are right," he said. "The police are on their way to arrest George Benny. The police chief will call us after they bring him in." Doctor Louis pokes out his chest and smiles. "Good work," he said.

It's ten in the morning when Salter's Point police reach Doctor Benny's home. They tumble out of their cars and sprint down the cobblestone side walk swarming the house like a pack of wild dogs. One officer, with a shot gun, hovers on one side of the door and another officer crouches on the other side ringing the doorbell over and over.

After several minutes pass, the officer kicks the door down. Armed officers follow him inside the house and they search every single room, closet, hole and cranny. They finally give up when there is no sign of either Doctor Benny or his lover, Susan Cole. The two of them are nowhere to be found.

Miles away, at SEA-TAC Airport, George Benny and Susan Cole have boarded their flight. Stuffing their carry-ons in the luggage bin. The flight, scheduled to leave any time now, is crowded and noisy. A loud booming voice bellows from the cockpit. "Good morning ladies and gentlemen," the pilot said. "Welcome to flight 700 on Delta Airlines. We will be leaving shortly, please take your seats and buckle up!"

Flight attendants scurry up and down the aisle like little mice, assisting passengers with their luggage, while two flight attendants at opposite ends of the aisle demonstrate emergency procedures for passengers seated at the plane's exit doors. Susan takes a seat next to the window and buckles her seat belt.

"I can't wait to see Paris," she said. "I'm so excited!"

"There's a lot to see there," Doctor Benny said taking the aisle seat next to her. He buckles his seat belt.

"I know," Susan said. "Will you take me to the Eiffel Tower?"

"Sure," he said. "As soon as we settle in our apartment."

"Our apartment?" she asked, looking very surprised. "How long are we staying there?"

"For a while," he said leaning over and kissing her on the cheek.

"What about your work?" she asked.

"I'm taking a sabbatical," Doctor Benny said.

"A sabbatical? What's that?" she asked.

He chuckles at her ignorance. "A sabbatical is an extended leave from work," he said.

"Oh," she said leaning back in her seat.

A security officer glides down the aisle, taking his time, with his light brown eyes darting back and forth from one passenger to the next. He then locks eyes with Doctor Benny and stops. The doctor sucks in his breath, holding it in. He begins to perspire and his face turns red hot. The officer stops at his seat and Doctor Benny panics. A warm sensation threatens his groin area and he bears down to keep from urinating in his pants.

"Good Morning sir," said the officer. "Are you alright?"

"I'm fine," said Doctor Benny with his voice hoarse.

The officer fixates his eyes on Susan. "Ma'am, you look familiar," he said. "Have we met?"

"I don't believe so," she said making brief eye contact with the officer.

"Well you look familiar," he said checking her out.

Doctor Benny fidgets in his seat and clears his throat. "Humph, Officer is something wrong?" he asked.

"No," he said, still eyeing Susan. He cranes his neck to get a better look at her. "Ma'am, are you a celebrity or something?" he asks. "I think I saw you on TV not long ago."

Doctor Benny almost peed on himself. He bears down harder to suppress it, holding his breath. Susan remains cool. "Officer I think you are mistaken," she said. "I'm no celebrity."

"Well you look very familiar," he said. "Sorry for the mistake."

"No problem," Susan said with her face damp.

She bends over and looks underneath her seat. She pulls out her handbag and places it in her lap. The officer moves on and makes his way to the back of the plane. Doctor Benny whistles out a long deep sigh.

"Whew," he said. "That was close."

"Yes it was," said Susan dabbing her face with a tissue. "I see why you wanted me to stay in the house. It's a good thing he mistook me for a celebrity. Otherwise, you would be in deep trouble," she said.

"I know," Doctor Benny said. "I know."

He leans over in the aisle. He can hear the officer having a conversation with one of the flight attendants in the back of the plane. The dialogue lasting only five minutes, but to him it seemed an eternity. The security officer then walks back to the front of the plane, passing him and Susan on his way there. He smiles at them as he passes with his gait very brisk. He stops and takes one more look around the plane and then he tips his hat and exits the plane.

Susan leans over and wipes Doctor Benny's cheek. "Honey, you are sweating bullets! Are you alright?"

"I'm okay," he said. "I'm just a little shaken up."

"Well, we are clear," she said. "Let's get some rest. We have a long flight ahead."

He smiles at her and she moves closer into him, nuzzling her head on his shoulder. The plane soon taxis out of the gate. He kisses her forehead. "We are off," he said. "Paris, France here we come!"

The flight attendants take their seats and the pilot turns on the loud speaker and makes an announcement, his voice roaring like a big lion.

"We will be in the air in a few minutes," he said. "This is an eight-hour flight destined to Paris, France. Buckle up everyone and flight attendants prepare for takeoff!"

Doctor Benny and Susan shared a passionate, lingering kiss as the plane picks up speed on the runway. They hold hands as the plane descends into the clouds, climbing thirty thousand feet, straight into the vast blue horizon. It will be years before George Benny and Susan Cole are heard from again. Until then, their infamous escape will be the talk of Salter's Point Regional for years to come.

Chapter Twenty-Three

An hour later, Doctor Beebe speeds like lightening through the crowded lobby of the police station, with the wheels on his wheelchair rumbling loud like a clap of thunder. Doctor Louis jogs behind him with a scowl on his face. George Benny's escape has him riled up. "I can't wait to see that idiot of a police chief," he mumbles to himself. "He has a lot of explaining to do."

Doctor Beebe, on the other hand, is disappointed but not surprised. He knew when he filed the arrest warrant his chances were slim, but he was hopeful and determined to put the whole debacle to rest. Now he's miserable because his efforts have failed.

"Will you slow down?" Doctor Louis asked, gasping for breath. "This is not a damn race!"

"Sorry," Doctor Beebe said looking glum. "I tend to get carried away in this chair when I'm in a hurry!"

"I can't believe those idiots didn't arrest him!" Doctor Louis growls.

"Louis, please don't show you're behind when we get there," Doctor Beebe said. "I don't have money to bail you out of jail!"

"Then don't," Doctor Louis scowls. "I can take care of myself," he said.

Doctor Beebe doesn't hear him. He's several feet ahead, whizzing down the hall like a bat on speed. Doctor Louis, short of breath, slows down to a brisk walk as he struggles to catch his breath. "Carl, slow your roll," he yells after him.

"Okay, okay," said Doctor Beebe putting on his brakes. He jerks forward and falls back in the chair. "Is this better," he said when Doctor Louis finally catches up with him.

"Smart ass," said Doctor Louis.

Doctor Beebe laughs. "Louis, face it. You are out of shape," he teases.

"Humph," Doctor Louis grumbles. He ignores the comment and continues to complain. "I can't wait to choke that police chief," he said. "He really botched this one up!"

"Louis, I'm warning you," Doctor Beebe said getting serious. "Keep your temper together! I don't want you ending up in jail!"

"Okay," he said. "But I'm not making any promises".

Soon they run into a black door with large gold lettering embolden across the front. "Does that say Police Chief's Office?" Doctor Beebe innocently asks.

"Geez, are you blind?" Doctor Louis smirks. He moves in front of Doctor Beebe and pounds on the door like a maniac.

"Will you stop acting like a nitwit?" asked Doctor Beebe looking exasperated. "Get a hold of yourself!"

"Carl, stop hassling me," he said shooting his boss an evil eye.

"Then calm down man," Doctor Beebe said backing up. The door swings open and an amazon looking woman, dressed in a red ruffled blouse, spandex pants and spiked red stilettos emerges in the doorway. Her dyed black hair is teased high into a beehive bun and her lipstick is florescent pink. She pops gum, every two seconds until the gooey substance turns into a bubble and pops all over her lips. She looks at the two men wary eyed as she bites and licks the sticky mess off her upper lip. "What do you fellas want?" she asked.

Doctor Louis grimaces. "Who in the hell are you?" he asked.

"I ask the questions here ratty head," she quips.

"What did you call me?" he asked, his face red as a cherry. He steps to her and Doctor Beebe yanks his coattail and pulls him back. Doctor Louis jerks away from him and scowls.

"Ma'am, we are doctors from Salter's Point Regional," he quickly said. "I'm Doctor Carl Beebe and this is Doctor Michael Louis. The police chief is expecting us."

"He is?" she asked, arching an eyebrow.

"Yes," said Doctor Beebe. "Can we see him?"

"It depends," she said smacking her gum. "Why do you need to see him?"

Feeling vindictive, Doctor Louis baits her. "It's none of your damn business," he said.

His words sting and she glares at him. "I need to check this out. I'll be right back," she said. She slams the door in their faces and locks it.

Doctor Louis' blood boils. He grabs the door knob and shakes it and then he pounds on the door. "Unlock this damn door, you witch," he said.

"Man will you stop," Doctor Beebe said yanking his coat tail again. "You are acting like a two-year old! You are making things worse!"

"Carl, that witch just slammed the door in our faces," he said looking like an overinflated orange balloon in the face. "I can't let her get away with that!"

"Let it go," Doctor Beebe said waving one hand. "We have bigger fish to fry!"

Doctor Louis pouts and backs away from the door. He folds his arms and paces back and forth, grumbling to himself. "That witch has a lot nerve," he said.

Seconds later, the door swings open and the same woman emerges in the doorway. Her spandex pants have slipped below her waistline exposing faded red panties. When she squats, and pulls her pants up, she almost tumbles over. "Oops," she said laughing. "I'm a little off balance."

"Off balance, my ass," Doctor Louis quips. "That heavy luggage you are carrying on your backside is your problem," he said.

She cuts her eyes at him and then she points to his head. "You got nerve," she said. "That animal you are sporting on top of your head is pretty damn scary!"

"You bit....," he said bristling up.

Doctor Beebe cringes and cuts him off. "Don't say another word," he said. Doctor Louis twists his lips and folds his arms. He rolls his eyes.

"Will you take us to the police chief?" Doctor Beebe asked, giving him the stink eye.

"Follow me," the woman said sticking her nose in the air. She takes off and the two men follow her. She tugs at her pants, squatting repeatedly every three minutes to adjust the material around her ample waist and thighs. Doctor Louis cracks up laughing. "Honey, spandex is not your friend," he said.

The woman stops and turns to face him. She pops her gum in a snappy staccato rhythm and her eyes narrow, not uttering a word. Then she spins on her stilettos and continues her journey.

"Louis," Doctor Beebe whispers. "Stop aggravating the poor woman!"

"Those tight spandex pants are aggravating her, not me," he jokes.

Doctor Beebe forces a smile. "Shame on you," he said.

Soon they stumble on a large open area filled with officers and administrative staff hunkered down in cubicles. Some of them shouting into telephones while others yell at each other across the room.

"Boy is it noisy in here," said Doctor Beebe casing the room.

The woman wiggles her way thru the cubicle maze, motioning for the men to follow her. Her pants slide down over her behind and she stops to pull them up. Doctor Beebe brings his wheelchair to a screeching halt. "What are you doing?" he asked with his tone high pitch. "I almost ran into you."

"Sorry, dude," she said tugging on her pants. "I just can't get these things to fit right."

"I told you spandex isn't your friend," Doctor Louis said under his breath.

Doctor Beebe shoots him another dirty look. "Will you be quiet?" he whispers. "She can hear you!"

"I don't care," he said. "Those pants are too little for her wide ass!" The woman moves across the floor in a rapid pace as her stilettos click hard on the linoleum floor. "We are almost there," she said.

"Finally," said Doctor Beebe taking a deep breath. It's not long before they approach a thick oak door. The woman stops there and knocks. "I don't see a name on the door," Doctor Beebe said looking perplexed. "Is this the police chief's office?" She doesn't answer.

The door swings open and a tall heavy set man with a pot belly and a receding hair line takes up the whole doorway. He grins with his hazel eyes expressive and quite inviting.

"Hello gentlemen," he said. "I'm Thomas Marshall, the police chief. Please come in and have a seat."

"Greetings," said both doctors.

"Let me get that door for you," said Thomas holding the door wide open. Doctor Beebe rolls his wheelchair past him and situates himself in front of Thomas' desk, which is an antique piece of furniture made from cherry wood.

"Thank you," he said.

"You're welcome," said Thomas.

Doctor Louis follows suit and shakes Thomas' hand. He then collapses in a black leather chair next to Doctor Beebe. He checks out the room. Every wall is decorated with awards and scenic pictures of trees and breath taking water fronts. The room is furnished with two black leather chairs, a big sofa and two shiny cherry wood end tables. Each table decorated with a potted green plant.

"Nice office," he said.

"Thanks," Thomas said.

A loud smacking noise is heard in the room and everyone turns around to look. The amazon woman, still playing with her spandex pants, is wedged in the doorway. She is smacking and popping her gum.

"Carla, you can go now," Thomas said waving for her to leave. "I'll buzz if I need anything else."

"Alright chief," she said.

She spits her gum out and balls it up in her fingers and then she throws it across the room, like a basketball, into the trash can.

She grins like a chess cat, winking at Doctor Louis who rolls his eyes in disgust. She then spins on her stiletto heels and steps out into the open office area, slamming the door behind her.

"She's nuts," Doctor Louis said under his breath. "She should never wear spandex again in life!"

Thomas roars. "I apologized for her behavior," he said. "She can be annoying at times."

"She's more than annoying," Doctor Louis said.

Thomas laughs again. "Well let's get down to business," he said. "Gentlemen, I am very sorry about this office's failure to arrest Doctor Benny this morning."

"What happened?" asked Doctor Louis with fury in his eyes.

"We acted on the warrant sir, but the doctor got away," Thomas said. "A neighbor saw him leave in a cab with his girlfriend early this morning," he said.

"His girlfriend is the missing patient," said Doctor Beebe now looking very pissed. "Her name is Susan Cole!"

"I'm so sorry," Thomas honestly said. "We really messed up this time!"

Doctor Louis bolts from his seat. "You sure in the hell did!" he retorts. He paces back and forth, his face beet red, mumbling to himself. "Damn, Damn, Damn," he said. "I can't believe this asshole got away!"

"We will find him," Thomas insists. "My people are already on it!"

"Your people are knuckleheads," said Doctor Louis, looking wolfish. "He's probably out of the state by now!" Thomas' face turns to stone. "Sir watch yourself," he warns.

Doctor Louis explodes and pounds on the desk sending books and papers onto the floor. Thomas lunges from his chair with his right hand on his holster. "Sir, calm down," he said. "You can get yourself into serious trouble. "

"Michael, he's right, you need to put a lid on it," Doctor Beebe quickly interjects.

"Sorry," said Doctor Louis returning to his senses. He goes to his seat and sits down. He fumes. Thomas takes his seat, but keeps his eyes peeled on the doctor.

"Your friend George Benny is clever," he surmises. "But we will find him, I promise you that."

"What happens if you don't?" asked Doctor Beebe feeling discouraged.

"We will contact the FBI," Thomas said.

"And what will they do?" asked Doctor Beebe.

"It's hard to say," Thomas said. "The warrant is flimsy, so even if we capture him, we won't be able to hold him."

"What?" Doctor Louis said jerking his head around like an owl. "Carl, what in the hell is he saying?"

"The judge thought the evidence against Benny was thin as piss," Doctor Beebe said. "He signed it after I told him he was keeping a missing patient in his home."

"The truth is, Susan Cole was a willing participant in her own disappearance," he adds.

"Damn, Damn, Damn!" Doctor Louis mutters shaking his head. "So really we have no case!"

"I'm sorry Louis, it's thin," Doctor Beebe said. "It's very, very thin."

Doctor Louis gets up. "I'm out," he said looking disappointed. He stomps out leaving Doctor Beebe in the office.

"Ugh," Doctor Beebe said rubbing his temples.

"I'm sorry the situation turned out this way," Thomas flatly said.

"Me too," said Doctor Beebe shaking his head.

"Do you think Doctor Louis will get over this?" Thomas asked.

"I don't think so," said Doctor Beebe. "He never liked George Benny in the first place."

He backs his chair up and rolls to the door. "Call me if you find the bastard," he said.

"I will," said Thomas rising from his seat. He meets Doctor Beebe at the door and holds it open for the doctor to exit. He watches Doctor Beebe speed across the room until he disappears through the exit. He sighs and shuts the door.

Back in her office, Jamie broods over her break-up with Anne. Emotionally tapped out, she is unable to concentrate on her work. When she receives two phone calls, one from Sally and then the other from Rachel, she is compelled, although reluctantly, to see what they want. She leaves her safe haven and goes to Rachel's office. "I am not in the mood for this crap," she mumbles trudging down the corridor.

Her appearance is vagabond-like with her hair stretched in every direction and her clothing, wrinkled and dark, hangs on her like a sack of potatoes. Her eyes, puffy and blood shot, stared blankly ahead as she struggles with her emotions. Feeling fine and dandy one minute and then balling her eyes out the next. She wrinkles up her nose when a pungent, rabid odor blasts by her. The odor becoming worse as she passes Doctor Hornsby's office. "What is that smell?" she wonders plugging her nose.

A patient, grimacing like a gremlin, walks by her in the corridor. "Whew it stinks," he gags. "It smells like horseshit!"

She knew it smelled worse than horse shit, but she didn't care. Anne occupied her mind and she was not able to focus. Minutes later she's tapping on Rachel's door. She opens it and sticks her head in.

"I'm here," she said fighting back tears.

"Girl, come in," Rachel said.

Jamie goes in and closes the door. She marches to the sofa and flops down next to Sally. She looks down in her lap, her mood sad. "So what's up?" she asked.

"Boy, you look a mess," Rachel said looking concerned. "You look like you are in mourning dressed in all of that damn black," she said.

"I am in mourning!" Jamie said raising her voice. "I just lost the love of my life!"

"We know," said Sally. "But we are not here to talk about Anne!"

"Then what is this meeting about?" Jamie asked, looking crossed.

"You're drinking," Sally said.

Jamie is pissed. How dare they trick her like that! She scoots down on the sofa and pouts, twiddling her index fingers.

"She's being salty toward us," said Rachel.

"I don't care," said Sally suddenly getting a burst of anger. "I have something to say!"

Jamie jerks her head around and chides Sally. "Then say it," she snaps.

"Every day you come to work reeking of alcohol," Sally said chastising her. "Girl, you have a serious problem and you need help!" "You think I have a problem?" Jamie asked, with her face twisted. "My drinking is not your business! Your ass drinks! Why are you on me?!" Rachel bolts out of her seat. "Don't you dare turn this around on Sally," she said. "Face it, you have a problem and it's affecting your work and everybody else's work!"

"Oh, really?" Jamie said with burning eyes. "Tell me, how is my drinking affecting your work?!"

"Oh let me tell you," Rachel said with her hands on her hips, her eyes buck wild.

"When you fight with Anne, you hide in your office all day drinking and sulking. I have to cover your cases and mine too," she said. "You are belligerent and rude and when you are like that it affects my work!"

Jamie falls back on the sofa as tears well in her eyes. Rachel's stinging words grip her and she knows her friend is right. Treatment, however, is the farthest thing from her mind. "I don't want help," she said. "I want Anne!"

"Jamie," Sally softly said. "Anne left you because of your drinking, remember?"

Sally's words haunt her like a nagging ghost and she breaks down balling. "I miss her," Jamie said.

"I know," said Sally. "But you need alcohol treatment; it's time to sober up!"

Rachel walks over to her and rubs her back. "Look, we are worried about you," she softly said. "We care what happens to you. We just want you to get help so you can be well and happy."

Sally reaches over and takes her hand. "Think about it girl," she said. "There are a lot of good treatment programs out there."

"Okay, I'll think about," Jamie said giving in, with her voice barely audible. "But promise me, you two will give me time to think this over."

"Okay we promise," Rachel said. "But don't think you are off the hook," she said. "We will jack you up again if we have to," she added smiling.

Jamie manages a smile. "I know you will," she said.

Out of the blue there is a hard knock on the door. Rachel rushes to the door and opens it. Beth Jones stands in the doorway tapping her foot. Her fierce green eyes peering over her bifocals. She appears two inches taller than usual in her purple, gold buckled, three-inch high boots.

"What's going on in here?" she asked, gesturing for Rachel to move out of her way. She steps pass Rachel and poses in the middle of the room. She checks out the three women and then she zeros in on Jamie. "What's wrong with you?" she asked. "You look like a barracuda!"

Jamie frowns. "Hello to you too," she said.

"Answer my question," said Beth looking fierce.

"Nothing is wrong," Jamie said. "I am fine," she said.

Beth rolls her eyes and decides to drop the subject. "Ladies, there's an emergency meeting in ten minutes in the conference room," she said.

"What's the meeting about?" asked Rachel, looking perplexed.

"Come to the meeting and find out," Beth said with her voice harsh. She marches out of the office, slamming the door behind her.

Jamie frowns, flipping a bird in Beth's direction. "She irritates me," she said. "Me too, "Rachel said.

"I wonder what's going on," Sally said.

"Well, ladies, let's find out," Rachel said already heading to the door. Sally and Jamie follow her.

On the way to the conference room, a rotten stench hits them as they pass Doctor Hornsby's office. "What is that smell?" Rachel asked, fanning her nose.

"Hell if I know," Jamie said wrinkling her nose.

"It smells like something died over here," Sally said stopping at Doctor Hornsby's office. She knocks on the door. There is no answer. "Has anyone seen her today?" she asks.

"No," Rachel said gagging.

Sally knocks on the door again and there is no answer. "I'll get housekeeping to check this out after the meeting," she said.

"Good idea," said Rachel. The women plugged their noses and hurried down the corridor.

Chapter Twenty-Four

Everyone packs into the conference room like a can of sardines, taking the first available seat as they settled in for the emergency meeting. Rachel, Sally and Jamie meander to the back of the room and take seats against the wall. Several nurses chatting, like hens in a chicken coop, sit together in a nearby corner.

Doctor Everett James, now sporting a black beret to compliment his dark sunglasses, leans against the wall checking everyone out as they stagger in for the meeting. Across the room, sitting on the floor Indian style with his hair wild all over his head like a mad scientist, is Hiram Gottschalks. He looks a mess with dingy white sleeves rolled up to his elbows and a tie twisted backwards around his neck.

Up front, sitting at a table and blowing big puffs of cigarette smoke into the atmosphere, is Beth Jones. She sucks drags off her cancer stick while she surveys the room. Doctor Louis soon joins her and whispers in her ear. Then he makes his way down the aisle to the front of the room. Nurses and techs check him out and giggle, while pointing at his head. His toupee, brown and greasy, has slid to the back of his head as he shoves it back to the top. His face is fixated in a permanent scowl.

"Do you see that?" asked one nurse, turning to face her friends sitting behind her. "That slimy rug on Doctor Louis' head almost fell off." They giggle and squirm in their seats while Doctor Beebe, looking very solemn, rolls his wheelchair to the podium. He parks it there and remains quiet, not uttering a word.

Rachel scoots over and whispers in Sally's ear. "What's wrong with Doctor Louis' hair?" she asked while giggling.

"Girl, he looks so damn ridiculous," she chuckles.

"A fool more like it," said Jamie listening within earshot.

Doctor Louis pats his toupee and then adjusts the volume on the microphone. It squeaks when he growls into it. "Good Afternoon, Everyone," he said turning down the volume. "We called this meeting because we have an announcement to make," he adds.

Nurses and Social Workers whisper among each other while Rachel cases the room looking for Doctor Benny. When she doesn't see him, she taps Sally's shoulder. "Where's Doctor Benny?" she asked.

"I don't know," Sally said. "He must still be out sick."

"Mmmm," said Rachel looking puzzled. "Something's not right," she said.

Doctor Louis takes a deep breath and begins the meeting. "Doctor George Benny is no longer an employee at Salter's Point Regional," he announces.

"What?!" Rachel said with her eyes big.

"My word," said Sally. "What the hell happened?" she asked. Loud talking erupts around the room and several social workers move closer to one another so they can gossip and converse.

"SETTLE DOWN!" said Doctor Louis, adjusting the microphone again. His toupee tilts on his head and he grabs it, shoving it to the top. Sprigs of greasy hair stick straight up like a porcupine.

Snickers break out across the room and a few social workers scoot to the edge of their seats to gossip with colleagues sitting in front of them. Doctor Louis continues with his comments despite the commotion. "We have learned that Doctor Benny and Susan Cole have been living together for the past few weeks," he said with his face beet red.

Gasps erupt around the room while Rachel, Sally and Jamie give each other knowingly glances. Not surprised by the startling news. The three of them had suspected the doctor anyway after observing his inappropriate behavior with female patients. "Quiet," said Doctor Louis getting inpatient. "I'm not finished!" The chatter tapers down except for a few nurses gabbing nearby in a corner. Several social workers fidget in their seats and make childlike faces. A male social worker farts and seconds later a whiff of rotten eggs consumes the room. Social Workers seated near him curse and plug their noses. Disgusted, they make a bee-line across the room, taking seats against the wall. Doctor Louis rubs his nose, ignoring the odor. He continues giving out information. "We believe Doctor Benny coerced Susan Cole into having an affair," he said. "We filed papers for his arrest, however, he skipped town."

"Doctor Benny, you scoundrel!" Hiram said hopping up and pulling his pants up. "What a way to go," he said. "We old guys know how to put it on them!" The men give Hiram a thunderous applause and he bows, grinning like a chess cat and enjoying the brief spotlight. Doctors Louis and Beebe glowered at him from across the room. "Alright, that's enough," Doctor Louis said. The applause dies down. "Hiram," he said his tone sharp. "Take a seat."

Hiram flips his hair back and drops to the floor. Giggles resonate around the room and Doctor Louis stares him down, with his temper flaring. Hiram, not intimidated, sits on the floor Indian style and picks his nose.

Looking flustered, Doctor Louis presses on. "The police are doing everything possible to find Doctor Benny and Miss Cole," he said. "This will probably be on the six o' clock news tonight, but if you have questions come to me," he said.

"I have a question," said one male social worker springing from his seat. He blasts out a series of farts and several social workers sitting in the vicinity groan and fan their noses.

"Doctor Louis, sir" he said pausing for a second. "Are you aware your toupee has slid to the back of your head?"

Loud laughter erupts around the room. Staff stomp their feet and point fingers at the doctor. His face turns ashy gray. He tries desperately to straighten his toupee, but to no avail. The hairy rug keeps sliding out of position. Out of shrill frustration, he snatches it off his head and stuffs it in his coat pocket. Staff roars with laughter and his blood boils. "The hell with you people!" he said. He stomps out of the room like a two-year old with Beth running after him.

Rachel, Sally and Jamie laugh so hard their stomachs hurt. Doctor Beebe rolls his wheelchair to the podium and snatches the microphone.

"I want everybody quiet," he said with his face puffed up like a blowfish.

The laughter soon fizzles out and Doctor Beebe zeros in on Luther.

"You weren't very nice to Doctor Louis," he said chastising the social worker. "You need to apologize to him the next time you see him."

"Sure thing," the social worker said with a smirk on his face. Snickers break out around the conference room again which upsets Doctor Beebe even more. "Stop it," He said. "I want quiet!"

Except for a few snickers here or there, everyone eventually quiets down. Doctor Beebe, visibly upset, blows on the microphone and speaks in a low voice. "Now I am open to questions," he said. "Do you have any?"

"I do," said a female social worker with a baby voice. She slides out of her seat, looking introspective and then she turns around in a complete circle breaking out in a huge grin.

"Doctor Beebe," she said her tone soft and polite. "Are you going to respond to the memo we sent you the other day?"

"What memo?" he asked, staring at her with fury in his eyes.

"The memo requesting permission to allow orthodox sex in the break room during work hours," she said smiling sweetly. "Inquiring minds want to know."

Everyone shrieks with laughter, stomping their feet, giving each other high fives. They chant in unison over and over, "We want Orthodox Sex! We want Orthodox Sex! We want Orthodox Sex! Hallelujah for Orthodox Sex."

Rachel's mouth drops open. "Do you believe this?" she asked shaking her head. "This place is way too much!"

"Crazy," said Sally shrugging her shoulders. "This whole meeting is out of control!"

Doctor Beebe, his face red like a chili pepper, throws the mic across the room, barely missing one of the nurses. "This meeting is over!" he shouts.

He flips his wheelchair around and rolls out of the conference room. The social worker chases after him, her stride short and quick. "Doctor Beebe, are you going to answer my question?" she hollers after him. "Hold up sir, I'm talking to you!"

Doctor Beebe speeds down the corridor as fast as he can. He whips around the corner and disappears, leaving her in the dust. Too exhausted to take another step, the social worker gives up and returns to her office. Rachel, Sally and Jamie, now heading back to their offices, are laughing hysterically.

"What was that?" asked Rachel doubled over.

"Girl, I wish I knew," Jamie chuckles.

"At least we know what happened to Susan Cole," Sally interjects. "The mystery is over."

"Doctor Benny… What a dog," Rachel said.

"Yep, a straight up dog," Jamie said.

"You think the police will ever find him?" Rachel asks.

"I hope so," said Sally.

"Don't count on it," Jamie said. "That slippery dog is long gone."

Chapter Twenty-Five

Jamie, Rachel and Sally head back to the admissions unit and they run into Peepers. The big cat crouches low in front of Doctor Hornsby's office door hissing and bearing his fangs. When he scratches the door, his sharp claws leave deep marks in the door's veneer. Soon patients and nurses gather in the hall holding their noses. The three women gag as they force their way through the crowd.

"Someone, please call housekeeping," Sally yells trying to push back a dry heave. "And someone please page Doctor Hornsby!"

A nurse hurries down the hall to the nursing station. She snatches the phone off its receiver and calls housekeeping and then she pages Doctor Hornsby.

"DOCTOR HORNSBY PLEASE COME TO THE ADMISSIONS UNIT!" she pages. She hesitates, gripping the counter, her face an ashy grey. Once the urge to vomit passes, she pages Doctor Hornsby again.

"DOCTOR HORNSBY YOU ARE NEEDED ON THE ADMISSIONS UNIT!" she belts out.

Five minutes later, Doctor Hornsby shows up, grinning from ear-to-ear. She strolls over to the crowd. "What's going on here?" she innocently asks, not the least bit bothered by the pungent odor.

"Don't you smell it?" asked Sally looking grave.

"Smell what?" asked Doctor Hornsby with a gleam in her eye.

"Don't you smell that freaking odor?" asked Sally. "It's coming from your office and its stinks!"

"My, my, aren't we out of sorts this afternoon," Doctor Hornsby said smiling.

"Stop playing with me," Sally hisses. "What do you have in there?"

"In where?" asked the doctor looking around. "You mean my office?"

"Yes, doctor, I mean your damn office," said Sally gritting her teeth.

"Yeah, what's in that office?" the crowd echoes, holding their noses. They move to one side creating a path for the doctor so she can get to her office. Peepers scratches the door at a fever pace, his long black claws scraping the paint off. He flashes his fangs and the hair on his back sticks straight up when Doctor Hornsby approaches. "Please move that cat," she said. A nurse picks up the cat and takes it down the hall. Doctor Hornsby faces the crowd. "I have been doing a little experiment," she explains.

"An experiment?" the staff groans. "What experiment?" they shout getting frustrated.

"Let me show you," she said.

She pauses briefly and then she unlocks the door and shoves it open. The odor hits everyone in the face like a ton of bricks and they back away, gagging and heaving. One patient vomits on the floor while another patient runs straight to the nearest bathroom. When housekeeping staff finally show up, they too are recoiled from the pungent odor.

Doctor Hornsby, unfazed by all the commotion, goes into her office and grabs a Tupperware container off her desk. She returns to the doorway and opens the container.

The odor is so bad, several staff throw up on the floor right in front of her, while some cover their mouths and run across the hall into the bathroom. Doctor Hornsby giggles like a hyena, shoving the container in Sally's face. She recoils. "What the hell is that?" she asked plugging her nose.

"A brain," said Doctor Hornsby.

"A brain?" Sally repeats, sounding like a parrot, as she begins to feel sick.

"A donated human brain," Doctor Hornsby said looking proud. She sniffs the contents of the container. "See it's not that bad," she said.

Rachel and Jamie head straight to the bathroom. The color in Sally's face disappears, turning a pasty, pale white.

"Why in the hell would you have this in your office?" she manages to ask, trying not to vomit. "Have you gone nuts?!"

"Now calm down dear," said Doctor Hornsby, trying to reassure her. "I was doing an experiment and forgot to return it to the lab this morning."

"You forgot to return it to the lab?" Sally asked, sounding like a parrot again, with her eyes wild. "You are out of your freaking mind! Get this out of here now!"

"Very well," said the doctor with a sly grin on her face. She seals the container and closes her office door. "Sorry my dear friends," she said. "I didn't mean to upset anyone."

She strolls down the hall, humming to herself, soon disappearing around the corner. Sally cups her mouth to keep from puking. She tells the housekeeping staff to disinfect the doctor's office and clean up the vomit on the floor. Across the hall in the bathroom, Rachel and Jamie are miserable. They hover over the sink puking their guts out until they have nothing left to give.

They slurp water out of the spigot rinsing the sour taste from their mouths. Rachel snatches a paper towel from the wall dispenser and dabs her lips.

"Why would anyone keep something like that in their office?" she asks, still feeling very nauseous.

"That woman is a nut," Jamie said, gagging and trying to catch her breath. "She's crazy as hell!"

"You got that right," said Rachel. "Do you think she did that shit on purpose so she can see us suffer?" she asked.

"Probably," Jamie said. "I always thought she was a little sadistic!"

Rachel pukes again while Jamie drops her head deep in the sink overwhelmed with dry heaves. Thirty minutes later, the two women feel better and head out of the bathroom. Peepers greets them in the doorway, with his yellow eyes engaging. Jamie picks him up and caresses his thick black fur and then she puts him down on the floor again. They make their way down the hall with the cat prowling behind them. Rachel clears her throat. "Girl, this has been a hell of a day," she said.

"Yep," said Jamie nodding her head. "Hellish indeed."

Later in the evening, around seven o'clock, Ray is having dinner and watching a basketball game on television when breaking news interrupts the game. The story of Susan Cole's disappearance is rehashed by the anchorwoman. The latest details of her love affair with Doctor George Benny and her escape out of the country is top breaking news. Susan Cole's picture flashes across the television screen and Ray chokes and stops eating. "I don't believe this," he said looking shocked. "Susan Cole? She was here right under my nose."

When he recalls his memory of Susan Cole, the nerve endings on his arms and legs tingle and he flinches trying to shake off the awful sensation. He wonders if Rachel is watching the news. He tries not to think about it, although, he knows he's fooling himself. "Damn!" he said.

He slides out of his chair and goes to the kitchen. He grabs a bottle of red wine from the refrigerator and pours himself a glass, filling it up to the rim. He gulps down the red liquid and pours himself another glass, with his mind rehearsing the past and sinking into deep thought. Soon Anne emerges and leans against the door frame. She folds her arms and studies him.

"Are you okay?" she asks, interrupting his thoughts. He flinches, surprised to see her.

"Yes," he lied. "I'm okay, why?"

"Just wondering," she said. "You seem a million miles away."

"I'm fine Anne," he said putting her off. He grabs the bottle of wine and walks past her out the door.

Meanwhile, back in Seattle, Rachel has just finished watching the evening news on television. She is surprised to learn the blonde woman she saw at Sully's a few days ago was Susan Cole herself. She knows the woman from somewhere, but she can't remember where. She racks her brain over and over trying to remember where she has seen the woman, but she can't recall and it bothers her.

Exhausted, she goes into her room and prepares for bed. She wiggles out of her clothes and gets in the shower. A few minutes later, she's out, drying herself off while still thinking about Susan Cole. As she shimmies into her pajamas, she freezes in place and screams.

She now remembers where she met Susan and she recalls the awful memory of Ray having sex with her. She flops on the bed and cradles her head in both hands. She never thought in a million years her checkered past would follow her to Washington State. "This is so crazy," she said burying her head in a pillow.

Sleepy, she turns off the light on the nightstand and pulls the comforter over her head. As she drifts off to sleep, she thinks about Ray again vowing never to see him again. As for Susan Cole, she will cross paths with the woman again. When she does, it will be under very bizarre, unusual circumstances.

Chapter Twenty-Six

It has been two long weeks since Doctor Benny and Susan Cole left the country. The police have stopped searching for the couple after running into too many dead ends. Frustrated, Doctor Beebe contacts the medical licensing board as his last resort and files a complaint against the doctor. He knows full well resolution of the matter will be caught up in red tape. He knows by the time his complaint comes up for a hearing, interest in the Susan Cole saga would have already fizzled out.

Meanwhile, Jamie, miserable and depressed struggles to sleep at night since her break up with Anne. Lately, Peepers has been her constant companion since Anne left and the big cat's presence has become a comfort to her. Still resistant to alcohol treatment, she avoids the subject every chance she gets by playing mind games with both Rachel and Sally. Promising to make that phone call with no intention of ever doing so.

The whole idea of alcohol treatment rubs her the wrong way as she constantly convinces herself she doesn't need it. After all she's a competent therapist who can solve her problem on her own. So, to keep the peace, she stays sober around them, forging a faulty plan that seems to work for the time being.

Hunkered down at her desk on a chilly Thursday morning, Jamie Lee sips on a cup of hot Starbucks coffee, with her head buried in the Seattle Times. She is reading her favorite comic strip, Charlie Brown. Suddenly there's a knock on the door. "It's open," she hollers barely looking up.

Anne eases in the door and sticks her head in. "Can I come in?" she asked, almost whispering. Jamie drops her newspaper and stares at Anne bug-eyed, very surprised to see her.

"Of course," she said waving her in.

Anne steps in and closes the door. "How are you doing?" she asked, with her voice shaking.

"Surviving," said Jamie, with her eyes still big.

Anne parks herself on the sofa next to Peepers. The big cat stretches out his long legs and then he rolls over into a sitting position. He sits there, staring at her with those big yellow piercing eyes.

"I need to talk to you," Anne said crossing her legs and clasping her hands together on one knee. "I hate the way I left the other night. It was cowardly of me to leave a note like that."

"Yep it was," said Jamie glancing down at her desk.

"I left because of your drinking," she said shrugging her shoulders. "I just couldn't take it anymore."

Jamie, looking bleak, sits there speechless. Anne swings her right leg back and forth. She is nervous but determined. She presses on, hoping to engage Jamie in a productive conversation.

"Jamie, I've been thinking," she said. "I think you should seriously consider going to treatment. You really do need help."

Jamie cringes. "Did Rachel and Sally send you here to talk to me?"

"No, No, No," Anne said shaking her head. "I came here on my own."

"Well, you are wasting your damn time! I am not going," Jamie said glowering.

"Alright," Anne said sighing in defeat. "It's your life," she said.

She drops her head and stares down at her lap. Ray crosses her mind and she contemplates on whether to tell Jamie about him. Fearing her reaction and not knowing if she can handle the news. She obsesses about it for a minute and then Jamie interrupts her thoughts.

"Where are you staying?" she asks.

"I'm staying with a friend in Tacoma for now," Anne said, being careful not to give up too much information just yet. "I plan to move into my own place by the end of the month."

"Sounds like you have things worked out," Jamie said with a smirk.

"Yes, I do," Anne said. "But......"

"But what?" Jamie asked, with her heart racing.

"There is something I have to tell you," Anne said.

"I'm listening," said Jamie. "What is it?"

Anne clears her throat. The tension in her stomach intensifies making her jittery. She wants to walk out, but she knows it will be cowardly to do so. She talks fast. "I have been seeing someone for the past month," she blurts out.

Jamie feels tears coming on. "I regret hurting you," Anne continues. "I didn't mean to. I'm so sorry."

Tears stream down Jamie's cheeks. Peepers leaps off the sofa and creeps over to her. He hops in her lap and purrs, nudging his massive head in the bosom of her breast. The largeness of his body takes up her entire lap as she embraces him while burying her face in his soft black fur. Anne gets up and searches for a box of tissue and finds one on the bookcase.

She tiptoes over to Jamie and offers her a tissue. Jamie takes one out of the box and dabs her eyes. Anne leaves the box on the desk.

"Look, I still care for you a lot and we will always be friends," Anne said trying to reassure her. "But I can't do this anymore. "I'm so sorry."

Jamie sobs, too hurt to respond. Peepers licks the tears off her face, with his eyes very sad. Not sure what else to say and feeling bad herself, Anne steps to the door.

"Jamie, I think I should go," she softly said opening the door. "Call me if you need anything."

Jamie sniffles and nods her head. She clutches Peepers in her arms, refusing to look her ex-lover's way. Anne steps out into the hall and shuts the door behind her. Jamie grabs another tissue and dabs her eyes. She opens her desk drawer and pulls out a bottle of Jack Daniels. She screws the cap off and sucks down several swigs of the liquor, coughing after each bitter swallow. She puts the bottle down on her desk and thick tears roll down her face again. The big cat gazes back at her and he whines, with his yellow eyes intense and sad. She caresses him and his soft black fur feels good to her fingertips.

She slumps down in her chair and leans back, laying her head on the headrest. She closes her eyes and thinks about her work load, not up to dealing with patients or anyone for that matter. "I think I'll go home," she said. So, she reaches for the telephone and dials Rachel's number.

Busy reviewing charts for tomorrow's court, Rachel wonders what Jamie is up to. She hasn't talked to her for a few hours. As she contemplates returning to her office to call Jamie, Doctor James swaggers into the nursing station. This time without his sunglasses and black beret. He grabs a chair and sits next to her with his afro wild and unruly.

"Good Morning, Miss Thomas," he said with his smile broad. "Busy this morning?"

"Yes," Rachel said, not cracking a smile and trying to remain business like. She glances at him out the corner of her eye and her heart flutters. "Who are you covering for today?" she finally asks him.

"I'm taking over for Doctor Benny," he tells her. "That means you and I will be working together."

"Oh," she said looking like a deer caught in head lights.

"You look surprised," he said.

"Yeah I am, "she said feeling off kilter. Inwardly, she panics, not sure how she will manage her attraction to him if they are forced to work together. "I can't do this," she thinks to herself.

"So who made this decision?" she asks, probing for more information.

"Doctor Beebe," he said.

"So how is this going to work?" she asked. "Are you going to handle all of the admissions?"

"No, the admissions will be split up between me and Doctor Louis," he said. "I understand from Doctor Beebe the hospital plans to hire another doctor soon."

She sighs with relief. "Good," she said looking away. "That's reassuring."

He senses her disappointment. "You don't seem happy with this arrangement, Miss. Thomas," he said.

"Oh, I'm fine with it, just feeling a little tired," she fibs. She hates his uncanny ability to read her. She wishes he wasn't so perceptive.

"Sounds like you need some rest, Miss Lady, "he said smiling.

"Probably," she said chuckling.

He grabs a chart and stands. "I'm going to interview Mosquito Bellamy," he said. "I hear he is upset about being here."

"Yeah I heard that," Rachel said.

"Be back in a few minutes," he said. Rachel nods her head.

He swaggers out of the nursing station and goes to Mosquito Bellamy's room. Mosquito, perched on a stack of pillows on the bed, is reading a comic book when Doctor James darkens his doorway. He's a peculiar looking fella, with a shiny bald head and wired frame glasses accenting his brown beady eyes. The features on his long narrow face resemble an insect's and his arms and legs are both long and skinny. He takes his beady eyes off his comic book and zeros in on Doctor James. "Who you be?" he asked.

"My name is Doctor James," he said. "Can I come in? I hear you are a little upset about your admission here."

"Sure doc," Mosquito said.

Doctor James struts into the room and sits near the foot of the bed. "I hear you were arrested yesterday," he said.

"Dooocccc! Let me tell you," Mosquito said pushing his eyeglasses up on his long thin nose with one index finger. "That raunchy hoe sold me some bad stuff," he said.

"Bad stuff?" asked Doctor James. "What bad stuff?"

"I'm talking about weed man," he said scooting off the pillows. "I paid good money for that weed and the shit was bad!" "What do you mean?" asked Doctor James raising an eye brow.

"I smoked the shit and it tasted like sardines man," Mosquito said snapping his overall straps. "And then I heard some Japanese voices telling me to unload the shit and get that raunchy hoe!"

"Japanese voices?" asked Doctor James trying to keep a straight face. "Do you speak or understand Japanese?"

"No doc, "Mosquito said taking off his glasses. He rubs his eyes with one index finger and then falls on his pillows.

"Then how do you know the voices were speaking Japanese?" asked Doctor James.

"Well, they weren't speaking English doc, I can tell you that," he said putting on his glasses. "They sounded like Japanese to me," he said.

Doctor James drops his head trying to stifle a laugh. "Tell me, Mr. Bellamy, how did you get arrested?"

Mosquito scoots off the bed and plays with his overall straps. "I went to the po-po station to report that hoe for selling me some bad shit," he said.

"You went where?" Doctor James asked, looking amazed.

"I went to the po-po station," Mosquito repeats twisting his lips.

Doctor James' eyes widen. "Tell me why you did that," he said.

"I needed the cops to help me get my money back," he said. "That raunchy hoe ripped me off man!"

Doctor James smiles "Then what happened," he asked.

"The po-po asked me if I had weed on me," Mosquito said, scratching his head. "I told him yeah. So, I pulled the shit out of my pocket and showed it to him," he said.

"Then what happened?" Doctor James asked, shaking his head. "The damn po-po arrested me," Mosquito said frowning up. "And maaan, that shit really pissed me off!"

Doctor James laughs out loud. He couldn't help himself. "Man, that weed must have been some pretty bad stuff for you to go to the police and snitch on yourself," he said.

"Doc, all I needed was my money back so I can buy some good shit," Mosquito said whining. He flops on the bed and scratches his head again. "Doc can you do something about these damn Japanese voices? he asked.

"The voices will disappear after the weed wears off," Doctor James said. "In the meantime, I'm sending you to drug rehab," he said.

Mosquito scoots off the bed again. "Ugh, doc, I don't need drug rehab," he protests. "What I need is some good shit to get rid of these voices!"

"I think you need to give up on the good shit," said Doctor James laughing. "It gets you into too much trouble so drug rehab it is," he said.

Mosquito pokes out his bottom lip. "How long do I have to stay there?" he asks.

"A few days," Doctor James said getting up to leave.

"Shit!" Mosquito said. He flops on the bed and grabs his comic book. "See ya doc," he said. Doctor James waves and leaves the room.

"How was your interview?" Rachel asked, when he returned to the nursing station.

"Mosquito Bellamy is a strange little character and he's not too bright," Doctor James chuckles.

"What do you mean?" asked Rachel, arching one eye brow.

"Some woman sold him bad weed. He reported it to the police and the dude got arrested," he said.

"Now that's the dumbest thing I ever heard," Rachel said laughing.

"Yep," said Doctor James sitting next to her. "Dumb as hell."

They both laugh out loud and their outburst catches Johnny Lewis' attention. He bounces up to the nursing station and hovers over the counter. He breaks out into a toothless grin and clutches the counter, swaying back and forth with his fingernails badly stained with brown tobacco.

"Doctor James," he shouts. "Can I get a cigarette?"

"No, it's not time yet," the doctor said. "The next smoke break is at ten o' clock."

"I want a cigarette now," he said frowning and getting agitated.

Doctor James glances at his watch. "It's not ten yet," he said. "You only have fifteen more minutes to wait, be patient."

"Nigga, your hair looks wild," Johnny blurts out. He cracks up laughing.

"Nigga your hair looks wild, nigga your hair looks wild, nigga your hair looks wild," he sings.

Doctor James bolts out of his seat, his face twisted like a pretzel. "What did you call me?" he asked.

Rachel braces herself with her eyes real big. Johnny flips the doctor a bird as he backs away from the counter.

He skips across the room, singing "Nigga, your hair looks wild, nigga your hair looks wild." "I'm going to lock his ass up," Doctor James mutters under his breath, while rushing around the counter with his fists balled up and his gait swift. "Come back here you little twit!" he said with fury in his eyes.

Johnny flips him another bird and runs down the hall disappearing into his room. Doctor James reaches over the counter for the phone and calls security. Minutes later, security guards swarm the nursing station like flies.

"What happened?" asked the lead guard, with his eyes bugged out.

"I want Johnny Lewis thrown into seclusion," Doctor James said his voice rough.

"Sir, what happened? Why seclusion?" the guard asked.

"I DO NOT have to give you an explanation," Doctor James yells. "Put the man in seclusion right now!"

Rachel is stunned. She empathizes with the doctor, but his decision to put Johnny Lewis in seclusion disturbs her. She contemplates intervening, but decides against it.

"What room is Johnny Lewis in?" asked the lead guard.

"Room 216," said Doctor James with his nostrils flaring.

"We are on our way sir," the guard said.

The guards sprint to Johnny's room and drag him out kicking and screaming. They carry him down the hall to the seclusion room. Johnny yells and curses at the guards, with his face apple red. They open the steel door and throw him in so hard his body bounces off the padded wall and he lands face first on the floor.

He hops up and makes a run for the door, but the lead guard slams the door in his face and locks it. Johnny bangs on the door like a lunatic, yelling at the top of his lungs.

"I'm going to sue you assholes!" he yells. "You just wait! I'm going to sue every one of your asses when I get out of here!"

The lead guard and his crew back away from the door leaving Johnny to his fit of rage.

He strolls back to the nursing station and leans on the counter. "He's in seclusion sir," he said with his smile bright.

"Good," said Doctor James still shaken up.

"Can you tell us what the poor man did?" the lead guard asks again.

Doctor James gives him a cold, glowering stare. "I don't want to talk about it right now," he said.

"There's no need to get nasty," said the guard backing away from the counter. Doctor James turns his back on him and walks around the counter into the nursing station. He situates himself in a chair and reaches for a chart. He opens the record and sulks.

"Let us know if there are any more problems," the guard said raising one eye brow.

"Huh, huh," said Doctor James not looking up.

"Okay men, let's go," the lead guard barks. "We are done here!"

The guards take off down the hall like a herd of elephants, sprinting pass each other on their way to the exit. The lead guard arrives at the exit first and unlocks the door. He shoves the door open and runs out with each guard right behind him.

When the last guard clears the exit the door slams shaking like an earthquake and locks. The unit is quiet. Doctor James fumes. Rachel is quiet. Soon the silence between them becomes too deafening for her. She decides to approach him. "Don't you think you over reacted a little?" she asked.

"NO!" he retorts flipping through a chart and refusing to look at her. Feeling offended, she glares at him and then she decides to leave him to his ornery mood. She grabs her charts and walks out of the nursing station. "You have a nice day," she said. He doesn't respond.

Chapter Twenty-Seven

By the time Rachel returns to her office, the phone is ringing off the hook. She unlocks the door and runs inside dropping the charts on her desk. She answers the phone out of breath. "This is Rachel Thomas," she said in a hurry. "Can I help you?"

"It's me," said Jamie.

"Hi girl," she said. "I haven't heard from you all morning! What's up?"

"I need to talk to you," Jamie said. "Can you come to my office?"

"Sure, I'll be right there," Rachel said.

She hangs up the phone and runs out of her office. It's not long before she's pounding on Jamie's door.

"Come in," Jamie said, sniffling.

Rachel opens the door and bounces in closing the door behind her. "What's up girl," she said flopping down on the sofa next to Peepers. The big cat sits up and yawns.

"Anne came to see me this morning," Jamie said. "She told me she's seeing someone."

"Oh my, I'm so sorry," Rachel said.

"Me too," Jamie said tearing up.

"Is there anything I can do? Maybe get one of my gangsta friends to kick her butt?" asked Rachel trying to lighten things up.

"You are so silly," Jamie said forcing a half smile and reaching for the Kleenex box. She snatches a tissue and blows her nose. She sighs and looks at Rachel, her eyes narrowing. "I have a favor to ask you," she said.

"Oh what is it?" Rachel asks looking concerned.

"I need to take a few days off, so I can get myself together," Jamie said. "Will you cover for me?"

"What do you mean get yourself together?" Rachel asked, looking surprised.

"I just need time alone.... To deal with the break-up," she said. "My emotional energy is so spent I can't be around patients right now."

"You are probably right," Rachel said. "I'll cover for you."

"Are you sure?" Jamie asked.

"Yes girl, go home," Rachel said. "I got things handled here."

"Thanks," Jamie said feeling relieved.

"You are welcome my friend," Rachel said.

Jamie reaches for her caseload list. "I have one patient scheduled for court in the morning," she said.

"Oh, who is it?" Rachel asked.

"Peter Pan," Jamie said.

"Who?" asked Rachel, with her brow furrowing.

"His real name is Michael Barrie, but he only answers to Peter Pan," Jamie said.

Rachel cracks up. "Is that the little knock-kneed dude I saw earlier in the dining room dressed like an elf?" she asked.

"Yep, that's him," Jamie said.

"Well, let's hope the judge keeps him in the hospital," Rachel said laughing.

"Don't worry, he will," Jamie said.

Rachel glimpses at her watch. "I need to get back to my office," she said. "I have a lot of charting to do today. Are you going to be alright?" "I think so," Jamie said with red eyes.

"You think so?" Rachel asked, mimicking her words. "Are you sure? I mean you don't look so good."

"Yes, yes, yes," said Jamie beckoning for her to leave her office. "Go, girl. I'll be fine."

"Okay," Rachel said hopping off the sofa. She hesitates and studies Jamie's face for a moment and then she heads to the door. "You call me if you need to talk," she said.

"I will," Jamie said.

"I mean it," said Rachel.

"Don't worry girl, I promise," she said.

"Okay, I'll see you later," Rachel said. She lingers by the door still checking her out.

Jamie waves her out the door. "Go! I will be fine, "she said.

Rachel opens the door and walks out. She heads to her office thinking about Jamie's decision. The thought of her being home alone, sulking, bothers her. She knows full well that Jamie will be spending her time there drinking, so she strategizes a plan. "I'll check on her everyday while she's out," she said. "That way I can keep an eye on her butt. She won't like it, but I don't care."

When Rachel steps on the admissions unit, a jazzy whistling tempo greets her at the door. She strains to hear and realizes the music is coming from the dining area. Curious, she bypasses her office and heads straight towards the area. As she approaches the area, the jazzy tempo becomes louder and louder.

Once in the dining area, she sees a little man playing a flute. He is dressed in a green elf costume, surrounded by a circle of patients clapping and dancing to the music.

Across the room, dancing a jig on top of the table, is a man about six feet tall dressed in a clown suit. Intrigued, she steps to the table to get a good look at the man. When she does, she cracks up laughing.

"Hiram have you lost your freaking mind?" she asked.

"I just love this little guy," Hiram said hopping up and down on one foot. "He can really play that flute!"

"Hiram, get down from there," Rachel said laughing. "You look like a fool!"

He turns his back on her and wiggles his behind to the music. Peter Pan skips around the room, playing his flute, as the patients dance behind him in a single line clapping their hands. Rachel laughs so hard her stomach aches. She gets herself together and runs to the nursing station. She calls security.

"Security," said the man on the other end of the phone.

"Listen, I need you to come to the admissions unit," she said giggling. "The patients are dancing a jig with Peter Pan and I can't get them to stop!"

"What did you say?" the lead guard asked.

"Peter Pan is causing a ruckus here in the patient dining room," she said. "He has hypnotized the patients with his flute!"

"Who?" the guard asked.

"You heard me," said Rachel laughing out loud.

"Okay, we will be right there," said the lead guard.

She hangs up the phone and waits for security to show up. Within minutes, they are on the unit, breaking up the dancing crowd. They usher the patients out of the dining area and into their rooms. One guard snatches Peter Pan's flute from him and the little guy tears up and pokes his bottom lip out.

"Give me back my flute," he said pouting. The guard shakes his head and locks the instrument in a nearby cabinet in the nursing station. "You can have it back when it's time for you to go home," he said.

Peter Pan shoves his thumb in his mouth and runs into a corner and pouts. Hiram, still high from the music, jumps off the table and skips down the hall, disappearing around the corner.

The security guards monitor the unit while Rachel gives the charge nurse a brief report. A half hour later she's back in her office. "This place never ceases to amaze me," she said. She reaches in her desk and pulls out a blank progress note. "Peter Pan you will be staying with us for a few days," she chuckles.

Late in the afternoon, barricaded in her office, Jamie updates her progress notes and arranges transportation home for two of her patients. She calls Beth and tells her she's taking time off and then she hangs up the phone and throws on her coat. Feeling tired and worn out, she leaves her office and hurries out the door. Making a dash to her mustang, she unlocks the car and hops in. She speeds home and when she's almost there, she remembers she forgot Peepers.

She makes a U-turn in the middle of the road and speeds back to the hospital. The security guard waves her through the gate and she speeds up the hill to East Campus Hospital. Half way there, she passes the rose garden and notices a couple making out on the park bench there. She slows down and sticks her head out the window, squinting to get a good look at the couple.

She gasps when she sees who it is. She brings her mustang to a screeching halt. Her body falls limp and she blinks back tears. Anne, the love of her life, is making out with a man on the park bench.

Blind with tears, she parks her car and turns off the ignition. She sits there sobbing. Believing her life is crumbling all around her, she starts the car up again and pulls away from the curb. She heads to East Campus Hospital and parks underneath a street light. She opens the glove compartment, grabs a tissue and wipes her face. Then she gets out of the car and drops her head. Tears stream down her face as she shuffles across the parking lot to the hospital entrance. She taps on the buzzer and the glass door slides open. She shuffles inside. She cases the lobby searching for Peepers.

"Here kitty, kitty, kitty," she whispers as she shuffles across the lobby. "Peepers where are you?!"

Soon, she spots the big cat sitting on a window pane in the reception area licking his black fur. "There you are," she said shuffling over to him. She grabs him and carries him to her office. Once there, she turns on the light and closes the door behind her. She puts the cat down on the floor and he leaps on the sofa. He sits there, staring at her. She rests in her chair and grabs her bottle of Jack Daniels out of her desk drawer. She inspects the bottle and discovers she has a little liquor left and then she finishes it off. She throws the bottle in a nearby trash can and tears well up in her eyes.

The big cat cocks his head to one side and his piercing yellow eyes study her face. She wipes her tears on her coat sleeve and then lays her head on the desk. Feeling woozy and depressed, she closes her eyes hoping to shut out the world and before she realizes it, she has drifted off to sleep.

Chapter Twenty-Eight

By the time Jamie wakes up from her alcohol induced slumber, it's nine in the evening. She yawns, feeling disoriented at first and then angry when she realizes she's still at work. "Damn it, I can use a drink right now," she said struggling to her feet. She grabs onto the edge of the desk as her head spins like a top. She glances across the room and Peepers, curled up in a big furry ball on the sofa, is snoring away.

She rubs her aching forehead and pulls open the desk drawer, taking out a pen and notepad. She scribbles on the pad, tears off the note and stuffs it in her coat pocket. She shuffles to the sofa and gathers Peepers into her arms. She cuddles with the cat, rubbing her nose against his warm thick fur. He yawns while waking up. She heads to the door, turns off the light and steps out into the hall. She locks the door and begins her hike down the dim corridor. Her head spins and she stumbles, almost dropping Peepers on the floor.

"Damn, this is some hangover," she said feeling disgusted. She leans against the wall for a few moments to catch her breath. She snuggles with Peepers and the big cat buries his head in her bosom. Soon the dizzy spell passes and she moves on, stopping by the mailroom. She drops the note she wrote in Rachel's box and then she shuffles out of the mailroom, across the lobby and out the door. The crisp night air hits her face like a brick and she welcomes it. The frigid, prickly breeze feels good against her skin. She gazes out into the parking lot.

The dim illumination from the street lights gives the smooth slab of concrete a ghoulish glow. She gazes up into the dark sky and notices it's unusually clear. Stars, twinkling like Christmas tree lights, brighten the dark clear sky. She moves on, as the cool breeze blows hard against her face and she shivers. She holds Peepers close, as his body heat blocks the frigid chill. She quickens her pace, staying close to the street lights so she can see her way to her car.

Big brown bats fly above her in droves. They ascend into the clear dark sky, land on the hospital roof and take up temporary residence there. Coyotes howl in bushes and owls hoot nearby. Jamie, unfazed by the presence of wildlife, continues to press forward with her mind focused on getting home.

When she reaches her car, she unlocks it and gets in. She drops Peepers in the passenger's seat and starts the car. She speeds out of the parking lot and turns on the radio. Led Zeppelin's song, "A Stairway to Heaven" is playing on the airwaves. She turns up the volume and begins her short trek home. A few miles down the road, her eyelids become heavy and she nods and bops her head, briefly dozing off. She comes to just in the nick of time before veering off the road. She straightens the car and rolls down the window. The cool air caresses her face waking her up. "Ahhhh, this feels good," she said.

Soon she feels dizzy again. Navigating the winding steep road of Salter's Point Cliff becomes a challenge for her. She swerves into the opposite lane, almost side swiping a BMW. The driver lays on the horn. The sound is shrill, like a train whistle. He speeds pass her and frowns, shaking his fist. "Oh go to hell," Jamie curses giving him the finger.

She ignores the twenty-mile speed zone and guns the accelerator, speeding down the road at forty miles per hour. She takes her eyes off the road for a brief second to adjust the radio and then in an instant she slams into a sharp incline jerking the car in the opposite lane. The car swerves back and forth across the entire winding road and then she crashes, hitting the railing. She screams, startled by the hard impact and the car spins around in a circle, jerking her body forward. Her head hits the windshield, shattering the glass.

Pieces of glass fly in the air and Jamie, still conscious, sustains a gaping red hole on her forehead. Red liquid drips in her eyes as she attempts to steers the car straight but to no avail. She finally crashes into a large boulder on the side of the road. The impact knocks her out cold and the car flips into the air. It sails over the cliff, throwing Peepers out the window into the darkness. The car tumbles down the side of the cliff, bouncing several times off the rocky terrain and then it disappears into the dark valley below.

Seconds later, the car explodes and bright flames illuminate the midnight sky. The flames light up the valley like a firework show and force hundreds of bats out of nearby trees. Their wings flap hard like a strong wind, as they fly high into the dark horizon disappearing over the cliff. There is another explosion and a fiery, hot blaze spreads like wild fire across the dark, deep valley. It consumes trees, bushes and every living thing in its path. Minutes later sirens are heard screeching in the far distance and Peepers, scared out of his wits, lands safe on all fours on the edge of Salter's Point cliff. He crawls along the edge, his claws gripping the rocky surface, until he finally finds a flat area to rest.

He sits on his hind legs and his big yellow eyes stare down into the midnight valley, craning his neck to see while the fiery blaze consumes every inch of Jamie Lee's mustang. Within minutes Jamie Lee's mustang is a charcoal shell of itself and the cat whimpers. He lies down and drops his massive head on his front paws, with his yellow eyes glassy and sad. He whines and whines and whines as his shrill outcry resonates in ripples across the vast valley.

Thirty minutes later, fire trucks and police cars arrive at the fiery scene, screeching to a halt on the edge of Salter's Point Cliff. Firefighters tumble out of their trucks and scale down the side of the rocky cliff like little ants, to the burning carnage below. The flames are so fierce several fire fighters jump back. The fiery blaze is hot like a furnace and within seconds, Jamie's car explodes again. The blast is so intense three fire fighters are thrown back into the bushes. "GET BACK! GET BACK!" they screamed as they run for cover away from the fiery scene.

They keep their distance while they drown out the fiery blaze with gallons of water. Twenty minutes later, the fire has died down. White and grey smoke creeps up from the charred carnage leaving a gruesome scene in its wake. Jamie Lee's mustang is nothing but a dark shell of itself and the odor of burning flesh reeks in the air. Jamie Lee's body is burned beyond recognition, but still intact. Her dark charred silhouette is slumped over in the driver's seat. As the firefighters begin to clean up the grisly mess, one firefighter notices Peepers perched on the edge of Salter's Point cliff.

His piercing yellow eyes were fixated on their movements. When Jamie Lee's charred remains are finally carted off, the cat whines loud and long. Moved by the cat's emotion, the firefighter sprints to the base of the cliff. He climbs the rocky terrain, taking great caution not to lose his footing. However, when he finally reaches the edge of the cliff, the big cat with the piercing yellow eyes is nowhere to be found.

Chapter Twenty-Nine

Friday morning, the news of Jamie Lee's death spreads like wildfire throughout the hospital. Social Workers and nurses huddle around a teary Joyce in the reception area while she explains the details of Jamie's death. Rachel, in tears, is unable to stay long enough to hear the whole story. She sprints like the wind to her office, unwilling to believe Jamie is gone. When she gets there, she unlocks the door and runs inside, leaving it wide open. She rushes to her desk and dials Jamie Lee's home number.

The phone rings and rings and soon the answering machine clicks on. She hears Jamie's voice telling her to leave a message and she breaks down, hanging up the phone. With her face, wet with tears and still not convinced her friend is gone, she picks up the phone again and dials Jamie's office number. The phone rings and rings and no one answers. She stares at the receiver for a minute and then she slams the phone down. She falls back in her chair and weeps like a baby.

Soon, she hears sobbing at her door. The door opens and Sally steps in with her eyes red and puffy. Rachel hops out of her seat and runs over to her. The two women hug each other and sob, rocking back and forth, with their grief unbearable.

"Rachel," Sally said. "Do you know what happened?"

Rachel breaks her embrace and stares into Sally's face. "Not really," she sniffles. "Joyce thinks Jamie's car ran off the road not far from Salter's Point Cliff," she said. "I didn't stay to hear the whole story. I just couldn't take it!"

"When was the last time you talked to her?" Sally asked, taking a tissue out of her coat pocket and blowing her nose.

"Yesterday," Rachel said with her eyes red. "She was really bummed out after Anne's visit yesterday. She told me she needed time off and she asked me to cover for her."

"Anne came to see her?" asked Sally, looking surprised.

"Yeah, she did," Rachel said. "She told her she was seeing someone and of course Jamie was very upset about it."

"What a bitch!" said Sally shaking her head as she plops down on the sofa. The two women sit in silence and tears stream down their faces. They share a box of tissues between them as they struggle with Jamie's sudden death. Soon there is another knock on the door and Sally gets up and opens it. Beth Jones, looking like a zombie, is standing in the doorway with her skin motley and pale.

"Good Morning Ladies," she said, her voice trembling. "I'm sure by now you heard the news." "Yes," Sally said. Rachel, still overcome with grief, doesn't respond or look up. "A meeting is scheduled in the conference room to update the staff on the details of Jamie's death," Beth sadly said. "It will start in ten minutes." "Okay," Rachel mumbles struggling to get herself together. Beth leaves and closes the door.

"Do you think I should call Anne?" Sally asks, taking another tissue out of the box." "NO!" Rachel said frowning. "She probably knows already and I personally don't have anything to say to her." "Okay," Sally said. "I was just checking."

The mood is quite solemn and quiet, as staff crowd into the conference room for the meeting. Sally and Rachel find seats in the back of the room.

Hiram, sitting Indian style in a nearby corner, stares into his lap with a blank look on his face, while twirling his thumbs. Social workers and nurses huddle in small groups, whispering to one another, while others sit in chairs alongside the walls alone in their thoughts. Cassie Marks tiptoes around the room offering tissue to everyone. Her fellow social workers, appreciative of the gesture take a tissue from her box to wipe their red and puffy faces. Once the box is empty, Cassie finds a seat and sits down.

Soon doctors Beebe, Louis, James, and Hornsby file into the conference room with Beth Jones on their heels. All the doctors, except for Doctor Beebe, take a seat at the table in front of the room. Doctor Beebe rolls his wheelchair to the podium and reaches for the microphone. It squeaks, with the sound shrill, as he adjusts the volume. Visibly upset, he clears his throat. "Humph," he said. "Good Morning, I'm sure everyone has heard about Jamie Lee. She was killed last night in a car accident."

No one utters a word. Faint sobs erupt around the room. Doctor Beebe continues as his voice trembles. "The police tell us she lost control of the car and drove off Salter's Point Cliff. They are still investigating the incident."

A deafening hush comes over the room. One social worker, her face wet with tears, raises her hand and rises to her feet. "Did she have a heart attack?" she asks, with her voice weak and shaky.

"We don't know," said Doctor Beebe.

"Do we know why she drove off Salter's Point Cliff like that?" she asks. "No, I'm afraid not," said Doctor Beebe. "We just don't know all of the details yet. We have been in touch with her family and they will notify us when funeral arrangements are set. Are there any other questions or concerns?"

"Was she drunk?" another social worker asks. "You know she drank a lot." Rachel's mouth drops open and rage consumes her. She bolts out of her seat with her face wolfish. "How dare you assume such nonsense!" she said glaring at the social worker. "You got a lot of nerve!"

"Calm down," the social worker said. "I'm just asking a question!"

"Let's not make assumptions," said Doctor Beebe trying to smooth things over. "Let's wait for the police to finish their investigation."

Rachel takes her seat and fumes. Sally hugs her. "Was her cat with her when this happened?" one social worker asks. "I haven't seen her cat this morning."

"Either have I," said several staff looking around the room.

"I don't know what happened to her cat," said Doctor Beebe. "Maybe he will show up soon."

Everyone sits quiet, glued to their seat. The only noise heard in the room, are faint sobs and a clock ticking on the wall. A male social worker suddenly leaves his seat and walks out the room. Soon everyone follows suit and exits the conference room but no one says another word. Sally and Rachel follow the crowd. They each go their separate ways and Rachel heads to the mailroom. When she arrives there, she scans the mailboxes. Her eyes stopped cold at Jamie Lee's mailbox and she blinks back tears. She goes to her mailbox and grabs her messages. She flips through each one and then Jamie's note catches her eye. Her heart races as she unfolds the crumpled-up note. She reads it, her eyes blind with tears.

"Are you alright?" asked a deep booming voice behind her. She flinches and turns around. Doctor James, holding a box of Kleenex, stares back at her. "Sorry to scare you," he said. "I thought you might like a tissue." She snatches a tissue from the box and wipes her face. She sniffles, shaking her head. "This note is from Jamie," she said handing him the note. "It's so disturbing."

He takes the note and reads it. "Disturbing indeed," he said nodding his head. "It's almost like she knew she was going to die," Rachel said tearing up again. "I agree," he said looking solemn. "Her note sounds suicidal," he adds.

Rachel frowns. "Don't say that," she tersely said, defending her friend. "Doctor Beebe is right! We really don't know what happened!"

"I don't mean to upset you," he said trying to be empathetic. "I'm sure the police will have something soon."

"I hope so," she said calming down.

He hands her Jamie's note. "Are you going to be alright?" he asked. "Is there anything I can do for you?"

"No," said Rachel walking pass him to the door. "I need to be alone, but thanks anyway."

"Try to have a good day," he said.

"You too," she said holding back tears. She drops her head and walks back to her office.

Chapter Thirty

It is Saturday morning, a week later. Cold blistery showers fall from the dark grey sky as hospital personnel with umbrellas high above their heads dash across the parking lot to Saint Mary's church for Jamie Lee's funeral. They pack in the church like a can of sardines forming a single line in the aisle each person taking a seat in the nearest pew. Haunting organ music whines in the back ground while men and women dressed in red and gold robes march into the pulpit one by one, taking seats in the choir stand. The minister, his face straight as an arrow, leans against the podium, checking out the crowd as they come into the vestibule taking their seats.

Rachel sits alone in a pew three rows from Jamie Lee's casket. She swallows hard, blinking back tears as she views Jamie's sealed casket loosely decorated with a wreath of red and black roses. The week leading up to Jamie Lee's funeral was rough on her. Her grief consumed her as she tried to wrap her head around her friend's untimely death. When she thought about saying her final good bye, she could hardly stand it, the emotional pain too much.

Doctors Beebe, Hornsby and Louis along with his wife, Sierra, sit quiet together in a pew five rows from the front of the church. Doctor James leans against the wall, looking dapper in his gray suit checking out the congregation behind his dark sunglasses. Beth Jones, sitting in a pew behind Doctor Louis and his wife resembles a wicked witch with her black floppy hat and matching lacey dress.

Loud whispers rumble throughout the church when Anne Cleveland is seen hurrying down the aisle in her gray tinted glasses a perfect match to her gray suit. She stops at Sally's pew and takes a seat next to her after the nurse reluctantly moves over to make room for her.

"Good Morning," Anne said looking glum.

"Good Morning," said Sally looking straight ahead.

Hiram, making an entrance, struts down the aisle like a proud peacock. He is looking like a Christmas tree ornament in his bright red neon suit and wide sombrero hat. He slides in the pew next to Rachel and crosses his legs. "Good Morning Missy," he grins.

"Good Morning Hiram," she said forcing a half smile, amused by the attorney's outlandish outfit and displaced cheerful mood.

Everyone waits with anticipation for the funeral service to begin, their mood very subdued. Except for the woman playing Amazing Grace on the whining organ, the church is eerily still. The song's sad melody whines and lingers in the air, tugging at the heart strings of every grieving soul there. The choir painstakingly belts out every word as their voices, at times, are drowned out by the congregation's sobs.

Finally, the song ends, much to everyone's relief and the choir sits down. The minister, his demeanor somber, rises from his seat with his movements purposeful and slow. He takes his place behind the podium and adjusts the volume on the microphone. He looks out over the congregation and begins the eulogy.

"Good Morning, family and friends," he said. "We are gathered........."

The minister belts out a long thought provoking prayer and then he tells the church Jamie Lee's life story.

When he finishes, family members take turns offering their remarks and telling stories about Jamie Lee's life. Several of Jamie's friends and colleagues take turns coming to the podium sharing their stories about their friendship with her.

When Anne takes the podium, boos breakout around the church. She attempts to tell her story but is interrupted by Marcy, who is a fellow colleague. "You are a bald face liar!" she hollers pointing her finger. Red-faced and tearful, Anne staggers off the podium and hurries down the aisle to the pew where she was sitting. She grabs her purse and heads to the door. Boos erupt everywhere following her down the aisle and the ushers move out of her way as she passes showing no empathy. She keeps her head down leaving the church in tears.

An hour later, the funeral service is over. The pallbearers carry Jamie Lee's casket down the aisle, with her family following behind, to the black shiny limousine waiting outside. Soon everyone follows suit, talking amongst themselves as they gradually move down the aisle heading toward the door. The rain pours down like bullets as people sprint to their cars parked alongside the street. Others make a mad dash across the street to the parking lot to their cars.

Soon a long funeral procession follows the black limousine down the road to Salter's Point Cemetery. The rain turns into a light drizzle and the cold wind picks up by the time the funeral procession reaches the cemetery. Everyone piles out of their cars with umbrellas over their heads making their way through the wet grassy terrain to Jamie Lee's burial site. When they arrive there, they form a big circle around the site, watching in silence as Jamie Lee's family escorts her casket to the dug up grave.

Faint sobs are heard over the whistling wind and the dark sky above threatens more heavy rain. As Jamie Lee's casket is lowered into the ground, the minster prays again. Rachel whimpers, moved by the minster's words as she tosses a black rose on top of the casket. She turns away, overcome with grief, walking as fast as she can to the back of the crowd. Several social workers take her place, jockeying for position so they can pay their last respects to their colleague.

Soon the family leaves the gravesite one by one with several mourners following their lead, returning to their cars. Rachel, still not ready to let go just yet, lingers a few feet away from the gravesite, dabbing her eyes with a handkerchief. She stands there, deep in thought. She remembers the good times she and Jamie had, the laughs they shared and the brief friendship they had. The thought of never seeing her friend again gnaws at her like a sore, piercing her very soul.

"Are you okay?" said a deep voice interrupting her thoughts.

Spooked, she hops a few inches off the ground. "You scared the hell out of me!" she said frowning at Doctor James. "You are always sneaking up on me!"

"Sorry," he said. "I'm just a little concerned, that's all. Are you alright?"

"Yes, I'm alright," Rachel said looking annoyed. "How about you, are you alright?"

"Yes," Doctor James said ignoring her flippant response.

He moves closer to her. They both stand side by side looking at the uncovered grave site, not saying a word. After some minutes pass by, Doctor James breaks the silence.

"Did you drive over here?" he asks.

"Uh, no," said Rachel. "I rode over here with that crazy Hiram, but as you can see he left me."

"Well, I can give you a lift back," he said.

"That will be nice," she said forcing a smile.

They both pay their last respects and then they trudge across the cemetery grounds to his car. It's not long before little droplets of water fall from the sky forcing the doctor to break out into a brisk jog. As the water droplets grow bigger and bigger, Rachel puts up her umbrella and quickens her pace. Soon thunder is heard crashing in a distance and she too breaks out into a brisk jog. She reaches the car just in time, before the sky opens and drowns the earth with buckets of water again. Doctor James opens the door for her and she hops in. He slams the door behind her and dashes to the other side of the car and hops in, with his suit damp from the rain's assault.

"Boy this rain is something else," he said as he starts up the car.

"Oh, this is normal," said Rachel forcing a grin. "It's just another typical day in the Great Northwest."

He grins at her and pulls away from the curb. "How about that dinner?" he asked as he speeds out of the cemetery gate.

She rolls her eyes. "You don't give up, do you?" she asked.

"Nope," he chuckles.

"Okay, let me think about it," she said.

Doctor James laughs. "Don't take too long," he said. "I'm not going to wait forever."

"I know," she smiles back. Lightning crackles across the dark, grey sky and water pellets the size of marbles bounce off the wet muddy ground.

Cemetery personnel work hard like beavers to cover Jamie Lee's grave. By the time they shovel the last bit of dirt on her grave site, the rain is so fierce, they take off running for cover. Fierce lightning blows up the universe like a fire cracker while the rain pelts down like a heavy brisk shower.

Out of nowhere, a big black cat with yellow piercing eyes creeps from around an evergreen tree with his stride measured and purposeful. The cat, unfazed by the heavy cold rain, whines loud. With his heart broken, the sound is shrill and haunting. He lies down on the muddy grave site and stretches his legs out laying his massive head on his front paws. When he whimpers, and closes his big yellow eyes, his chest heaves up and down in two second intervals for several long minutes. Soon his breathing becomes labored and slow and then in a few seconds the big cat is still. The hard, cold rain beats down on the cat's lifeless body pounding it deep into Jamie Lee's grave until it finally disappears underneath the muddy terrain and is seen no more.

THE END

68343464R00146

Made in the USA
Charleston, SC
13 March 2017